HARRY KEMELMAN's first novel, *FRIDAY THE RABBI SLEPT LATE*, became something of a publishing phenomenon. Universally praised by reviewers, it was the choice of a major book club; publication rights were snapped up in half a dozen countries; and it was awarded the coveted Edgar of the Mystery Writers of America as best first novel of the year. Now here is his second novel, and the exciting news is that it's even better than its bestselling predecessor.

"Herry Kemelman has come through as a winner again . . . A good tale well told."
—*The New York Times*

"Another Sholem Aleichem . . . An excellent storyteller . . . Here is detective work at its best." —*Detroit News*

"Detailed with humor and intelligence. Top quality!" —*Bestsellers*

"Wise and witty." —*Saturday Review*

Fawcett Crest Books
by Harry Kemelman:

FRIDAY THE RABBI SLEPT LATE
SATURDAY THE RABBI WENT HUNGRY
SUNDAY THE RABBI STAYED HOME
MONDAY THE RABBI TOOK OFF
TUESDAY THE RABBI SAW RED
and
THE NINE-MILE WALK

HARRY KEMELMAN

Saturday THE RABBi WENT HuNGRY

A FAWCETT CREST BOOK

FAWCETT PUBLICATIONS, INC., GREENWICH, CONN.

To Anne

A Fawcett Crest Book reprinted by arrangement
with Crown Publishers.

Library of Congress Catalog Card Number: 66-15114

Alternate Selection of the Book-of-the-Month Club, 1966

Printed in the United States of America

1

. . . On the tenth day of this seventh month is the day of atonement, a holy convocation shall it be unto you, and ye shall fast . . . and no manner of work shall ye do on this day . . . it shall be a statute forever throughout your generations in all your dwellings. A sabbath of rest it shall be unto you, and ye shall fast: on the ninth day of the month at evening shall ye begin, from evening unto evening shall ye celebrate your sabbath.

This year the Day of Atonement coincided with the weekly Sabbath, so that the ninth day of the month in the Hebrew calendar fell on a Friday and the tenth on Saturday. It did not make the day any holier—that was impossible—but it enabled most Jews to observe the holiday without interrupting their normal work week. Late Friday afternoon the Jewish community of Barnard's Crossing, like Jews everywhere, was making ready for this most holy day of the year. The women were preparing the evening meal, which traditionally was more elaborate than usual not only to set off more sharply the twenty-four-hour fast that followed but to give the sustenance needed to endure it. The men had left work early to give them time to bathe, change into holiday clothes, dine, and still get to the synagogue before sundown when the chanting of Kol Nidre ushered in the Holy Day.

David Small, the young rabbi of the community, had finished dressing and now stood for inspection in front of the critical eye of his wife, Miriam. He was of medium height, but although in excellent health he was thin and pale, and behind his glasses his eyes were dark, deep-set, and brooding. He carried his head slightly forward as though peering at a book; his shoulders had a scholarly stoop.

His wife was tiny and vivacious with a mass of blonde hair that seemed to overbalance her. She had wide blue eyes and an open, trusting countenance that would have seemed ingenuous were it not offset by a determined little chin. There was a certain childlike quality about her that not

5

even the protuberant belly marking her final month of pregnancy could dispel.

"Your suit, David—the jacket doesn't hang right somehow. Stand up straight and throw your shoulders back."

He made the effort.

"It's that top button. It's a good half inch off and pulls the lapel askew."

"It fell off and I sewed it on myself. You were at a Hadassah meeting."

"Well, give it to me and I'll resew it." She examined the button critically. "Why did you use blue thread when the suit is gray?"

"Actually it's white thread. I colored it with my fountain pen. Besides, my kittel will cover it during services."

"And what about on the way to the temple? And talking to the members afterward? And your shoes are dusty."

He started to rub his shoe against the calf of his trouser leg.

"David!"

"They'll only get dusty again when we walk to the temple," he said apologetically.

"Use the shoe brush."

He uttered a faint sigh of protest but went to the back hallway, and presently she heard sharp staccato whisks.

When he returned she helped him on with his jacket, adjusting the set on his shoulders like a tailor, and then buttoned it. She patted the front of the jacket. "There, that looks better."

"Am I all right now? Do I pass muster?"

"You're handsome, David."

"Then we'd better get on with it." From his wallet he extracted two one-dollar bills and gave her one and kept one for himself. Automatically he started to return the wallet to his back pocket, then thought better of it and went inside and put it away in his bureau drawer. He did not carry money on the Sabbath.

He came back with a prayer book in hand. Flipping the pages with index and second fingers, he found the place and handed her the open book. He pointed. "There's the prayer."

She read the Hebrew passage that explained that this money was for charity in partial atonement for her sins. Then she folded the bill and inserted it in the opening of the blue tin charity box that she kept on a shelf in the kitchen.

"Is a dollar enough, David?"

"It's just a token." He slipped in his own folded bill. "You

6

know, my grandfather who lived with us a few years before he died, used for his offering a live rooster, which, I understood, was given to the poor. According to the custom, a man would use a rooster and a woman a hen. You now, in your condition, would be expected to use a hen and an egg."

"You're joking."

"No, seriously."

"And what would happen to the egg?"

"Oh, I suppose we'd eat it."

"It sounds cannibalistic."

"Now that you mention it. My folks used money, of course, usually in some multiple of eighteen. My father would accumulate coins for the purpose, dimes, as I recall, and he and my mother each would use eighteen. As a youngster I was given eighteen pennies."

"Why eighteen?"

"Because in Hebrew the two letters in the alphabet that represent the numerals eight and ten spell *chai*, which means life—a bit of cabalistic nonsense, really. Come to think of it, today is the eighteenth of September, which gives it even added significance. I should have arranged to get some coins."

"I've got a bunch of pennies, David—"

"I think the poor would appreciate a dollar more than eighteen cents. We'll let it go this time and try to remember next year. But now if we don't want to be late we'd better eat."

They sat down and he pronounced the blessing. The telephone rang. The rabbi, who was nearer, picked up the instrument.

From the receiver came a loud voice. "Rabbi? Rabbi Small? This is Stanley. You know, Stanley Doble from the temple."

Stanley was the temple janitor and general maintenance man, and although he saw the rabbi almost every day he still found it necessary to identify himself as Stanley Doble from the temple—like some heraldic title—whenever he phoned. Although he had an instinctive knowledge of all things electrical and mechanical, apparently he considered the phone wire a hollow tube through which he had to shout to be heard.

"I'm sorry to bother you, Rabbi, but the public-address system is on the blink."

"What's the matter with it?"

"It don't work right. It don't work right at all. It howls."

"Maybe by tonight it will straighten itself out," suggested

the rabbi, who regarded all mechanical devices as a mystery; they got out of order owing to some perversity and might right themselves if let alone. Then hopefully, "Maybe a minor adjustment?"

"I checked the wiring. I couldn't find anything. I think it's the microphone. I think maybe it's broken."

"Is there anyone you can call for service? How about the company that installed it?"

"It's a Boston outfit."

The rabbi glanced at his watch. "Then there's no sense in calling at this hour. What about someone in Lynn or Salem?"

"It's pretty late, Rabbi. Most places are closed by now."

"Well, I'll just have to talk a little louder then. Perhaps you had better call the cantor and tell him."

"Okay, Rabbi. Sorry to bother you, but I thought you'd like to know."

The rabbi returned to his soup which his wife had set before him. He just started on it when the phone rang again. It was Mrs. Robinson, president of the Sisterhood. "Oh, Rabbi, Sue Robinson." Her voice had a breathless quality as though she had sighted him at a distance and caught up with him only at the corner. "Forgive me for interrupting your pre-Holy Day meditations, but it's frightfully important. You *were* going to make an announcement on the floral decorations, weren't you?" She sounded accusing.

"Of course. Just a minute." He opened his prayer book to a sheet of paper he had inserted. "I have it right here— Floral decorations, courtesy of the Sisterhood."

"Well, there's a change. Do you have a pencil and paper handy? I'll hold on."

"All right."

"Rose Bloom—no, you had better make that Mr. and Mrs. Ira Bloom, in memory of her father David Isaac Lavin—"

"Lavin?"

"That's right, she pronounces it Lavin, L-a-v-i-n, with a long A. She insists that's nearer the original Hebrew than if she spelled it the usual way with an E. Is that right, Rabbi?"

"Yes, I suppose it is."

"Well, of course if you say so, but it still sounds affected to me. Anyway, Floral decorations, courtesy of Mr. and Mrs. Ira Bloom. You don't want to make a mistake on the names, Rabbi," she said sharply. "I would have called earlier, but she called me only half an hour ago."

8

"I won't forget." He read the announcement back to her from his scribbled notes.

"Splendid. Oh, and Rabbi, you might tell Miriam. She'll want to know."

"Of course. I'll tell her."

He carefully copied over the hastily penciled note, printing the names neatly so he would make no mistake when making his announcements from the pulpit. Back at the table, he took a few spoonfuls of soup and shook his head. "I don't think I care for any more," he said apologetically.

"It's probably cold by now." She removed the plate.

The phone rang again. It was a Mrs. Rosoff. "Tell me, Rabbi," she said, and tried to keep her voice calm, "I don't like to disturb you at this time, but how much does the Torah weigh? You know, the Scroll?"

"Why, I don't know, Mrs. Rosoff. The Scrolls are of different sizes, so I suppose they would vary quite a bit in weight. Is it important? I imagine most of ours would be about thirty pounds apiece, but that would be only a guess."

"Well, I think it's important, Rabbi. My husband got a notice last week that he was to have an honor for Yom Kippur. They said he would be *hagboh*. And I just found out what it means. It means, Rabbi, that he is supposed to lift the Scroll up by the handles way over his head. Is this the kind of honor you give to a man who had a heart attack not three years ago, and who to this day wouldn't think of going out into the street without his little bottle of nitroglycerine pills? Is this how you give out honors, Rabbi? You'd like to see my husband have a heart attack right there on the altar?"

He tried to explain that the honors were distributed by the Ritual Committee and that he was sure they had no knowledge of Mr. Rosoff's condition. "But it's really nothing serious, Mrs. Rosoff, because *hagboh* is one of a pair. There's *hagboh* and *glilloh*. *Hagboh* lifts the Scroll, and *glilloh* rolls it up and ties it. Your husband has only to say he would prefer the honor of rolling up the Scroll instead of lifting it, and the other man can do the lifting."

"You don't know my husband. You think he'll admit he can't lift the Scroll after you have announced he will? My big hero would rather take a chance on a heart attack."

He assured her he would take care of it, and rather than rely on his memory immediately dialed Mortimer Schwarz, president of the congregation, who announced the honors from the pulpit.

"I'm glad you called, Rabbi," he said after he had taken the message. "I wanted to phone but I hated to disturb you at this time. You heard about the public-address system?"

"Yes, Stanley told me."

"It isn't as bad as he probably said it was. When you talk right into it there's a low hum, but you can pretty much tune it out by turning down the volume. It's only when you don't talk into it directly that you get a kind of howl. So if you can remember to talk into it directly—"

"I doubt if I could, Mr. Schwarz, but on the other hand I don't think I really need it."

"I was thinking about tomorrow. The going will be a lot tougher. That's a full day's service and on an empty stomach."

"I'm sure we can manage. The hall has good natural acoustics."

"Suppose I could get hold of a mechanic to work on it right after our service tonight—"

"Oh, I'm afraid that's out of the question," said the rabbi quickly.

"Well, perhaps you're right. It would cost us an arm and a leg, and people might notice that there was a light on in the temple. You're sure you don't mind?"

He returned to the table. "Mortimer Schwarz being solicitous," he remarked. "The effect of the Yom Kippur spirit, no doubt."

He was halfway through his roast chicken when the phone rang again. Miriam started for it purposefully, but her husband waved her aside. "It's probably for me," he said. "It seems as though I've been on the phone all evening talking to people who don't want to disturb me."

He lifted the receiver: "Rabbi Small."

"Oh, Rabbi, how fortunate to find you in. This is Mrs. Drury Linscott. I am not of your faith, but both my husband and I have the highest opinion of your people. As a matter of fact, my husband's principal assistant, a man in whom he has the highest confidence, is a full-blooded Jew." She waited for him to be duly grateful.

"I see," he murmured.

"Now my husband reports that Morton—that's my husband's assistant, Morton Zoll—do you know him?"

"I—I don't think so."

"A very fine man, and really quite dependable. Well, my husband claims that Morton told him that starting at sundown tonight he is not supposed to eat or drink, not even water, until sunset tomorrow. Now I find that hard to believe, and I am sure that Mr. Linscott must have misunderstood."

"No, it's quite true, Mrs. Linscott. We fast from sunset to sunset."

"Indeed? And he must not do work of any kind during that time?"

"Quite true."

"Oh!"

The rabbi waited.

"Very well then." And she hung up.

The rabbi looked quizzically at the instrument and then gently replaced it on its cradle.

"What was that all about?" asked Miriam.

He reported the conversation.

"I'll answer the phone from now on," she said. Almost immediately it rang again.

She waved him away and picked up the receiver. She cupped her hand over the mouthpiece. "It's Cantor Zimbler," she whispered.

"I better take it."

The cantor sounded frantic. "Rabbi, have you heard about the public-address system? Stanley called me and I came right over to the temple. I'm calling from there now. I just tested it and it's terrible. I started singing my *Hineni heoni memaas* and it sounded like an old-fashioned phonograph with a dull needle. If I turned my head the least bit, it went awooh, awooh, like a fire alarm. What are we going to do, Rabbi?"

The rabbi smiled. He wondered if the cantor had put on his robes and tall white *yarmulka* to make the test. He was a short fat man with a little black moustache and goatee, who looked like the chef in a spaghetti advertisement. They shared the same enrobing room, and the cantor insisted on affixing a full-length mirror to the door. Only the year before last he had served in an Orthodox congregation, and in applying for his present job he sent along with his résumé one of the posters he used in advertising special concerts. There he had referred to himself as Yossele Zimbler. Since then, he had had new ones printed up in which he called himself the Reverend Joseph Zimbler.

"With a voice like yours, Cantor, I shouldn't think you'd need a public-address system."

"You think not, Rabbi?"

"No question of it. Besides, you are Orthodox in outlook, aren't you?"

"So?"

"So I shouldn't think you would want to use a public-address system at all. As I understand it, it's an electric system where the circuit is made and broken by the inflections of your voice."

"So?"

"So it's like turning the electric light on and off all through the service."

"We-el . . ." the cantor obviously was not convinced.

"That's why many of the Orthodox congregations don't use it at all during the Sabbath, and of course Yom Kippur is the Sabbath of Sabbaths."

"That's true, Rabbi," said the cantor slowly. Then, "But we used it last Yom Kippur."

"That's because we are a Conservative congregation and the Conservative synagogue permits it. But this year the Holy Day comes on the Sabbath, so this year it is the Sabbath of Sabbaths of Sabbaths," and he rotated his free hand in slow circles, Talmudic fashion, to indicate the ever-increasing sanctity of Sabbath piled on Sabbath. "You could argue that if the rule applies for the Sabbath for the Orthodox synagogue, then it should apply for us Conservatives on Yom Kippur, and on a third-degree Sabbath such as we're having this year, it ought to apply even to Reform congregations."

The cantor's chuckle told him he was won over. The rabbi returned to the table. His wife shook her head with a smile. "That was a terrible pilpul."

"You're probably right," the rabbi said wryly. "However, since pilpul is a fine, hairline distinction the rabbi has used for a couple of thousand years to prove a point his common sense has already told him is right, this serves the purpose —and in the present case I have converted into a blessing something that has to be tolerated anyway. It made him feel pious and devout instead of aggrieved." He laughed. "They're like children—so many of these cantors. Maybe that's why they always call themselves by their diminutives—Yossele, Mottele, Itzekel."

"Maybe if I call you Dovidel, I can exercise enough authority to keep you at the table until you finish your meal. Remember, there's a long fast ahead."

The telephone did not ring again and he was able to drink his coffee in peace. Miriam cleared away and washed the dishes and got dressed. "You're sure you don't mind the walk?" he asked solicitously.

12

"Of course not. The doctor wants me to get plenty of exercise. But let's start now to avoid any more idiot calls."

It was half-past six, and although the sun was not due to set for another hour the service started fifteen minutes earlier. It was only a twenty-minute walk to the temple, but tonight it was well to get there early. They were on their way out the door when the telephone rang.

"Let it ring, David."

"And wonder all evening who it was? Don't worry, I'll cut it short."

"Rabbi?" The voice was low and hoarse and urgent. "This is Ben Goralsky. I've got a favor to ask of you. Could you stop at my house before going to the temple? It's awfully important. It's my father. He's very sick."

"But we're just leaving to walk to temple and haven't much time. And your house is not en route."

"Rabbi, you've got to come. It's a matter of life and death. I'm sending a car for you, and I can drive you to the temple afterwards. It's all right to ride over, isn't it? It's only after services that you don't want to ride. Don't worry, you'll get there the same time you would if you walked."

"Well . . ."

"He's already started out. He'll be over your place in minutes."

2

Hugh Lanigan, chief of police of Barnard's Crossing, pulled back his chair and, plumping himself down on its leather seat, swiveled around to face his visitor. He was a stocky man with a pleasant Irish face and snow-white hair. "What can I do for you, Padre?" he said genially.

The man in the visitor's chair was young—not more than thirty-five. He was tall with broad shoulders and a deep chest. A pillar of neck supported a handsome, craggy face surmounted by blond, curly hair that was just beginning to thin out in two peaks above the forehead. In spite of the clerical collar and black silk rabat, he looked more like a football player than an Anglican minister. And indeed, Peter Dodge had been an All-American guard on the Wabash var-

13

sity and played professionally for several seasons before the call to enter the ministry.

"I am Peter Dodge, assistant to Dr. Sturgis at St. Andrew's," he said in a deep baritone.

Lanigan nodded.

"I've come to lodge a complaint against a couple of your men."

"Oh? Who are they?"

"I don't know their names—"

"Badge numbers?"

"I don't know those either, but they were the two men riding the patrol car Wednesday night."

Lanigan glanced at a chart on the wall. "That would be Loomis and Derry. They're both good men. What did they do?"

"There was a fracas of some sort at Bill's Cafe over near the Salem line—"

"I know where it is."

"Of course. Well, there was some sort of trouble and Bill, er—the proprietor—asked some of the participants to leave. They did so without argument, but I gather they hung around outside and when customers drove up urged them not to go in. They made nuisances of themselves, but I'm sure there was nothing vicious in it. It was all quite good-natured, without animosity."

"Even though they were urging customers to stay away?"

"I spoke to the proprietor and he assured me he did not take the matter seriously—"

"Oh, then you weren't there at the time."

"No, I came along some time afterward."

"In the course of your regular evening walk?"

The younger man showed his surprise. "You know that I take a walk every evening? Don't tell me I'm under police surveillance?"

The chief smiled. "This is a small town, Padre, but we've got a lot of territory to cover and not enough men to do a thorough job. Other towns are the same way. If you want to cover the area with foot patrolmen, you need a lot more men than the town is willing to pay for. And cruising cars or motorcycles miss a lot. So we use a combination of the two, and take up the slack by trying to know things before they happen. You're new here—couple of months?"

Dodge nodded.

"And I suppose you come from a big city"—he hesitated— "from the Midwest judging by your accent—"

14

"South Bend."

"Well, that's a pretty big city. People who live in cities usually aren't aware of their police until they actually need them. The police are a service they expect will function when they need them the same way they expect water when they turn on the tap or electricity when they flip a switch. But in small towns like this, police are still people. They're neighbors and friends and you know them the way you do any other neighbor. It's part of our job to know what's going on. We see a man walking along the street after dark, and the patrolman on the beat will make a point of speaking to him." He looked at the young minister quizzically. "Weren't you ever approached by a policeman?"

"Oh, shortly after I came, but he only asked if he could help me. I suppose he thought I was looking for a street number."

"And you explained that you always take a walk after dinner?"

"Oh—"

"You start out from Mrs. Oliphant's where you board, and you go up Oak Street just beyond Colonial Village, and then you swing down Main Street over to the Salem line, and then along the waterfront and home."

"So that's how it's done?"

"That's how it's done."

"And if instead of this collar, I had been wearing—well, ordinary clothes?"

"Then he would have been just as polite, but probably he would have asked a few more questions. And maybe if you had explained you were just walking to the bus station, he might have suggested you wait for the cruising car to give you a lift."

"I see."

"Now my guess is that you came by Bill's place about half-past eight and found the boys standing around, full of indignation, and asked them—"

"One of them goes to our church. And according to him, and the others agreed, your two policemen were abusive and unnecessarily rough. There were two Negro lads in the group. You men were especially abusive to them."

It crossed Lanigan's mind idly that his own pastor, Father O'Shaughnessy, would have referred to them as "colored boys" but doubted Dodge would understand no offense was intended. "Your complaint then is that my men were unnecessarily rough? Did they hit them? Did they use their clubs?"

"I want to make it clear, first of all, that the cruising car was not called; it just happened by."

"Yeah, we check Bill's place two or three times a night."

"Which would indicate that nothing very serious had happened there."

"All right."

"I'm mostly concerned about the particular abuse that was meted out to the Negro lads. This isn't Alabama, I hope."

"So that's it. You're connected with the Civil Rights movement, aren't you?"

"I certainly am."

"All right. Now what happened to the colored boys that upset you?"

"Well, for one thing, I protest their having been singled out. They were pushed and one of them fell. Your men were vituperative, and as public servants I don't think—"

"Maybe that's the point, Padre, I mean that they are public servants. But they think of themselves as servants of the Barnard's Crossing public rather than the public in general, and those two boys were not from our town."

"How do you know?"

"Because we have no colored families in Barnard's Crossing. And before you go jumping to conclusions, let me assure you that it isn't because we don't want them or because we have some sort of gentlemen's agreement to keep them out. It's just that real estate prices around here are high and most Negroes can't afford it."

He wondered whether it was worthwhile trying to explain to this outlander how things were in Barnard's Crossing. "You've got to understand the situation here, Padre. Ed Loomis, and I guess it must have been Ed, has no prejudice against blacks, or against any other ethnic group. We don't have much of that kind of thing in this town. The spirit of the town is live and let live, and after you've been here a while, you'll realize it. It was settled by people who left Salem because they didn't want the theocracy there telling them what they could do and couldn't do. And for a long time we had neither church nor minister here. They were a rough lot, but they were tolerant, and I'm inclined to believe that both traditions have carried down some to the present. The fact that my people, Irish Catholic, could settle here during colonial times will give you some idea of the spirit of tolerance that prevailed. Those two boys were from Salem, and I suppose there is a kind of prejudice against outsiders, and that would include anyone not born here. They call them foreigners. But I assure you that Ed Loomis meant nothing personal. If it's wrong for Barnard's Crossing police to shoo out-of-towners a little more forcefully than they would local youngsters, at least it's understandable."

"So you condone it?"

"I don't condone it, but I understand it."

"I don't think it's enough. Mr. Braddock, the chairman of the Board of Selectmen, is a member of our church and I intend to speak to him about it."

Lanigan pursed his lips. Then he glanced at the clock on the wall and leaned back in his swivel chair far enough to see down the connecting corridor to the sergeant's desk. "Will you contact the patrol car, Joe?" he called out. "See that they get right down to the temple to help with the traffic. I spoke to the rabbi, and he said they'd start arriving around half-past six and that traffic would be heaviest between a quarter of and a quarter past seven. They can leave after that and Lem'l can stay on for another half hour. Then they can circle back and pick him up."

He straightened up in his chair and smiled at his visitor. "You go right ahead and talk to Alf Braddock about Ed, Padre. He knows Ed Loomis pretty well. Ed crews for him during Race Week."

3

Colonial Village was the first real-estate development in the Chilton area of Barnard's Crossing. The usual jokes about developments did not apply to Colonial Village; no danger here of the husband returning home and blundering into the wrong house. Although all floor plans were identical, Colonial Village had three different exteriors and no two adjoining houses were built in the same style. There was no confusing the Moderne with its flush door and three small diagonal panes of glass with the Cape Cod, which had a white paneled door flanked by two long narrow windows—or either with the Renaissance, which had a massive-looking door hung

17

on two wrought-iron hinges generously studded with hammered iron nails and a small square window set in a black iron frame. In each case the porch light and railing leading to the front door carried out the motif. And inside too, as the agent went to pains to point out, light fixtures and hardware matched perfectly. The Cape Cod had glass doorknobs and crystal chandeliers; the Renaissance, hammered copper hardware and square lanterns of pebbled stained glass set in frames of hammered iron; and the Moderne featured polished brass doorknobs and light fixtures composed of a shallow curve of polished brass.

And though the house lots were modest—five thousand square feet for the most part—they afforded privacy while offering the added advantage of a closer relationship between neighbors. Shared barbecue meals were common in Colonial Village during summer, and several times a season there were block parties on Saturday nights.

The older inhabitants of the town tended to be supercilious toward Colonial Village. They came from a background of ugly but solid and spacious Victorian houses, and referred to Colonial Village as "cracker boxes" and joked about their indoor swimming pools in sneering reference to flooded cellars after a rainstorm. This was unfair. Not all Colonial Village cellars were subject to flooding—only those at the lower end of the development.

Nor was it true that only Jews lived in the village. Almost as many non-Jews lived there. Bradford Lane, where Isaac and Patricia Hirsh lived, for example, may have been solidly Jewish at their end of the street, but the other end had a Venuti, an O'Hearne, and Stan Padefsky who was Polish.

Right now, on the eve of Yom Kippur, there was a bustle of activity in many Colonial Village households as families got ready for temple. The Hirsh home, however, was relatively quiet. Patricia Hirsh, a tall, statuesque woman in her thirties, with red hair and freckles and bright blue eyes, had already had her supper and cleared away the dishes. She frequently ate alone since there was no telling when her husband would get home from the lab. Normally she did not mind, but tonight she had promised to baby-sit across the street for Liz Marcus so she could go to the Kol Nidre service. Her husband's tardiness was annoying, especially since Pat had told him to be sure to get home early. His place was laid in the tiny dining area, set off from the rest of the living room by a two-tier painted bookcase. (Renaissance had a wrought-iron railing, and Moderne a low wall of glass brick.) She glanced at the clock and was considering calling the lab to see if he'd started out when she heard his key in the lock.

In contrast to his attractive young wife, Isaac Hirsh was short, fat, and fifty. He had a fringe of grizzled iron-gray hair around a bald head, and a short bristly moustache under his bulbous, red-veined nose. She bent forward to kiss him perfunctorily, then said, "I told you I was going to baby-sit for Liz Marcus. I promised to be over early."

"You have plenty of time, baby. They don't start services until after seven, maybe not till quarter past, just before sundown."

"How would you know?" she said. "You haven't gone in years."

"Some things you don't forget, baby."

"Well, if you can't forget it, why don't you go?"

He shrugged his shoulders and sat down at the table. "I mean it's like Christmas, isn't it? I don't go to church and we never did much back home, but I always feel I've got to celebrate Christmas. When Ma and Pa were alive, I always made a point of trying to get back to South Bend." She began serving his dinner. "It's like that, isn't it?"

He considered. "Yes, for some it's like that. But for most, it's like anything religious—a kind of superstition. And I just don't happen to be superstitious."

She sat down opposite him and watched him eat. He spoke between mouthfuls. "There are some Jews who let on to be awfully proud of being Jews, although they had nothing to do with it and it certainly wasn't of their own choosing. . . . And there are some that are sorry they were born Jews. It's the same feeling really, just turned inside out." He waved his spoon at her. "Nothing so much resembles a hollow as a swelling. So they do what they can to change it—poor buggers."

She took the plate away and brought him another.

"If they go out of town, they change their names," he went on. "If they remain in their hometown, it's not so easy but they work at it. I'm a Jew, and I'm not proud of it and I'm not sorry for it. I don't try to hide it, but I don't glory in it either. It's what I am because it's what I was born. It's just a pigeonhole, a category, and you can make categories any way you like—shift them up or down, one side or the other."

"I don't understand."

"Well, you come from South Bend. Are you proud of it? Do you regret it? You're a female—"

"There have been times when I've been sorry for that, I can tell you."

He nodded. "All right, maybe I've been sorry a couple of times. It's only human." He grew reflective. "At that, I guess I've been lucky. In science it doesn't matter so much. If I had gone into business or one of the professions like medicine where a lot of doors are closed to you if you're Jewish, maybe I would have regretted it more and then I might have tried to do something about it—hide it, or gone the other way. But in my field, in math research, it's no particular liability. In fact, some people even think we've got a special knack; it gives us an edge, like an Italian looking for a job with an opera company."

"My, aren't we getting philosophical."

"Maybe. Fact is I'm bushed. That can make a man philosophical—just being tired."

"Has Sykes been bearing down on you?" she asked, at once sympathetic. "He called you, by the way."

"Sykes? When did he call?"

"About ten or fifteen minutes before you got home. He wanted you to call him back."

"All right."

"Aren't you going to call him?"

"No, I'll run up later and see him at the lab. That's probably what he wanted."

"But you're tired," she protested, "and it's your holiday too."

"Oh, Sykes knows I don't go to the synagogue. The old man has been chewing him out so naturally he's on my tail."

"Is something wrong, Ike?" she asked anxiously.

He shrugged his shoulders. "The usual headaches. You get an idea and it looks good. So you work on it and work on it, and then it turns out sour."

"That happens all the time in research, doesn't it?"

"Sure, and for the boys in pure research at the universities, it doesn't make any difference. But with us, where we're working for industry, and you've got to charge the customer, it can become a little sticky. This job was for Goraltronics, and they're not easy people to work for at any time. Right now, for some reason, they seem jumpier than ever, and it rubs off on everyone else down the line. Well, let the big

20

boys worry, I'm just one of the peasants. I do my work and draw my pay."

"Then you'll be working late?"

"Maybe a couple of hours. Why?"

"Peter Dodge called earlier to say he might drop by."

"To see me or to see you?"

She colored. "Oh, Ike—"

He laughed at her embarrassment. "I'm just kidding, baby. C'mere."

She came over and he put his arm around her and nuzzled her thigh while massaging her buttock with his hand.

"He's just friendly because we're from the same hometown," she said defensively.

The phone rang and she left him to answer it, saying over her shoulder, "That's probably Sykes again wondering why you didn't call back."

But it was the petulant, metallic voice of Liz Marcus. "Hey, Pat, I thought you promised to get here early." Turning to her husband, she said, "Got to go, dear. Try not to let him keep you there too late."

"Right, baby."

From the door, she pursed her lips in a token kiss.

4

To native Barnard's Crossers the sprawling Goralsky showplace was always referred to as "the old Northcliffe estate." It had passed to the Goralskys three years before, and Myron Landis, the local realtor who had negotiated the sale, never tired of telling how the purchase was made. "Cinny Northcliffe—that's the young one, although she was the last one and was a good sixty or sixty-five at the time— gave me an exclusive in this area on the estate, and I ran an ad in the Boston papers. A hundred-twenty-thousand-dollar proposition, I figured it was worth a fifty-dollar ad. So the next day, in come these two characters: an old geezer with a beard, and this feller, his son, maybe fifty years old or so. And the old guy says—he does the talking, and he's got an accent you can hardly understand him—'You the agent the Nortcliff place?'

"So I says, 'Yes, sir.'

"So then he says, 'So how much they asking?'

"And I say, 'One hundred and twenty thousand dollars.'

"So then he gives his son a nod and they go over to the corner of the room and they argue a little. I could hear what they're saying, but it's not in English so it don't do me any good. So then they come back to the desk and the young man writes out a check and he gives it to the old man to sign. And the old man he takes off his glasses and he puts on another pair. And he reads over the check, his head moving from side to side and his lips moving like he's spelling it out. Then he takes out a fountain pen, one of those old-fashioned kind that you fill, and he shakes it a couple of times and then writes his name like he has to draw each letter. Then he hands it to me and it's a check for a hundred thousand dollars signed by a Moses Goralsky.

"So I say, 'This is for a hundred thousand. The price is a hundred and twenty thousand.' Which is a kind of crazy thing to say, because of course you don't buy property that way. Without even showing the place or answering questions. To say nothing of arranging financing, a mortgage, a second mortgage. I mean I never sold property like that before. A check for five thousand, or even a thousand as a binder, or even an option—that would be normal, you understand. So he says, 'You get in touch with your seller. Say you got a check for a hundred thousand dollars. I can have certify if you want.' So naturally I got in touch with Miss Northcliffe and she says to go ahead. I told her, 'Miss Northcliffe, where they offer a hundred I'm sure they'll go the other twenty.' And you know what she says? She says, 'Landis, you're a damn fool, and you don't know the first thing about business. Take his offer.' And that's how it went."

It was a large gray stone mansion, set well back from the street by a few acres of lawn, and encircled by a high iron fence. The rear of the house faced the sea, in fact was part of the sea wall, and as the car approached the front gate Rabbi Small and Miriam could hear the pounding of the surf against the wall and feel the chill ocean air.

The car circled the driveway and stopped at the front door. The chauffeur jumped out and opened the door for them. Almost immediately they were joined by Ben Goralsky, a tall, heavy man, swarthy, with bluish jowls and heavy black eyebrows.

He grasped the rabbi's hand and wrung it gratefully. "Thank you, Rabbi, thank you. I would have come for you myself but I didn't like to leave my father." He turned to the chauffeur. "You can go now, but leave the car here. I'll drive them back." To his guests he explained, "All the servants except the housekeeper have tonight and tomorrow off. My father's idea that they mustn't work because they are of our household. But I'll drive you to the temple myself. Don't worry, you'll get there in time."

"How is he?" asked the rabbi.

"Not good. The doctor just left about half an hour ago. We had Hamilton Jones. You've heard of him, I'm sure. The biggest man in the field—professor at Harvard."

"Your father's conscious?"

"Oh, sure. Sometimes he dozes off for a little but he's conscious all right."

"Was this something sudden? It seems to me I saw him only recently at the minyan."

"That's right, Tuesday—Tuesday he went to the minyan. Then Wednesday he's a little out of sorts, and Thursday he runs a little fever and he's coughing, and then today when it keeps up I figure I better bring in somebody. It's a strep infection, the doctor says. And you know how it is, he's an old man —at his age, any little cold it can become serious."

They paused in the ornate foyer. "Do you mind waiting here, Mrs. Small?" asked Goralsky. "The housekeeper is upstairs—"

"Certainly, Mr. Goralsky. I'll be all right. Don't mind me."

"This way, Rabbi." He led him to the wide marble staircase, which had a thick-piled red carpet running down the middle.

"When did he ask for me?" the rabbi asked.

"Oh, he didn't ask for you, Rabbi. It was my idea." Suddenly Goralsky seemed embarrassed. "You see, he won't take his medicine."

The rabbi stopped and looked at him incredulously.

Goralsky too stopped. "You don't understand. The doctor said he had to take his medicine every four hours—all through the night. We even have to wake him up to give it to him. I told the doctor I didn't like to wake him up, and he said if I wanted my father to live I'd wake him. They have no heart, these doctors. To him, my father is just a case. This is what I tell you to do—do it or don't do it, that's your business."

"And you want me to give him his medicine?"

Goralsky seemed desperate to make the rabbi understand.

"The medicine I can give him, or the housekeeper. But he won't take it because it's Yom Kippur and it will mean breaking his fast."

"But that's nonsense. The rule doesn't apply to the sick."

"I know, but he's stubborn. I thought maybe you could convince him. Maybe he'll take it from you."

They had come to the first-floor landing, and now Goralsky led him down a short corridor. "Right here," he said, and pushed open the door.

The housekeeper rose when they entered, and Goralsky motioned her to wait outside. The room was in marked contrast to the rest of the house, or that portion the rabbi had been able to see as they went up the stairs. In the center of the room was a large, old-fashioned brass bed, in which, propped up by pillows, the old man lay. A large roll-topped oak desk, scratched and scarred and piled high with papers, stood against the wall, and in front was a mahogany swivel chair of the same vintage; on top of its cracked leatherette cushion was another of well-worn tapestry, long removed from some ancient sofa. There were a couple of straight-backed chairs covered in green plush that the rabbi assumed probably had been part of the Goralsky dining-room furniture.

"The rabbi has come to see you, Papa," said Goralsky.

"I thank him," said the old man. He was small with a pale, waxen face, and a straggly beard. His dark eyes, sunk deep in bony sockets, were bright with fever. One thin hand picked nervously at the coverlet.

"How do you feel, Mr. Goralsky?" asked the rabbi.

"Nasser should feel like this." He smiled in self-deprecation.

The rabbi smiled back at him. "So why don't you take your medicine?"

The old man shook his head slowly. "On Yom Kippur, Rabbi, I fast."

"But the regulation to fast doesn't apply to medicine. It's an exception, a special rule."

"About special rules, exceptions, Rabbi, I don't know. What I do, I learned from my father, may he rest in peace. He was not a learned man, but there wasn't another one in the village in the old country who could touch him for praying. He believed in God like in a father. He didn't ask questions and he didn't make exceptions. Once, when I was maybe thirteen or fourteen years old, he was in the house saying his morning prayers when some peasants pushed open the door. They had been drinking and they were looking for trouble. They shouted to my father he should give them some *bromphen*, brandy. My mother and I, we were frightened, and she hugged me, but my father didn't look at them and he didn't even skip a word in his prayer. One of them came up to him, and my mother screamed, but my father went on praying. Then the others, they must have got nervous, because they pulled their friend back, and then they left the house."

His son obviously had heard the story many times for he made a grimace of impatience, but his father did not notice and went on. "My father worked hard, and he always managed to feed us and clothe us. And with me, it's the same way. I always obeyed the rules, and God always took care of me. Sometimes I worked harder and sometimes there was trouble, but looking back it was more good than bad. So what I'm told to do, I do, and this must be what God wants because He gave me a good wife who lived till she was full of years, and good sons, and in my old age He even made me rich."

"Do you think that the regulations—to pray, to keep the Sabbath, to fast on Yom Kippur—do you think these are good-luck charms?" the rabbi said. "God also gave you a mind to reason with and to use to protect the life He entrusted to your care."

The old man shrugged his shoulders.

"In fact, if you are sick, the regulation specifically states that you must not fast. And it's not an exception either. It's a general principle that is basic to our religion."

"So who says I'm sick? A doctor says I'm sick, that makes me sick?"

"All day he goes on like that," said Ben admiringly. "A mind like a steel trap." To his father he said, "Look, Papa, I asked Dr. Bloom who we should get and he tells me Dr. Hamilton Jones is the best there is. So we get Hamilton Jones. He's not just any doctor; he's a professor, from Harvard College."

"Mr. Goralsky," said the rabbi earnestly, "man was created in God's image. So to disregard the health of the body that was entrusted to our care, God's image, Mr. Goralsky, this is a serious sin. It is *chillul ha-Shem*, an affront to the Almighty."

"Look, Rabbi, I'm an old man. For seventy-five years at least—seventy-five years I can give you a guarantee—I fasted on Yom Kippur. So this Yom Kippur you think I'm going to eat?"

"But medicine is not eating, Mr. Goralsky."

"When I take in my mouth and I swallow, by me this is eating."

"You can't beat him," Ben Goralsky murmured in the rabbi's ear.

"Do you realize, Mr. Goralsky," said the rabbi seriously, "that if, God forbid, you should die because you refused medication, it could be considered suicide."

The old man grinned.

The rabbi realized that the old man was enjoying this, that he was deriving a perverse sort of pleasure from debating with a young rabbi. David Small wanted to smile, but he made one last effort and managed to sound somber and portentous. "Think, Mr. Goralsky. If I should judge you a suicide, you would not receive formal burial. There would be no eulogy over your grave. There would be no public mourning. No Kaddish would be recited in your memory. According to strict interpretation of the Law, you might be buried in a corner off to one side of the cemetery—you couldn't even be placed beside your dear wife—and your children and grandchildren would be shamed—"

The old man held up a thin, blue-veined hand. "Look, Rabbi, in all my life I never did anybody any harm. I never cheated; I never bore false witness. Fifty years I'm in business for myself and show me one person who can say I took from him a penny. So I'm sure God will take care of me and not let me die tonight."

The rabbi couldn't resist the gambit. "If you are on such good terms with the Almighty, Mr. Goralsky, then why did He let you get sick in the first place?"

The old man smiled as though his opponent had fallen into the trap he had set. "Such a question! If He didn't let me get sick, so how could He make me well?"

"He can stop you like that every time," said the son.

"Don't worry, Rabbi," said the old man. "I'm not going to die tonight. Benjamin, send in the woman. You better go now; you'll be late for Kol Nidre." He closed his eyes in dismissal.

As the two men walked down the stairs, the rabbi said, "I'm afraid I wasn't of much help." He looked at his host curiously. "But I would have thought he would listen to you—"

"When does a parent ever listen to a child, Rabbi?" asked Goralsky bitterly. "To him, I'm just a boy. He's proud when other people say nice things about me. Last year, I was written up in *Time* magazine and he carried the clipping in his wallet and pulled it out and showed it to people whenever my name was mentioned. And if it wasn't mentioned, he'd bring it up himself: 'Did you read about my son, Benjamin?' But when it comes to taking my advice, that's another story. In matters of business, at least, he listens; but when it's his own personal health—talk to the wall."

"Has he been well all along?"

"He's never sick. He doesn't see a doctor from one year to the next. That's the trouble: he thinks he is indestructible and when something like this happens, he won't do anything about it."

"He must be pretty old."

"Eighty-four," said Goralsky proudly.

"Then maybe he's right," suggested the rabbi. "After all, you can't argue with success. If, at his age, he is well and never sees a doctor, then he's probably learned instinctively how to take care of himself."

"Maybe, Rabbi, maybe. Well, thanks anyway for trying. I'll drive you and Mrs. Small to the temple now."

"Aren't you coming to services?"

"No, I think tonight to be on the safe side I better hang around here."

5

A light panel truck bearing the sign Jackson's Liquor Mart drove up to the Levensons across the street from the Hirsh house. The driver got out and stood at the front door with a small parcel under his arm. He pushed the doorbell and waited. He rang again, his fingers drumming a nervous tattoo on the aluminum cover of his voucher book. Just then he saw Isaac Hirsh leave his house and start for his car. He hailed him and walked over.

"You live in that house, Mister?"

"That's right."

"You know"—he peered at the name on the package—"Charles Levenson?"

"Sure. That's his house right there."

"Yeah, I know." Suddenly the driver was exasperated.

"Look, this is my last delivery today and I'm running late. And tomorrow all my deliveries are on the other side of town. There's no one home, and I hate to leave this where anyone can get at it, if you know what I mean. Would you mind taking this and giving it to Mr. Levenson when you see him tomorrow?"

"Why not?"

"Fine. Sign here."

Tweaking the belly of the toy troll suspended from the rearview mirror, Hirsh set it dancing on its elastic. "Wasn't that a gurgle we heard, Herr Einstein?" The little figure with its wild mop of hair seemed to nod in agreement. "This needs looking into, I should say," and suiting the action to the word, he carefully opened the package and extracted a bottle. "A fifth of vodka no less, and of the right brand." He held the enclosed card under the dashboard light and read, 'To Charlie Levenson for a Happy Birthday.' "Very touching, don't you think, Einstein, old friend? I am strongly tempted to drink a toast to our friend and neighbor Charlie Levenson. But first let us consider. It's been six months since we've had a drink. What's that you say? Nearer eight months? Well, perhaps you're right. Either way, it's a long time between drinks. On the one hand, it's a shame to spoil the record, but on the other hand, only a lout would refuse to drink good old Charlie's health. Did I hear you say something? You say I don't know when to stop once I begin? You've got a point there, old friend, but how do we know unless we test ourselves every now and then? After all, we didn't ask for this; we didn't go looking for it. We were just minding our business, setting out for the lab, and this comes along, out of the blue, you might say. Now I'd call that an omen. And on this night, particularly. And suppose we do overdo it a little, what's the harm? Tomorrow is Saturday and we can sleep as late as we like. You say Levenson will miss his bottle? Why, that's the beauty of the thing, old friend. Charlie's off to temple and won't be home till late. Being it's Yom Kippur he won't or he shouldn't—feel like taking a drink. Then tomorrow before he gets back from services all we have to do is buy another bottle and he'll never know. I say, we should vote on it. All in favor say Aye. All opposed Nay—The Ayes have it."

He unscrewed the cap and took an experimental nip. "Just as I said, Einstein, old friend, it's the right brand."

28

He took another drink and then recapped the bottle. "Yes, sir, it seems to be clearing the cobwebs out of the brain. And tonight of all nights we need a clear head." He set the car in motion.

Several times along the way he stopped to toast Charlie's good health. Behind him, he heard the loud blare of an automobile horn. He swung his car to the right; the wheel grated against the road divider and he swung left. Once again there was the blare of a horn, and a car swept around him and hung alongside for a moment as the driver cursed at him.

"You know what, Einstein? Traffic here on Route 128 is moving just a little too fast for us. The old brain is clear as a bell, but the reflexes are a bit slow. What say we stop for a while? There's a turnout ahead just a couple of hundred yards before we get to the lab where we can let things kind of catch up."

He pulled to a stop. He fumbled clumsily with the wrapper of the bottle. Then, in annoyance, he ripped off the wrapping paper and cardboard box and with a lordly gesture threw them out the window. "The big trick is to time yourself. You time yourself, and there's no problem." He turned off the motor and headlights. "Better wait half an hour or so, grab a little shut-eye maybe, and then go on to the lab. You mark my words, Einstein, old friend, if past experience is any guide, when I wake up the old brain will be ticking like a regular computer."

6

The Smalls arrived at the temple just in time. The rabbi left Miriam to make her way through the front door where stragglers were still coming in, and hurried to a side door that led to the vestry and the narrow staircase to the enrobing room adjoining the altar. The room had become something of a catchall for old prayer books, florists' baskets used to decorate the altar, piles of cantorial music, and two coils of BX cable left by the electricians when the building was constructed some three years before. The rabbi hung up his topcoat and hat and put on his skullcap and the white robe

29

which was the conservative compromise on the orthodox kittel or grave vestment. Then bracing against his locker—there was no chair—he changed from street shoes to white rubber-soled canvas shoes, a modern compromise on the ancient Mishnah ban against wearing shoes during the day of prayer. Lastly he draped his silk prayer shawl over his shoulders, and after a glance in the mirror opened the door that led to the altar.

On either side of the Ark were two high-backed red velvet chairs. The two on the far side were occupied by the vice-president and cantor; the two nearest the anteroom were reserved for himself and the president of the congregation, Mortimer Schwarz. He came forward and shook hands with the president, then crossed in front of the Ark to shake hands with the cantor and Ely Kahn, the vice-president. He returned to his chair and looked around at the congregation, nodding to members who happened to catch his eye.

"You cut it rather fine, Rabbi," said Schwarz. He was a tall, youngish-looking man of fifty, with thin gray-black hair slicked back as if to emphasize his high forehead. He had a long thin face and a thin, high-bridged nose. His mouth was small and the lips full and round, almost as though pursed or kissing. He was an architect; and something about his dress, the long points of his shirt collar, the thickly knotted tie, suggested some connection with the arts. He was good-looking, even handsome; and his posture and general movements—not studied, but controlled—suggested he knew it. With the rabbi he maintained an armed truce which manifested itself in a kind of jocose teasing that occasionally developed an unpleasant edge.

"For a Hadassah meeting, or a Sisterhood committee meeting," he went on, "understandable. Ethel tells me that they don't even expect you to remember. They have an unofficial Rabbi Delivering Committee whose job it is to keep reminding you of the meeting date, and if necessary to go fetch you. She thinks it adds spice to the meeting: will the rabbi turn up in time or not? It's a convenient trait, since I suppose it enables you to miss an occasional meeting. But Kol Nidre, Rabbi! I wonder you were able to find a parking place."

"Oh, Miriam and I plan to walk home. I'm a little old-fashioned about these things."

"You walked? Why didn't you tell me and I would have arranged to get you a ride?"

"I did ride. As a matter of fact, I rode in style, in a Lincoln

Continental, I believe. Just as I was leaving the house, Ben Goralsky called and insisted I had to see his father. A matter of life and death, he said. So I couldn't very well refuse. Ben drove me down afterward."

Schwarz sounded suddenly concerned. "Something's the matter with the old man? It sounds serious if they sent for you."

The rabbi grinned. "He wouldn't take his medicine."

Schwarz frowned his disapproval of the rabbi's levity. In his relation with the rabbi, humor was a one-way street. "This is serious business. Tell me, is something really wrong?"

"Any time a man that age gets sick, it's serious, I suppose. But I think he'll be all right." He went on briefly to describe his visit.

The frown did not lift from the president's handsome face; if anything, it grew more pronounced. "You mean to say you threatened old man Goralsky with a suicide's grave, Rabbi? You must have offended him."

"I don't think so. I think he rather enjoyed fencing with me. He could see that I was more than half fooling."

"I certainly hope so."

"Why this tremendous interest in Mr. Goralsky? He's a member, to be sure, but a relatively new one and rather a cantankerous one at that."

"Yes, they're new. When was it they joined? About a year ago, wasn't it, when the old lady died and they bought the big center lot in the cemetery? But with their kind of money, they're important. Surely I don't have to tell you, Rabbi, that when you're running an organization like this, you need money. And if you don't have money—and what synagogue does?—the next best thing is to have members who do."

"I've heard something to that effect. But surely it must be the son, Ben, who has the money."

Schwarz's face brightened and he looked straight out at the congregation. Then he leaned toward the rabbi and said, "You'd think so, wouldn't you? But actually the father is everything, and the son, at least while the father is alive, is just a messenger boy."

"And the father is willing to give and the son is not?"

"You don't get the picture, Rabbi." He gestured with his hands spread as if to frame the picture. "The money, they're both prepared to give. When you accumulate the kind of money they have, you're prepared to give some of it away. It's expected of you. It goes with your status like Continentals and a uniformed chauffeur. Now the old man has been a pious Jew all his life. As you know, he comes to the minyan almost every day when the weather permits. So a man like that, his idea of giving away money is to give it to a temple.

"But Ben? Ben is a businessman through and through. When a businessman decides that the time has come to give charity, he views it as a business proposition. He is buying *kovod*, honor. And naturally he wants to get the most for his *kovod* dollar. If he uses the money to build a chapel—say the Goralsky Memorial Chapel—who will see it? Who will know about it except the folks here in Barnard's Crossing? But," he lowered his voice, "suppose he were to donate a laboratory to Brandeis or even to Harvard? The Goralsky Chemical Research Laboratory? Eh? Scientists and scholars from all over the world would get to hear of it."

The congregation had quieted as people began to settle down, their eyes now on the altar in anticipation. The rabbi glanced at the clock and said he thought they had better begin.

The two men rose and beckoned the cantor and the vice-president on the other side of the Ark with a nod. The cantor pulled the cord that parted the white velvet curtains in front of the Ark. As he slid back the wooden doors of the Ark to expose the precious Scrolls of the Law, the congregation rose.

The president, reading from a slip of paper, called the names of half a dozen of the more important members of the congregation to come forward, and they ascended the steps to the altar and the cantor handed each of them a Scroll. When all the Scrolls were received, the men clustered around the reading desk facing the congregation and the rabbi recited first in Hebrew and then in English the ancient formula that traditionally introduces the Yom Kippur service: "By the authority of the Court on high, and by the authority of the Court below, by permission of God and by permission of this holy congregation, we hold it lawful to pray with the transgressors."

Then the cantor began the mournful yet uplifting chant of the Kol Nidre. Three times he would chant the prayer, and by the time he had finished the sun would have gone down and the Day of Atonement, the Sabbath of Sabbaths, would have begun.

"How did the public-address system work out?" asked

Miriam as they walked home from the service. "Did it put much of a strain on your voice?"

"Not a bit. I just spoke a little slower." He chuckled. "But our president was quite upset. Every time he got up to announce the names of those who had honors, they had difficulty hearing him. The Ritual Committee sends out notices indicating the approximate time a man will be called, but we were running a little late and there was some confusion. A Mr. Goldman, who sits well back, didn't hear his name, so Mr. Schwarz took the next name on the list and that upset the whole schedule. Did you get that bit at the end? When Marvin Brown was called?"

"Yes, what happened?"

"Well, I guess he didn't hear his name, but instead of calling up a substitute as he had been doing all evening, Schwarz kept repeating the name. I suppose because Marvin is a special friend of his and he didn't want him to miss his honor, even though it was just to open the Ark. Finally, after he called Mr. Brown, Mr. Marvin Brown, two or three times, the vice-president came over and opened the Ark himself. Our president was a little annoyed with him for it."

"It seems a small thing to make a fuss about."

"Mr. Schwarz evidently didn't consider it so. As a matter of fact, he kept grousing a good part of the evening about the acoustics. At first I thought it was professional jealousy, but then I got the feeling he had something else in mind. Especially when he said something about expecting us at his house tomorrow after we broke our fast. Did Mrs. Schwarz call you?"

"This morning. Ethel invited us for dessert and coffee. Isn't it the usual custom? Don't we always go to the president's house for coffee after Yom Kippur?"

"I guess we do at that. But somehow, when Mr. Wasserman and even Mr. Becker were president, I didn't think of it as a custom. I felt they asked us over, as they did on other occasions, because they wanted to see us. But I don't feel it's quite the same with Mortimer Schwarz. You know, in your present condition, we could easily duck it."

"There'll be a lot of other people there, David; we won't have to stay long. Ethel seemed particularly anxious for us to come. Maybe they're just trying to be nice and show they want to let bygones be bygones."

The rabbi looked doubtful.

"You both seemed quite friendly up there on the platform."

"Naturally, we're not going to sit there and glare at each other. On the surface everything is fine. We even joke with each other, although it's apt to be rather patronizing on his part—the way I would imagine he jokes with his junior draftsman. When I answer in kind, I get the feeling he regards it as an impertinence, although of course he wouldn't say so."

She was troubled. "Aren't you perhaps imagining a lot of this because he opposed renewing your contract when it came up before the Board?"

"I don't think so. There were others who opposed me, and when I was voted my five-year contract they came up to congratulate me. When my five years are up they may oppose me again, but in the meantime, they will remain neutral and work with me. With Schwarz, on the other hand, I have the feeling that if he could get me out tomorrow, he would."

"But that's just the point, David, he can't. You have a five-year contract that has four more years to go. And his term of office is only one year. You'll outlast him."

"It really isn't much of a contract, you know," he said.

"I don't understand."

"It's a service contract, which means they can't drop me as long as I behave myself. What constitutes proper behavior is up to them to decide, while nothing is said about *their* behavior. They can do all kinds of things against which I have no recourse. Suppose they decide to make some change in the ritual that I couldn't possibly live with. What happens then? The only thing I could do would be to resign."

"And you think Schwarz might do something like that?"

"Just to get me out? No. But we could disagree about something, and he might use that as an excuse. And to give him his due, he'd probably feel it was for the good of the congregation."

7

Just before midnight the call came in. "Barnard's Crossing Police Department," the man at the desk said. "Sergeant Jeffers. Yes, I see . . . Do you want to give me the name again? . . . H-I-R-S-H, no C . . . Mrs. Isaac Hirsh."

He repeated as he wrote, "Bradford Lane . . . that's in Colonial Village, isn't it? . . . Now what time did he leave? . . . Well then, what time did you call the lab? . . . I see . . . Can you give me a description of the car and the license number? . . . Any marks on the car? . . . All right, ma'am, I'll notify State Police and local police departments to be on the lookout. And I'll have the cruising car stop by at your house. . . . In a few minutes. Will you put your porch light on, please . . . We'll do everything we can, ma'am."

The patrol car answered his signal right away. "Take this down, Joe. Chevrolet, four-door sedan, light blue, rusty dent on left rear fender. License number 438,972, repeat, 438,-972. Isaac Hirsh, 4 Bradford Lane. It's next to the corner. The porch light will be on. His wife just called in. He works at the Goddard Lab on Route 128. She was out baby-sitting for a neighbor, and when she got back he had gone. Nothing unusual, he's apt to run down to the lab and work at night. But she called the lab a little while ago and he wasn't there and hadn't been there. Stop over and talk to her. See if she's got a picture of him we can broadcast."

"Okay, Sarge. Say—Isaac Hirsh—isn't that the guy who went on a toot some months back and we finally located him in a dive in the South End in Boston?"

"Yeah, come to think of it. I'll notify Boston police to keep an eye out for him. That's probably what happened—got thirsty again. When you go over, kind of suggest that she look around and see if anything is missing, like the cooking sherry or his aftershave bay rum. Those guys will drink anything when it hits them."

"Got it, Sarge." He turned to his partner. "Let's go, Tommy boy."

"What is it, a missing drunk? Why don't we stop at a couple of places downtown first, The Foc'sle and the Sea and Sand, and see if he's there."

"Not that kind of drunk, Tommy. He's some hot-shot scientist. He don't drink, except every now and then he goes on a big toot that lasts for days, even weeks. Last time, at least last time we know about on account of the missus calling in, he was missing three days. It must have been all of eight months ago, maybe more. The Boston police finally found him holed up in a filthy little dive of a hotel in the South End. He was lying in bed fully dressed with a pile of dead soldiers on the floor. I don't think he had eaten in all that time. Mark my words, when we turn him up, it'll probably be another such place. Ah, here we are, the house with the porch light. I recognize it now, we took him home in the ambulance last time. You wait here in case the sergeant calls in."

Patricia Hirsh opened the door before he had a chance to ring. "Thank you for coming so quickly, Officer." Although she was obviously agitated, her voice was controlled.

"Just as soon as we got the message, ma'am." He took out his notebook and pencil from the thigh pocket of his uniform. "Now, can you tell me what your husband was wearing?"

"Oh." She went to the hall closet. "A light topcoat—it's gray, dark gray herringbone. And—no, his hat is here. Underneath he had on a regular business suit—dark brown."

"And can you give me a description of him, height, weight, and so on?"

"He's quite plump. He weighs about a hundred and ninety pounds and is about five three." As he looked up involuntarily, she said, "Yes, he's shorter than I am. He's also quite a bit older. He's fifty-one, and bald," she added defiantly, "with a moustache."

"You got a picture of him, ma'am?"

"Yes, upstairs in the bedroom. Would you like me to get it?"

"If you please." As she started for the stairs, he called after her, "I'll just give this information to my partner outside so he can call it in right away."

At the car he asked Tommy if there had been any calls. His partner shook his head, then said: "Better check out the house, Joe. The garage door, I notice it's down. When we first came on duty about eight o'clock a number of them were up. Probably because so many people were over at the temple."

"Okay, I'll check it. Meantime, call in this description." And after repeating what Mrs. Hirsh had told him, he went back to the house. She was waiting for him with the picture. He took it, studied it for a moment, then said gently, "You haven't noticed anything missing, have you?"

"I haven't looked. Like what?"

"Well, like whiskey—"

"We don't have it in the house."

"Cooking sherry?"

"I don't use it."

"Maybe bay rum or rubbing alcohol?"

"No, nothing like that."

36

"All right, ma'am. We get right on to it. Why don't you just go to bed. I'll let myself out through the back."

"That only leads to the garage."

"Never hurts to look around, ma'am."

"You'll call me—no matter what time, won't you?"

"Sure will." Making his way through the kitchen to the garage, he opened the back door, and then quickly closed it behind him. The car was in the garage, and on the front seat, on the passenger side, was Isaac Hirsh.

Even slim as he was, it was a tight squeeze for Joe between the wall of the garage and the car, but he managed. He opened the front door and leaned across the driver's seat to touch the man. By the light of his flashlight he noted the position of the key in the ignition switch. He noted the half-empty vodka bottle. Then he withdrew and closed the car door. Squeezing his way to the front of the garage he raised the overhead door just enough to duck under, and pulled it down after him.

He got into the cruising car, but as the driver started to shift into gear he held onto his hand. "No, Tommy, we're not going anywhere. I've found him. He's in the garage."

"Dead to the world?"

"Yeah, only this time it's for good."

8

The daylong Yom Kippur services began at nine with the recital of morning prayers. Only a handful of people were in the temple, mostly the older men, and on the platform only the rabbi was in his seat. Even the cantor had not yet arrived, since it was customary to have someone else lead the morning service to give him a measure of relief. The honor usually went to Jacob Wasserman, the first president of the temple and the man who more than anyone else had organized the congregation. His voice made up in genuine fervor what it lacked in volume, and the rabbi enjoyed his chanting with its traditional quavers and trills more than the studied effects of the cantor who surreptitiously would stoop and tap his tuning fork and hum the pitch before beginning a chant.

37

The congregation kept drifting in all morning. Shortly after the cantor took his seat, Mortimer Schwarz appeared. He shook hands ceremoniously with the rabbi, and then crossed over to shake hands with the cantor. He returned to his seat and whispered that, just as he had expected, Marvin Brown called last night.

"You mean about the honor he missed?"

"Well, Rabbi, he didn't come right out and say so, but I know that's what it was."

"I wouldn't have thought it meant so much to him."

"Oh, I don't think he's particularly religious. But he's a salesman first, last, and always. And, something like that, he builds it up in his mind as kind of good luck. And if he should somehow miss out, it could throw him off stride. Do you understand?"

"I can understand how he might feel that way," said the rabbi.

"Well, I don't mind saying I felt Ely Kahn kind of jumped the gun by going ahead and opening the Ark when Marvin didn't come down right away. Nothing terrible would have happened if we'd waited a few minutes. Anyway, today I'm going to be extra careful. I'll call out these names good and loud, and we'll wait until we're sure the person is not in the temple before picking a substitute."

By a quarter past ten, when the Scrolls were removed from the Ark for the Reading, the sanctuary was full. Some chose to regard this point in the service as a recess; and while a few left, most remained. For the Memorial Service for the Dead that followed, the Yizkor service, the sanctuary filled up again. Many came just for this portion out of a sense of respect for departed members of their immediate family. Traditionally it was considered bad luck for anyone whose parents were alive to be present, but the rabbi, like most Conservative rabbis, felt this to be idle superstition. He began by explaining that it was proper for all to attend, that since those who had died in the Nazi holocaust were going to be memorialized, everyone could consider himself bereaved; but here and there he could see some of the older congregants brought up in Orthodoxy urge their children to leave.

However, after Yizkor he could not help feeling pleased to note a large portion of the young people return, presumably to hear his sermon. One portion of the Holy Day service described the way the High Priest of ancient times purified himself and his family before making the sacrifice to atone for the sins of his people. The sermon discussed this portion of the service, comparing this with the attempted sacrifice of Isaac by Abraham—a reference to the New Year Reading on Rosh Hashanah, the beginning of the ten Days of Awe. With many a rabbinic allusion, he explained that the sacrifice of Isaac was a stern injunction *against* the human sacrifice that was universally practiced at the time, and then went on to show how the whole concept of sacrifice and atonement had gradually changed from sacrificing a live scapegoat to the modern attitude toward prayer, which meant begging forgiveness—from the Lord for sins committed against Him as well as from individuals for sins committed against them.

As in all his sermons, the tone and style was instructional and informal, like a college lecture. He himself thought of his sermons as theses in which he attempted to explain seeming contradictions in the Law, rather than as exhortations. He knew some members of the congregation, including the president, grew restive during his discourse, and would have preferred a more oratorical, hortative style, but he felt his type of sermon was more in keeping with his basic function of teacher, implicit in the word "rabbi."

The service continued, the day wore on; people came and left, some to go home for a nap or perhaps even a hurried snack, while outside, boys and girls stood about in their new clothes, laughing and flirting. The very young played on the temple grounds, their high shrill voices sometimes disturbing the decorum inside, requiring one of the ushers to go out and lecture them for making noise while the service was in progress.

At four o'clock, it became apparent that they were proceeding too rapidly and the service was in danger of ending before sunset. The rabbi approached the reading desk, "We're running ahead of time, Cantor Zimbler. Can you slow it down?"

The cantor shrugged his shoulders. "What do you want me to do, Rabbi, hold the notes longer?"

The rabbi smiled. Then: "I guess we'd better have a recess." He announced that the congregation was praying with such fervor that they were outrunning the sun. "So we'll have a half-hour break."

There was a murmur of grateful laughter from the congregation but only a few left since those present at that hour represented the hard core of worshipers who came with the intention of remaining through the day. But they appreciated the respite and engaged their neighbors in a few minutes' conversation before returning to the concluding portion which ended with the blowing of the shofar.

The president stretched on his thronelike chair and turned to the rabbi. "You know, apropos of your sermon, it occurs to me I made a sacrifice of my own. This is the first year in a long time that I have fasted, and I feel fine, just fine. Other years, I didn't exactly eat, I mean, I didn't have a regular meal. I'd have some juice in the morning, and then around noon I might go home for a cup of coffee and a sandwich, but this year I felt, being president, I ought to go the distance. And though I feel a little weak, otherwise I'm just fine."

"Mr. Goralsky told me he had been doing it for seventy-five years, and it doesn't appear to have hurt him any."

"Gosh, I forgot all about the old man. Have you heard how he is? I haven't seen Ben around."

"I'm sure he hasn't been here or I would have seen him."

"That sounds bad, Rabbi. The old man must be very sick —Ben would have come for Yizkor at least, with his mother dead only recently, within the year."

"Not necessarily. They're quite Orthodox and according to custom those recently bereaved, who are still in the year of mourning, do not attend the Yizkor service."

"That so? Then, maybe that's it. I certainly hope so."

The rabbi regarded him curiously. "Are you really so sure of getting a large contribution from Mr. Goralsky?"

"I've talked to the old man—informally, you know," Schwarz said smugly. "No definite promise, of course, but I can tell he's receptive to the idea."

"And how big a contribution do you hope for?"

Schwarz looked at him in some surprise. "I told you about it last night, Rabbi. A memorial chapel."

"You mentioned it, but I thought it was just by way of example. You mean he really is interested in building a Goralsky Memorial Chapel? What kind of money would be involved?"

"Oh, a hundred thousand dollars—to a hundred and a half."

The rabbi pursed his lips in a soundless whistle. "They're in electronics?"

"That's right, electronics and transistors. They've got a big new plant on Route 128. They're loaded. Right now, I understand, they're planning to merge with some big outfit out West, and their stock has been going up like a skyrocket. It's doubled in the last couple of weeks. And they started in the poultry business."

"The poultry business?"

"The absolute truth. My grandmother used to buy fresh-killed chickens from their store in Chelsea, and the old man himself used to wait on her in a blood-smeared white apron and a straw hat. Then they got a little ahead of themselves and began to gamble in futures and made quite a bit of money. So they had spare money when a chance came to invest in a transistor company and they were on their way. They bought out their partner, the man who started the business, and after that they really began to expand. They were lucky enough to go public right at the boom, and the rest is financial history. Maybe you saw the write-up on Ben Goralsky in *Time* magazine?"

The rabbi shook his head.

"A column and a half plus picture. I tried to put him on the Board, but he said he was too busy." He sounded gloomy.

"And do you think if you got him on the Board he might be inclined to favor a chapel over a chemistry lab?"

"At least it would get him interested in our organization and its problems."

"But do we need a chapel? It seems to me we have plenty of room right now—"

Schwarz looked at him. "Rabbi, a growing organization *never* has plenty of room. If it's enough for today, then it's not enough for tomorrow. Besides, next to the high school, our sanctuary is the biggest auditorium in town. Once or twice in the past we've been asked for the loan of our facilities by outside organizations. Now, how does it sit with you to have a secular organization like Kiwanis, say, transacting their business right here in front of the Holy Ark?"

"Well—"

"But suppose we had a small chapel built right onto the wall behind us, a small jewel of a chapel that you could tell was a chapel and not a barracks or a light and power company office building?"

"You don't like this building?"

Schwarz smiled condescendingly. "Remember, Rabbi, I'm an architect by profession. Look, are you and Miriam coming over tonight after you break your fast? Ethel is expecting you."

"If Miriam is up to it."

"Good. I'll show you something that will knock your eye out."

From where she was sitting, Miriam signaled her husband with a nod. He left the pulpit and joined her as she made her way out of the sanctuary.

"Something wrong, dear?"

"I feel a little done in. I guess I've got used to napping in the afternoon. Alice Fine is going home, and I thought I'd get a ride with her."

"You'll make yourself some tea, won't you? Or perhaps a glass of warm milk would be even better. I think you should eat something. You sure you're all right?"

"Believe me, David, I feel fine."

"Anything wrong?" asked Schwarz when the rabbi returned to the pulpit. He told him Miriam felt a little tired.

"Well, it's understandable. I hope she's not fasting."

"She was, but she promised to eat something."

The sun began to set, and many of those who had left earlier returned to take part in the final congregational confession of sins, "We have trespassed, we have been faithless . . ." and to ask once again for forgiveness, "Our God and God of our fathers, pardon our iniquities on this Day of Atonement. . . . Accept, O Lord our God, thy people Israel and their prayer. . . ."

The sun set as they began to read responsively the *Ovenu Malkenu,* "Our Father, our King." Then in a voice of fervor and exultation, they declaimed, "Hear, O Israel: the Lord our God, the Lord is One," followed by "Blessed be His Name, whose glorious Kingdom is forever and ever," recited three times. Then seven times, the cantor and the congregation exclaimed, "The Lord, He is God," each time louder and more passionately, the last time climaxed by a long blast—eerie, piercing, and exultant—of the shofar, the ram's horn, signifying the end of the long day of Atonement and the ten Days of Awe.

The Mourner's Kaddish remained to be said, and a benediction by the rabbi, but the members of the congregation were already folding their prayer shawls and shaking hands with their neighbors and wishing them a healthy and happy New Year.

The rabbi shook hands with Mortimer Schwarz, with the cantor, and with the vice-president.

"See you tonight, Rabbi?" asked Schwarz.

"If Miriam feels well enough."

9

Reluctantly Jordan Marcus went to the telephone, but before picking up the instrument he made one more appeal. "I tell you, Liz, I still don't think we ought to get mixed up in this. We're new members, for one thing."

"So?" his wife said. "You paid your dues, didn't you?"

"You know damn well I did, and don't think that hundred bucks didn't hurt plenty, plus fifty bucks on top of that for two tickets—"

"So? So what did you want to do on the High Holidays? Go to the movies?"

"You didn't even have to show your tickets. We could have just walked in—"

"And when you got in you'd be invisible? The Levensons, the Baylisses—they wouldn't see you? And wouldn't know you're not a member?"

"We could have gone to my folks' place in Chelsea. It would have cost me ten bucks apiece for the tickets, and I would have saved myself a hundred and thirty bucks."

"And next year, when Monte has to start religious school, you'd take him to Chelsea three days a week, I suppose."

"So we could have joined next year. And that's a sweet little racket, by the way, making you join the temple so your kids can go to the religious school."

"They all do it, all the new temples. I guess they got to. Besides what's the difference if we join this year or next year?"

"A hundred and thirty bucks' difference."

"You want everybody to know you only joined at the last minute because you had to? You want everybody to think we're cheap?"

"Well, by God, I'd just as soon. I'm getting sick and tired of worrying about whether people think I'm cheap. I put in wall-to-wall broadloom for almost a thousand bucks so people wouldn't think I was cheap; I swapped the Chevy for a Pontiac so people wouldn't think I was cheap; and when Henry Bayliss suggests going to the Checkerboard for a bite after the movie, I got to say, Fine—swell idea, because if

I mention someplace where you can get a hamburg and coffee for under a buck, that means I'm cheap."

"So? That's gracious living. You're in Barnard's Crossing now. When in Rome you got to do like the Romans. We got a responsibility to the kids, and that's why you joined the temple. But now that you're a member in good standing, you got rights like anybody else. So stop stalling and call the rabbi."

"But, Liz, he's just got back from the temple. He's probably at dinner and must be starved. Besides, there's more involved than you realize. The bylaws say you got to be a bona fide member to be buried in the cemetery. Now you want me to ask the rabbi to forget the bylaws and make an exception for a friend of mine whose wife isn't even Jewish. That's what I mean I'm a new member. To ask a favor like this, you got to be one of the big shots. If it were a relative of mine, that's one thing. But this guy Hirsh, I hardly knew him. Maybe all the time we've been living here I've said Hello to him three times. I say we shouldn't get involved."

"But we are involved. Patricia Hirsh was right here in this house taking care of your kids while her husband was dying in his garage not a hundred feet away. Besides, didn't we tell her to have him buried by Jewish law?"

"You did; I didn't. As a matter of fact, seems to me she was already planning to anyway before we even got there. You just said, the way I remember, you thought it was a wonderful idea and we could talk to the rabbi. And she said that this Dr. Sykes, her husband's boss, was going to make all the arrangements, he planned to call the rabbi himself. If he's going to, why do we have to?"

"You keep forgetting I am practically her best friend around here and she was baby-sitting for us. It was all I could do to get you to go over to see her when we heard."

He had indeed been reluctant. He dreaded the weeping, the depressing conversation he associated with a house of mourning. But it turned out to be not so bad. Except for the Levensons across the street, the others present had all been Gentiles. Dr. Sykes, Hirsh's section head, seemed to be in charge. At least, he had come to the door and introduced them around. There was someone in a gray suit and Roman collar, the Reverend Peter Dodge, who seemed to know the family because he and Hirsh were both active in the Civil Rights movement. The MacCarthys who lived down the street were just going when they came in. Liz ran over and threw her arms around Mrs. Hirsh, and both of them had been teary for a minute, but then Mrs. Hirsh got control of herself. When the question of a Jewish ceremony came up, Dodge had even got her to smile when after saying he knew Rabbi Small well, they were both in the Ministers' Association, he added: "But I don't think it would be proper for me to ask him to officiate at the burial, Pat, not where we're business competitors, so to speak." And that's when Dr. Sykes said he was going to arrange everything.

Once outside, Jordon told his wife he had to hand it to her. "I was afraid we'd be stuck there all morning."

"When I saw what the situation was, I wasn't going to hang around," she answered primly. "This Dodge fellow, Pat knew him from South Bend where she came from. You notice he called her by her first name? He's not married. You notice how he was looking at her?"

"How was he looking at her?"

"You know, kind of hungry."

"Oh, Jesus. You dames, all you got on your minds. The guy isn't even buried yet, and you're already trying to marry her off."

As he dialed he rehearsed in his mind what he would say to the rabbi. "Rabbi Small? . . . Oh, Mrs. Small? Am I disturbing your dinner?"

"Is that the rabbi's wife?" Liz took the instrument from him. "Mrs. Small? This is Liz Marcus. I sat right behind you at the Hadassah meeting, and you asked me about taking off your hat when the film began? . . . Well, a very good friend of ours—she's not Jewish, but she's got a real Jewish heart. . . ."

"The Marcuses," Miriam explained as she returned to the table. "They're recent members—"

"Yes, I know. Joe, no, Jordan Marcus?"

"That's right. They called about an Isaac Hirsh who died last night. As a matter of fact, that's the second call. A Dr. Sykes called just after I got back from the temple. He wanted to see you about this same Isaac Hirsh. I made an appointment for him for tomorrow. Do we know an Isaac Hirsh?"

"He's not a member of the congregation. I don't think we even have an Isaac." He smiled. "Too bad, because around here, it's an old Yankee name. Isn't the Town Clerk Isaac Broadhurst?" He nodded at her middle. "How about Isaac for the coming Small?"

"You know we decided on Jonathan," she said with determination.

"I know, but it has been bothering me. It suggests David.

Now I'm David, and it might give the young man the idea that we were pals, friends, contemporaries—David and Jonathan. I'm afraid the young man might presume."

"Well, Isaac is out of the question," she said again. "Your uncle is named Isaac, and your family would never agree to another Isaac Small while he is still living."

"I suppose not. I'm inclined to believe the Christians are a little smarter than we in the matter of names. When they can't decide what to call a child, they can always use Junior. And then Second and Third. David Small the Third. Now there's a name for you!"

"It could be a girl, you know."

The rabbi appeared to consider. Then he shook his head. "I'm afraid not. My mother is a strong-minded woman. She has decided that the first one will be a boy. I don't think she'd countenance the change."

"I'm kind of strong-minded myself, and recently I've been thinking that perhaps I'd prefer a girl. I think you'd like a girl, David. Girls are gentle and kind and—"

"Strong-minded."

"Of course, if it were a girl," she went on, "I'd have to name her after my Aunt Hetty. I'd *have* to. Uncle Zachary would never forgive me if I didn't."

"And I'd never forgive you if you did. It's too big a handicap for a girl, and it's asking too much of a new father. Perhaps if the fifth or sixth child should be a girl— By then I'd be an old hand as a parent and more able to take the name in stride."

"But Aunt Hetty has been dead barely a year, and there's no one else who can name a child for her. Certainly Dot is not likely to have any more children. Even if it's a boy, and we name him Jonathan, I'll have a hard time explaining to my uncle why we didn't call him something like Harry or Henry or Herbert."

"And how would that constitute naming him after your Aunt Hetty?"

"Well, it's the same initial."

"Talk about silly superstitions. When we name a child, the father is called up for the Reading of the Torah, and then a blessing is made in the Hebrew name of the child. The Hebrew name is always a combination of the given name and the name of the father. Your aunt's name was what? Hepzibah? So she was Hepzibah *bas* Joshua. She was your father's sister, wasn't she?"

"His oldest sister."

"Fine. Now if we named our boy after her, he would have to be something like Hillel—Hillel *ben* David. Now does Hillel *ben* David in any way match Hepzibah *bas* Joshua?"

She was troubled. "But if the baby should be a girl, we could name it after my aunt and call her Harriet or Helen—"

"Or we could call her Sally and say that we were matching the last letter of the name rather than the first."

She glanced at him doubtfully. "Would that be quite the same?"

"It would certainly be just as sensible." His face softened. "As you know, every Jewish child has two names: a Hebrew name which is used in the temple and is primarily for religious purposes, such as for naming or being called up to the Reading, or Bar Mitzvah, or marriage; and an English name which is normally the English equivalent, such as Moses for Mosheh. When we go beyond that simple rule, we are apt to do something silly, as when we give children the name Harold or Henry from Zevi because Zevi means deer and the Yiddish-German word for deer is Hirsh. Harold, however, means something entirely different. It means champion. So we call a child a champion when we intended to call him a deer because the Yiddish word for deer begins with an H. Or take this name, Ytschak. The normal English equivalent is Isaac, but a lot of Jews, feeling Isaac sounded too Jewish, used Isidore instead because it had the same initial, not realizing that the only Isidore of any historic significance was the Archbishop of Seville. That's almost like naming a child Adolph instead of Aaron from the Hebrew Aharon.

"The English name is the one that the child will use for ninety-nine percent of his life. So the obviously intelligent thing to do is to select a name you like that will not be a burden to the child and will be fairly euphonious in conjunction with his surname. Then pick a Hebrew name on the same principle and don't worry whether the two match or not. So if it's a girl, you could call her Hepzibah, which is a very pretty name in Hebrew, and that would take care of your Aunt Hetty. And you could use precisely the same name for her English name, or you could call her Ruth or Naomi or any other name you happened to like."

"Minna Robinson suggested we ought to use a Hebrew name for both—I mean, give the English name the Hebrew pronunciation instead of translating it. It's rather fashionable now."

"You mean call him Yonason instead of Jonathan? And

how about the surname, Small? In Hebrew that's *koton*. There's an idea—Yonason Cotton, or even Jonathan Cotton. Now there's a real New England name for you. Say, I wonder if Cotton Mather was originally Little Mather."

"Look, if you don't finish so we can get over to the Schwarzes, your name will be neither Small nor Cotton, but Mud. We were due there ten minutes ago."

10

"And now," said Schwarz, "I want to show you two something."

There had been a great crush of people when they arrived, but the crowd thinned out until around midnight just the two of them were left. Ethel Schwarz served tea and cookies as they sat around the dining-room table and held a general post-mortem on the High Holy Day services: on the rabbi's sermons, on the cantor's singing, on the faulty public-address system, on the disorder during the Reading. And through it all, much to the rabbi's surprise, Schwarz had been pleasant and cordial; but now, he felt, they had come to the real reason the president insisted they remain after the others had gone.

"This is my study," Schwarz called over his shoulder as he led them down a hall. "I do a lot of work here." He stood aside to let his guests enter. The room had no books but against one wall there were a large tilt drafting table and a broad cabinet with drawers for storing blueprints. But what attracted their attention was the table in the center of the room—on which was a pasteboard replica of the temple done to scale. Even the landscaping had been reproduced, the grass made of green fuzzy material, the shrubbery of twigs and wrapped wire, the wall setting off the parking lot a piece of cardboard painted to represent rough fieldstone. There were even a few plaster of Paris manikins to give some idea of the size of the structure.

"It's lovely," exclaimed Miriam.

"Seventy hours of work," said Schwarz. "But you haven't seen the best part." He led them around the table. Abutting the rear wall of the temple was a small structure which the rabbi guessed was the chapel Schwarz had mentioned. Slightly lower than the parent building, it had a parabolic dome suggesting the architecture in the Holy Land. A portico in front was supported by a row of columns—twin cylinders, obviously intended to represent Torah Scrolls.

"How do you like it?" asked Schwarz. And without waiting for an answer, he went on, "It's rich; it's classic. It's simple and it's elegant. How about using the Scrolls as supporting columns? Could anything be more natural, more right? You've seen Jewish temples and synagogues using Greek columns, and Byzantine temples and Colonial temples. And all the time we've had the Scroll, which couldn't be more suitable—and beautiful. The cylinder, of course, gives the greatest support with the greatest economy of material. It is naturally graceful. So why do we have to borrow from the Greeks when we have in the Scroll a double cylinder, if you please—the greatest symbol of our religion?

"Next, look at the portico. Have you ever thought of the significance of the portico, Rabbi? In our present building we have a door that's all." His voice was contemptuous. "You're either in or you're out. How does that jibe with our services and prayer habits? On the High Holy Days, for example, we're in and out all day long. And on Friday nights or Saturdays, don't we stand around after the services and *schmoos* a while? Now do you see the significance of the portico? It's in *and* out. It's a stopping-off place, a lingering place. It expresses our reluctance to leave the temple when the service is over."

"It certainly is an—interesting concept," the rabbi said. "But doesn't it—well, change the general effect of the original building?"

"You bet it does," said Schwarz. "But it doesn't clash, it blends with it. That was part of the problem. If I had a free hand, if I didn't have to take into account Christian Sorenson's phony modernism—" he broke off abruptly. "You know, when the temple was first organized and they selected committees I was a little surprised not to be put on the Building Committee. Surprised, and frankly a little annoyed. After all, I was the only member of the congregation who was a practicing architect. Once I even mentioned it casually to Jake Wasserman, and he said he suggested my name but the committee said we'd be putting up a permanent building in the not too distant future, and since I would probably be called on to submit a design, how would it look if I were on the committee that made the final selection? Fair enough.

49

So then they decide to build. I couldn't very well submit a design, out of the blue, so to speak. After all, I'm not a youngster just out of college—I'm an established architect; I expect to be invited to submit. You'll hear around that Mort Schwarz is only interested in the buck, but I assure you I didn't care about this commission for the money in it. I wouldn't have charged them one red cent beyond my out-of-pocket expenses. But not a whisper, not a murmur. After a while, I swallowed my pride and made a few inquiries and was told the project was still a long way off—they were holding things close to their chests, the gang that was in power the first year. And the next thing I knew, they had engaged Christian Sorenson, a Gentile if you please, to build the temple. You get it? I can't serve on the Building Committee because I'm an architect and would naturally be called on to submit a design, and then I'm kept from submitting a design."

Miriam shook her head sympathetically.

"I'm not blaming Jake Wasserman. He's all right, threw me a bone, as a matter of fact, and put me on the Board because of all the work I'd done for the temple—but that runaway Building Committee . . . Did you ever stop to think, Rabbi, what it means to a Jewish architect? The anti-Semitism that was common, at least up until recently, in medicine, or in banking, or in big business—it was nothing compared to my field, architecture. It's a little better now, I understand, but do you know what chance a Jew had of getting placed with one of the big firms of architects? Just exactly zero, and it wouldn't make any difference if he were top man in his class, yes, and was willing to start as a draftsman."

"I had no idea it was that bad," said Miriam.

"You bet, and it was the time of the Depression, too, which didn't help any. But you struggle and somehow or other you serve your apprenticeship and you get your experience, and you finally take the plunge and open up your own office. You're full of ideas and artistic ideals. You want to build something worthwhile, that people will see, that might be written up and pictured in architectural journals. You're trying to make a reputation. And what do you get? A block of stores, a job of redesigning standard plans for a bunch of cracker boxes in a cheap real-estate development like Colonial Village, a factory, a warehouse. And it can't be experimental because then your client starts to worry whether the bank will advance the mortgage money, or whether it won't detract from the price if he should want to sell." -

50

"But isn't that true of many people?" the rabbi asked gently. "They have to compromise to make a living."

"Right, Rabbi. It's a living and you're not hungry anymore, but suddenly you're fifty years old. You're not a youngster anymore and you've drawn a lot of plans in your time, and you're not satisfied. And then your chance comes along. Your own community is going to build a temple. In the trade journals you've seen pictures of big new projects, some of them designed by people you went to school with and didn't think much of. Now at last you've got a chance to show what you can do. And what happens? They bring in a phony, and because he's associated with a well-known firm that has built a couple of churches he gets the job."

"Well—"

"But now I'm president of the temple, and that makes me chairman ex officio of the Building Committee and I will not be denied." And he slammed his hand down on the table.

The rabbi was embarrassed by the president's emotion. "But a building like that, I would imagine would cost a lot of money."

"Old man Goralsky will provide it. I'm sure of it. I've spoken to him; I've described and explained my design, and he likes the idea."

"And do we really need it?"

"How can you talk that way, Rabbi? It isn't a matter of mere need. This is a thing of the spirit. For a community to build an edifice like this is an act of religious dedication. Visit the great cathedrals of Europe and ask yourself how many were actually needed. Ethel and I went to Europe last summer with the Wolffs. Took the grand tour, and believe you me it was an eye-opener. And you know what really got me—me a believing Jew and president of a temple, at that? The churches, the cathedrals! And not just because of the architecture, although naturally that interested me. It was something else. You'd come into some church like Santa Croce in Firenze—that's Florence—and on the walls there are Giotto frescoes, and the ceilings are painted beams, and the walls are lined with tombs of famous artists and scientists —Michelangelo, Rossini, Galileo—Charlie Wolff said to me, and he's only a dress manufacturer, 'Mort, that was to me a religious experience.' And I felt the same way. And Ethel did too, didn't you?"

"Oh, I did, Rabbi. I felt—how shall I put it—spiritually uplifted."

"So I thought, why them and not us? Why can't we—why

51

can't I—build a temple that will give our people some of that same feeling, that same uplift, as Ethel says? That's something that's been missing in our temples. The old ones are nothing and the new ones are like Sorenson's phony designs."

"Sometimes," the rabbi said slowly, "we tend to confuse aesthetic with religious experiences."

"I'm afraid, Ethel," said Schwarz with a bitter smile, "our rabbi is not too enthusiastic about our project."

The rabbi colored. "It would be hypocritical of me if I were to say I had no interest in the appearance and size of the synagogue where I was serving. The physical plant is a rough indication of the size and importance of the community, and naturally as a young man not without ambition I prefer to be associated with a large, growing, vigorous community rather than one on the decline. When friends of mine, former classmates at the seminary, come to visit me, I am not unmindful of their appreciation of our synagogue with all that implies. But size for the sake of size? When there is no need? Not even in the foreseeable future? Barnard's Crossing is a small community, and even at Kol Nidre, when temples and synagogues are traditionally crowded, we have empty seats. And that is only one night in the year.

"That you want to perform an act of spititual dedication does you great credit, Mr. Schwarz, but it is only fair to point out that what you propose is not in the general direction of our tradition. Those churches, full of marvelous statues and paintings—to the worshipers they are holy. The buildings themselves are holy. The ground on which they stand is hallowed ground. But this is not our way. We are subject to the commandment, Thou shalt not make unto thyself any graven image. Our synagogues and temples—the piles of masonry, I mean—are not in themselves holy, only the words that are said there. For a long time, we got along very well housing the Ark of the Lord in ōnly a tent."

"I'm not interested in sermons, Rabbi," said Schwarz coldly. "Are you trying to tell me that you plan to tout Goralsky off the project?"

"I certainly have no intention of seeking him out, but if he were to ask my opinion I would have to be candid with him."

"You'd say you were opposed to it?"

The rabbi temporized. "It would depend on what he asked."

"And what do you mean by that?"

52

"If he were to ask if I had any objection to the new chapel I would tell him, of course, that adding it to the main structure is not contrary to either our doctrine or our tradition." He shrugged. "If, however, he were to ask if I thought it necessary, I could not in all conscience say I did. And if he were to ask if I thought it was a worthy project, a worthy use of the money, I would have to tell him that I could think of dozens of uses to which the money could be better put."

"Of all the smug, sanctimonious!—" Schwarz shook his head angrily. "You know, that's what comes of giving a man too much security. When they first proposed giving him a five-year contract, I opposed it, and by God I knew what I was doing."

"He doesn't mince words, our rabbi," said Ethel as she loaded the dishwasher. "What I don't understand is that it's all meant for him. I mean, that sanctuary would really be his—I'd think he'd like his own chapel instead of the public auditorium."

"That's just the point. In a sense I *was* doing it for him. At least, he's the one who will benefit most from it. Why wouldn't he want it? I'll tell you why—it's just to defy me. There can't be any other reason."

"Well, I don't know what he had in mind, but it seems pretty bad manners on his part. I mean, as our guest, the least he could have done was say it was nice. Even if he didn't like it, he could have been sort of noncommittal."

"That's what I'm telling you. That's just my point. He went out of his way to be unnecessarily unpleasant. And that can only mean that he was opposing me on personal grounds. Maybe he's sore about my voting against him on the new contract, and is trying to get back at me."

"Do you think he'll talk to Goralsky about it?"

"He'd better not, that's all I can say. He'd better not. Because if he does, then contract or no contract, this place will be too hot to hold him."

"It wouldn't have hurt to show some enthusiasm, David. He was trying so hard to be nice and friendly, the least you could have done was to compliment him on the design."

"Honestly, Miriam, I tried, but the words stuck in my throat. I kept thinking how ridiculous the temple would look with that what did he call it? rich, simple, elegant, classic monstrosity along with his *schmoosing* gallery, and the words wouldn't come out. Sorenson's design may not be much, but it is simple and it has an austere grace that Schwarz wants to spoil just so he can show he can build something besides a supermarket. We need a chapel about as much as we need a bowling alley. We don't need the extra space. And when the sanctuary is used for secular purposes, there's no reason we can't put a simple screen in front of the Ark as they do in other synagogues. Don't you see, he wasn't interested in improving the temple—only in advertising himself."

"All I see is that he was trying to be friendly, and you turned him down."

"I couldn't buy his friendship on that basis. I don't think for a moment that Goralsky would ask my opinion, but if he did I couldn't give him a false impresson just to curry favor with Schwarz." He could see she was still unconvinced. "Look, Miriam, as the rabbi of the congregation, a sort of public figure, I have to be nice to all kinds of people. I have to pretend an interest in things that truthfully don't interest me at all. I have to busy myself with matters that aren't worth the time I spend on them. And I do it. No matter how much I resent it, I do it. I do it because in some small way, they help the congregation or the community. But if I gushed all over Schwarz about how wonderful his design was, and how wonderful it would be for the congregation to have a little jewel of a chapel which could never be profaned by anything mundane or secular, and if I assured him that I would back him to the hilt in dealing with Goralsky, then I'd be doing it just to get in good with him, to make my job more secure, and that I couldn't do."

"I don't think the design is really so bad," she said tentatively.

"By itself, no. It's a little fancy for my taste, but well within the range of acceptability if it stood alone. But when you slap it up against the wall of our present structure, don't you see what the effect would be? The two buildings don't blend. They clash. And because our present structure is simple with clean lines, and the proposed building is ornate and fancy, he's hoping that people will make the comparison. What he's saying in effect is, 'See what you would have got if you had engaged me originally.' "

Still she did not answer. Her silence made him uncomfortable. "What is it, Miriam? What's troubling you? Are you worried about what Schwarz can do?"

"Oh, David, you know I've gone along with you in every important decision. After you got your degree, when you turned down that job in Chicago that paid so much money because you didn't like the kind of congregation it seemed to be, I didn't say a word although we were living on my salary as a typist—that and whatever occasional fees you got as a fill-in rabbi for the High Holy Days in small towns. And then there was the job at a good salary down in Louisiana that was the right kind of congregation but which you refused because you felt you couldn't serve effectively in the South. Then there was the job as assistant rabbi in that Cleveland temple that paid more than most full rabbi jobs, but you said you didn't want to serve under someone else and have to subordinate your own thinking to his. It was near the end of the hiring season, and you yourself felt that Hanslick was getting tired of offering you jobs you kept turning down. And it was I who urged you to turn it down; I told you I didn't mind continuing my job and that I loved our little one-room basement apartment that was so cold in the winter and hot in the summer, and doing all the shopping and the cooking—"

"I did some of the shopping and the cooking," he protested.

"But when you did it, the clerks always gave you the worst —the vegetables that were just starting to rot—and the butcher, that kosher butcher on the corner—I'll bet his eyes lit up when he saw you come in—all the fat and bones and gristle, and you couldn't even remember to take off the roast until it started to burn—" She began to laugh. "Do you remember that time when you started to cut away the burnt part and I said I liked meat well done, and you said you could eat any kind of meat but you couldn't stand a liar, and you went out and bought some delicatessen?"

"Yes"—and he, too, started laughing—"and remember the time—" He broke off. "But what are you getting at?"

"Just that in those days it didn't make any difference."

"And now is it different? Since living in Barnard's Crossing, have I been buying two-hundred-dollar suits and alligator shoes?"

"You need a new suit, and the collars on half your shirts are frayed—"

"Stick to the point, woman," he cried in exasperation.

"The point is, that was all right when there were just two of us. But I'm carrying a child and I feel responsible for it."

"For *him,* and I'm responsible. Are you worried that I

might lose my job and not be able to make a living for my wife and child? Don't worry. As long as we haven't developed a taste for luxury, then if not this job, another. And if not another pulpit, then a teaching job. And if I can't get that, then a job as a bookkeeper in an office, or a clerk in a store. These days there's always some job for a man who is willing to work. Remember, a rabbi doesn't have to have a pulpit to be a rabbi. Traditionally, we don't even approve of being paid for one's learning. 'One should use the Torah as a spade to dig with.' But don't think that I haven't thought about it.

"I'm aware of my responsibilities. And I'm aware of the added burden that will fall on our child as a rabbi's son. I am a rabbi's son and I know what it means. Because your father is a public figure, everyone expects more of you, and you feel guilty when you don't come up to expectations. As a youngster, you can't imagine how often I wished my father owned a shoe store or went to work in an office like the fathers of the other boys. Believe me, I envied the boys whose fathers earned a living in the ordinary way. But there were compensations, and much of it was fun. When I went to the synagogue on a Friday night with my mother, and I saw my father in the pulpit conducting the service, delivering his sermons, I always felt that the synagogue was ours, that I was being taken there as other boys were occasionally taken to their father's offices on Saturday.

"But when I got a little older and would overhear, and partly understand, the talk of men such as Schwarz—and don't think my father didn't have his Schwarzes—every rabbi does—then it wasn't so pleasant. A rabbi is a public servant, and anyone who has many masters can't expect to please them all. Once I asked my father about something I overheard—some controversy he was having with the members of his synagogue at the time—and he smiled at me and said, 'In this life you sometimes have to choose between pleasing God and pleasing man. And in the long run, it's better to please God—He's more apt to remember.' After that, I wasn't bothered so much. Whenever I heard an uncomplimentary remark about my father, I figured he had chosen to please God again."

"Oh, David, I don't want you to do anything you think is wrong. Only—" she looked up at him—"please could we please God *after* the baby is born?"

11

Precisely at noon the next day a cab pulled up to the door and out stepped a slim, boyish-looking man in his early forties. Dr. Ronald Sykes had a long narrow face with thinning dark hair; it was an intelligent face with shrewd knowing eyes and a ready smile. He was wearing stout English boots, gray flannels, and a tweed jacket. If the hair had been a little thicker, the face a little fuller, and the eyes somewhat less knowing, he could have passed for an undergraduate.

"I came to see you in behalf of my late friend and colleague, Isaac Hirsh," he said when they were seated in the rabbi's study. "You heard of his death, of course."

"I don't believe I knew an Isaac Hirsh," the rabbi said with a tinge of embarrassment. "He wasn't a member of my congregation, was he?"

"No, Rabbi, but he did live here and was part of the Jewish community, so I thought you might know him."

The rabbi shook his head slowly.

"Well, he died Friday night, and his wife, or rather his widow, would like to arrange for him to have a Jewish funeral. Is that possible—I mean where he was not a member of your congregation?"

"Oh, yes. Although our cemetery is reserved for members of the congregation, we make provision for Jews in the community who are not members. Upon paying a small fee they are accorded nominal membership, which of course is exclusive of the price of a lot. However, as a resident of Barnard's Crossing, Mr. Hirsh can be buried in the town cemetery, Grove Hill, which is nonsectarian. I don't know what fees would be involved, but I could give him Jewish burial there just as well."

The doctor shook his head. "No, I think Mrs. Hirsh would want him buried among his own kind. Mrs. Hirsh is not Jewish."

"Oh."

"Does that make a difference?" Sykes asked quickly.

"It might." The rabbi hesitated. "In that case, I'd have to

be sure that the deceased had in fact been a Jew—that is, had remained a Jew."

"I'm not sure I understand. His wife considers him a Jew. As long as I knew him, which is only this past year, to be sure, he never pretended to be anything else."

The rabbi smiled. "It's a religious rather than an ethnic distinction. Anyone born of a Jewish mother, not father if you please, is automatically considered Jewish, provided"—he paused to emphasize the point—"that he has not repudiated his religion by conversion to another religion or by public disclaimer."

"To the best of my knowledge he belonged to no other church."

"But you said Mrs. Hirsh was not Jewish. Was she Catholic or Protestant?"

"I don't know. Anglican, I think, originally. At least the Anglican minister came to pay his respects while I was there."

"Well, you see how it is. If they had come to me and asked me to marry them, I would have refused unless she converted. So perhaps the late Mr. Hirsh was converted when they were married. Tell me, why didn't Mrs. Hirsh come, or send for me herself?"

"The shock of her husband's death, Rabbi. As a matter of fact, she's been kept under mild sedation. So as his section head, his boss you might say, she naturally turned to me to make the arrangements. And as for his religious status, I can only say I very much doubt if he would have undergone even nominal conversion to marry. He never cared much for all this mumbo jumbo—" he checked himself. "I'm sorry, rabbi, but those were his words; I was quoting him." He had a sudden thought. "His name, Isaac, is essentially Jewish. He didn't change that, so wouldn't that indicate how he felt?"

The rabbi smiled. "You must have noticed when Mrs. Small opened the door that we are expecting a child. So our interest in names is more than just academic. We were just talking about that and decided the name Isaac, these days, is as likely to be pure Yankee."

Sykes spread his hands in token of defeat. "Well, all I can say is that I feel he had no religious affiliations. Poor devil, he would have been better off if he had. He might have been alive today if he like the rest of the Jews had gone to temple Friday night."

"Then his death was unexpected?"

58

"He was found dead in his garage Friday night. Patricia Hirsh notified me the next day, and I came right over."

"Heart attack?"

"Carbon monoxide poisoning."

"Oh." The rabbi, who had been lounging back in his chair, now leaned forward. His face became thoughtful and his fingers drummed a soft tattoo on the desk.

"You're thinking of suicide, Rabbi? Would that make a difference?"

"It might."

"I suppose it could be suicide," said Sykes slowly, "although there was no note, and if he were going to take his own life, you'd think he'd have left some word for his wife. He was very fond of her. The police officially called it accidental death. You see, he had been drinking heavily—"

"You mean he was drunk?"

"Must have been. He had gone through half a bottle of vodka, about a pint, in a pretty short time. He probably blacked out, and the motor kept running."

"He was a heavy drinker?"

"He was an alcoholic, Rabbi, but as long as he had been with us he was all right. It's not that they drink much—only that when they start, they can't stop."

"And this did not interfere with his work? By the way, what was his work?"

"He was a mathematician in my unit at the Goddard Research and Development Laboratory."

The rabbi nodded thoughtfully. "Our people don't run to alcoholism. I am rather surprised that considering this—this affliction, that you hired him."

"Well, there aren't too many mathematicians kicking around, at least not of the stature of Isaac Hirsh. It may help to explain our attitude, and perhaps his problem, when I tell you that he was on the original Manhattan Project and worked with Fermi. When we dropped the bomb on Hiroshima, it raised hell with a lot of men there."

"In that case, he must have been well along in years."

"Early fifties, I should say. He got his Ph.D from M.I.T. in 1935. I got mine same place in '43, in case you are wondering."

"And yet you are the head of the unit and he was your subordinate?"

"Just that I got there first. I went to Goddard as soon as I got my degree."

"Tell me, what did you call him?"

"Eh? Oh, you mean how did I address him?" He flushed. "Mostly, I'd call him Doctor. You see, he was quite a bit older than I. But sometimes when we were just sitting around talking—what was the expression he used? *schmoosing*, that's Yiddish, I guess. He used a lot of Yiddish words from time to time—well, then he would sometimes call me Ronald or Ron, and I'd call him Ike. Most of the time it was Doctor, though, because there are always technicians around and you use first names indiscriminately and after a while the technicians start calling you by your first name and there goes the discipline. At least, that's our director's idea. He's an old army man."

"I see." He thought for a moment. "It would help if I could visit Mrs. Hirsh. Would it be all right if I dropped over this afternoon?"

"I'm sure that will be fine."

"Then perhaps you had better make your arrangements for the cemetery plot. You would have to see the chairman of our Cemetery Committee. If you like, I'll call Mr. Brown. Do you know him, Marvin Brown, insurance business?"

Sykes shook his head. "If he can see me now I'd go right over there. Would you mind calling me a cab?"

"Of course." The rabbi started out the door and then hesitated. "Oh, and by the way, if money is a consideration to the widow, and I suppose it is, a plain undecorated pine box is most correct according to our traditions."

Marvin Brown was a live wire, a go-getter. He was a wiry terrier of a man who knew that time was money and that there were a hundred cents to every dollar. He had long ago learned the supreme lesson of salesmanship, that if you made one sale for every ten calls you could make two sales by making twenty calls. This doctrine he not only preached, he practiced. Over the years, his wife had learned to adjust to his pace. She planned her evening meal for six o'clock, knowing that Marve might not get to it until nine and then he might tell her he had grabbed a bite somewhere and wasn't hungry.

"How do you stand it, Mitzi?" her friends would ask. "It would drive me up a wall if my husband didn't get home at a regular time for his meals. And how does he stand it? Marvin's no youngster, you know. He ought to begin taking it easy."

And it worried Mitzi every now and then, because Marve was almost forty and it seemed to her he was working harder than ever. He had been a member of the Million Dollar Club for four years running now, and although nearly every year his sales earned him a trip to Florida or Mexico or Puerto Rico, even on his vacations he wouldn't relax. Every day he played golf and went for a swim, and then he would see people around the hotel and talk business.

But, as Mitzi reflected, when Marve was out, or when he called to say that he would be home late, she was always sure it was insurance business, not monkey business. As a matter of fact, not only insurance business kept him busy; there were also the temple, and the Parent-Teacher Association of which he was vice-president, and the Community Fund of which he was a district leader. When she protested that with all his own work it was foolish of him to take on more, he pointed out it was really all insurance business. It meant that many more contacts, and the insurance business was all a matter of contacts. But she knew better—she knew he did these things because he liked to be active, he liked to race around. And she had to admit it seemed to be good for him.

"Honest," she would say to her friends, "the children hardly know their father. The only time they can count on seeing him is Sunday morning when he takes them to Sunday school. The rest of the time, they're usually in bed asleep when he gets home." But secretly she was pleased. He was her man and he was working night and day to make a good living for her—just how good was attested by the winter trips, her mink stole, and the shiny black Lincoln they had finally worked up to.

Marvin Brown's success was not due simply to his many contacts. He never went to see a prospective client cold. As he never tired of saying to the salesmen in his office, "Before you go to see your prospect, find out all you can about him." So when his wife told him that a Dr. Sykes would be calling on him, and that the appointment had been arranged by the rabbi, he immediately phoned to find out what it was all about.

"He's acting for the widow of Isaac Hirsh who died Friday night," said the rabbi.

"Did you say Isaac Hirsh? My God, I sold him a policy less than a year ago."

"Really? A life insurance policy? Do you remember for how much?"

"Not offhand. I think it was about twenty-five thousand dollars, but I could look it up. Why?"

"Tell me, Mr. Brown, did he have any difficulty passing the physical?"

"Not that I know of. That doesn't mean anything, though. Some of these doctors don't even touch the patient with a stethoscope. They ask him a few questions and if he looks all right and has a pulse, they pass him. What's it all about, Rabbi? Was it a heart attack?"

"I think the police ruled it accidental death."

"Uh-oh—there's a double indemnity clause for accidental death on most of our policies. It's only a small additional fee, so we usually write them. I guess the widow is mighty happy—I mean, it's a lucky thing for her that he decided to take out the policy, although, as I remember it, I didn't have to do much selling."

"Well, Dr. Sykes is acting for the widow. Mr. Hirsh was not a member of our temple, but his wife would like him buried in a Jewish cemetery according to Jewish rites. She herself is not Jewish."

"I get the picture, Rabbi. Don't worry about a thing. Just leave everything to me."

12

Nothing Sykes said had prepared the rabbi for Mrs. Hirsh. He found her surprisingly young, in her early thirties, for a man in his fifties. And she was tall. Even though her blue eyes were swollen from weeping he found them attractive, and her red hair was striking. At first he thought she looked flashy. Although she was dressed in black, her silk dress had flounces and lawn sleeves hardly appropriate for mourning—but then he realized she probably had not bought it for the occasion and must be wearing it because she had nothing more suitable. Normally of a gay and happy temperament, this would be reflected in her wardrobe.

He introduced himself.

"Oh, come in, Rabbi. Dr. Sykes phoned to say you were going to drop over. Peter Dodge was here earlier, he said he knows you. And the Lutheran minister, Pastor Kal—Kalt—"

"Pastor Kaltfuess."

"That's it, and then there was the Methodist minister

and the Unitarian minister, I guess. I sure got a lot of spiritual comfort today."

"They came to console you."

"Oh, I know. And are you, too, going to tell me that Ike's soul is in Heaven or in a better world?"

Because he was aware that grief can take many forms the rabbi was not offended by her bitter flippancy. "I'm afraid we don't peddle that kind of merchandise," he said.

"You mean you don't believe in life after death, in a Hereafter?"

"We believe that his soul lives on in your memory and in the remembrance of his friends and in his influence on their lives. Of course, if he had children, he would live on in them, too."

"Well, that's pretty obvious."

"It doesn't make it any the less true." He paused, reluctant to broach the real reason for his visit. No matter how much experience he had with death, he still had not acquired the professional touch.

But she helped him out. "Dr. Sykes said you wanted to ask me some questions about my husband."

He nodded gratefully. "Burial is a ritual, Mrs. Hirsh, and I must be sure that your husband was a Jew according to our Law. And since he married out of the faith—"

"Does that make him any less a Jew?"

"Not that in itself, but the circumstances might. Tell me, who officiated at your wedding?"

"We were married by a justice of the peace. Do you want to see the license?"

He smiled. "I'll take your word for it."

Impulsively she said, "Forgive me, Rabbi. I've been bitchy, haven't I?"

"A little, and now you're trying to shock me."

She smiled. "All right, let's start again. Ask me any questions at all."

He settled back in his chair. "All right, why do you want to give him a Jewish burial?"

"Because Ike was a Jew. He never thought of himself as anything else."

"And yet he never practiced our religion, I understand."

"Well, he always said there were two ways of being a Jew. You could be one by practicing the religion or just by being born and thinking of yourself as Jew. Was he wrong?"

"No," said the rabbi cautiously, "but a Jewish funeral is a religious ceremony. Would he have wanted that?"

"I know it can be done by a funeral director, but what connection would he have with Ike? No, this is what he would have wanted. We never discussed it, of course. For himself, he probably wouldn't have cared. But out of respect for my feelings, I think he would have wanted some kind of ceremony. And what could have any meaning for him except a Jewish ceremony?"

"I see. All right, I'll perform the service. It's customary to say a few words at the grave. But I didn't know your husband. So you'll have to tell me about him. He was quite a bit older, wasn't he? Were you happy together?"

"Twenty years, but we were happy." She thought a moment. "He was good to me. And I was good for him. As for his being so much older—well, I had had enough of the other before I met him. He needed me and I needed him. Yes, I think we had a good marriage."

The rabbi hesitated and then took the plunge. "I understand his death was due indirectly to his—to his drinking. Didn't it bother you—his drinking, I mean?"

"That really bugs you people, doesn't it? Well, it bothered Ike a lot, too. Oh, of course it made things hard sometimes. He lost jobs because of it, and sometimes we had to move and that's not easy, making new arrangements and finding a new place to live. But it didn't frighten me the way it might some. He was never ugly when he was drunk, and that's what counts—more weak and silly like, and would cry like a child. But never ugly and never nasty to me. And it didn't really bother me. My father was a heavy drinker, and my mother was no teetotaler. So I was kind of used to it. Later on, when he got worse and began to black out—that was frightening, but I was frightened *for* him because there was no knowing what might happen to him."

"And did that happen often?"

She shook her head. "The last couple or three years he never touched a drop, except once or twice when he got started and couldn't stop. I mean, he didn't drink regularly. He was on the wagon, but whenever he fell off it was all the way. The last time was months and months ago."

"Except for Friday night."

"Yes, I forgot about that." She closed her eyes, and the rabbi was afraid she was going to break down. But she opened her eyes and even managed a smile.

He rose, as if to signify he had finished. Then he thought of something. "Could you tell when one of these spells was coming on?"

She shook her head.

"Can you account for his suddenly starting to drink? Was something bothering him?"

Again she shook her head. "I guess he was always bothered about something. That's why people drink, I suppose. I would try to comfort him—you know, make him feel I was always there and would always understand."

"Perhaps you were better for him than he was for you," suggested the rabbi gently.

"We were good for each other," she said emphatically. "I told you he was always kind to me. Look, Rabbi, I was no innocent when I met Ike. I had been around. He was the first man I had known who was nice to me with no strings attached. And I was good to him; I took care of him like a mother."

"And yet he drank."

"That started before I met him. And I'm not sorry," she added defiantly, "because that's how I met him."

"So?"

"He had holed up at this little hotel where I was working on the cigar counter in the lobby. If he hadn't been on a bender, how could the likes of me have met a man like him?"

"And you feel you got the best of the bargain?"

"It was the best kind of bargain there is, Rabbi, where both parties feel they've got the best of it."

13

"Yeah, this is Ben Goralsky talking. All right, I'll hold on . . . Hello, hello . . ." At the other end he could hear someone talking, and then he realized the voice was not talking to him but to someone else in the other room at the other end.

"Mr. Goralsky? Ted Stevenson speaking."

"Oh, hello Ted, nice to hear your voice. Where you calling from?"

"From our offices."

"On Sunday? Don't you guys ever stop working?"

"There are no regular hours and no days off for top management in this company, Mr. Goralsky, not when there's important business to be done. And if you join us, you'll work the same way."

Goralsky had an inkling of the purpose of the call, and the implication of the "if" was not lost on him.

"We were going to call you yesterday, as a matter of fact," Stevenson went on, "but we knew it was your holiday and assumed you would be at your synagogue."

"Well, as a matter of fact, I didn't go. I was right here all the time. My father took sick, and with a man that age—"

"Oh, I'm sorry to hear that. How is he?"

"He's all right now, but for a while it was kind of like touch and go."

"Well, I'm delighted to hear he's on the mend. Give the old gentleman our regards and best wishes for his recovery."

"Thanks. He'll be pleased."

The voice at the other end shifted gears abruptly. "We have been somewhat disturbed over here, Mr. Goralsky, over the action of your stock in the last week or so."

"Yeah, well, Ted, you know how it is. Rumors of a merger get out. We tried to keep it mum at this end, and as far as I know no one here has leaked. But when your crew came down, someone may have recognized somebody in your party—I tell you, when it first got back to me, you could have knocked me over with a feather. But I guess that's the way it is in these things—"

"No, Mr. Goralsky, that's not the way it is. We know that there always are rumors preceding a merger, and that can affect your stock. But your stock has climbed so precipitously, we did a little investigating. We inquired among some of our good friends in the market down in Boston, and we learned that the reason for the climb was not the rumor of a merger with us but some new process."

"Well, that turned out to be a dud, I guess," said Ben unhappily.

"So we discovered on further inquiry. Of course these things happen from time to time in any R and D program, but if we thought that it was deliberately engineered for the purpose of increasing the value of your stock preliminary to the merger, we would regard that as—er—sharp practice, and would be forced to reconsider the entire proposition."

66

"And I wouldn't blame you Mr. Stevenson, but I give you my word—"

The other cut him off unceremoniously. "We're not interested in explanations or excuses. What we want from you is . . ."

When Ben finally hung up, he was dripping with perspiration. For a long time thereafter he sat staring at the telephone.

14

The rabbi had intended to go right home after seeing Mrs. Hirsh, but once outside and behind the wheel of his car he found himself driving in the opposite direction, downtown, and presently he was caught in the maze of narrow crooked streets of Old Town. After two turns he got lost and turned up one street and down another in the hope of finding himself on familiar ground; but each time he thought he spotted a house he knew, the road curved another way. Perched on a hill tantalizingly close he could see the town hall which was on familiar territory, yet none of the streets seemed to lead toward it. All the while, he caught kaleidoscopic glimpses of lovely old-fashioned gardens hidden behind charming weather-beaten houses, most of them with a golden eagle over the door lintel, interesting shops of handcrafters and artists, and most fascinating of all, the ship chandler's shop with its windows stuffed with fascinating gear—brass compasses, coils of nylon rope, bells, curiously shaped nautical fittings of mysterious function, and, incongruously, a pair of stout rubber boots.

Suddenly he found himself on an extremely narrow street which had cars parked on both sides and traffic going in both directions. He slowed down to worm his way through and his car stalled. Horns blared behind him as he twisted the key viciously; the only response was the high-pitched whine of the starting motor. As he pumped the gas pedal in vexation, a voice at his side said, "You've probably flooded it, Rabbi."

He looked up and was tremendously relieved to see Hugh

Lanigan. The local chief of police was wearing a sport shirt and chinos, and under his arm he had the Sunday paper.

"Here, let me try it."

The rabbi set the brake and moved over so that the other could get in. Whether because those behind recognized the chief or they realized the offending driver was in genuine difficulty, the blaring horns stopped. The chief pressed the accelerator all the way to the floor, turned the key, and miraculously the motor caught.

He grinned at the rabbi. "How about a drink at our place?"

"I'd love one. You drive."

"All right." Effortlessly Lanigan threaded the maze between oncoming and parked cars, and when he reached his house he ran the right wheels up on the sidewalk to obstruct as little of the road as possible. Opening the gate of his white picket fence he marched the rabbi up the walk and short flight of steps that led to the verandah. He shouted through the screen door, "We got some company, Gladys."

"Coming," his wife shouted back from inside, and a moment later appeared at the door. She was dressed in slacks and sweater and looked as though she had just finished helping her husband with the lawn. But her white hair was carefully combed and her makeup was fresh. "Well, this is a pleasant surprise, Rabbi Small," she said and held out her hand. "You'll join us in a drink? I was just fixing Manhattans."

"That will do very nicely," said the rabbi with a grin.

"I can't help thinking," said the rabbi, as she left to prepare them, "that on the few occasions I have called on you it always starts with a drink—"

"Spirits for the spiritual, Rabbi."

"Yes, but when you dropped in on me, I always offered you tea."

"At the rate I was coming around it was just as well," said Lanigan. "Besides, I was usually on business, and I don't drink during business hours."

"Tell me, were you ever drunk?"

The chief stared at him. "Why, of course. Haven't you ever been?"

The rabbi shook his head. "And didn't Mrs. Lanigan mind?"

Chief Lanigan laughed. "Gladys has been kind of high herself on occasion. No, why would she mind? It isn't as though I've ever been really blind drunk. Always it's been on some special occasion where it's kind of expected. Why? What are you getting at?"

"I have just been to see Mrs. Hirsh—"

"Ah-hah."

"And I'm just trying to understand. Her husband was an alcoholic, and that's something I haven't had much experience with. We Jews don't run to alcoholism."

"That's true, you don't. I wonder why."

The rabbi shrugged his shoulders. "I don't know. The Chinese and the Italians also have low incidences of alcoholism, yet none of us are teetotalers. As far as Jews are concerned, all our holidays and celebrations involve drinking. At the Passover feast, everyone is expected to drink at least four glasses of wine. Even the young children partake. It's sweet, but the alcoholic content is there nonetheless. You can get drunk on it, but I can't remember any Passover when anyone did. Maybe the very fact that we do not forbid it enables us to enjoy it in moderation. For us, it doesn't carry the joys of forbidden fruits."

"In France, I understand, they drink wine as freely as water, but they have a lot of alcoholism there."

"That's true. I don't suppose there's any single explanation. There are certain similarities among the three groups that do encourage speculation. All have a strong family tradition that might provide a sense of security other people may look for in alcohol. The Chinese, especially, feel about their elders somewhat as we do. You know, we have a saying that other people boast of the beauty of their women; we boast of our old men."

"Well, that might apply to the Italians, too—respect for elders, I mean, although they seem to lean more toward the mother than the father. But how does that help?"

"Simply that the embarrassment of being seen drunk might act as a deterrent in societies where elders are greatly revered."

"Possible," Lanigan said judiciously.

"But there's another explanation—and here we share a similarity with the Chinese. Their religion, like ours, emphasizes ethics, morals, and good behavior; and like us they attach less importance to faith than you Christians. This helps to keep us from being guilt-ridden."

"What's faith got to do with it?"

"In Christianity, it's the key to salvation. And faith is not easy to maintain at all times. To believe is to question. The very act of affirming implies a doubt."

"I don't get it."

"We don't have that much control of our minds. Thoughts come unbidden—unpleasant thoughts, awful thoughts—and if you believed that doubt could lead to damnation, you'd be apt to feel guilty a good part of the time. And one place you might find solace would be in alcohol."

Lanigan smiled easily. "Yes, but any mature, intelligent person knows how the mind works and discounts it."

"Any intelligent, mature person, yes. But how about the immature?"

"I see, so you think one reason Jews don't become alcoholics is because they don't have guilt feelings?"

"It's a theory. I'm just speculating idly while waiting for a drink."

"Gladys," Lanigan bawled. "What are you doing in there? The rabbi is dying of thirst."

"Coming."

She appeared with a tray of glasses and a pitcher. "You can replenish your glass whenever you've a mind to, Rabbi."

"And how about Isaac Hirsh?" asked Lanigan as he raised his glass in silent toast to his guest. "As I understand it, he didn't have any interest in the Jewish religion, let alone the Christian."

"But he may have felt guilt. At least so thinks his superior, a Dr. Sykes. He suggested he may have become an alcoholic because of the work he did on the bomb dropped on Hiroshima."

"That so? And how are you involved? Was Hirsh a member of your congregation?"

"No, but his widow thought he should be buried in our cemetery."

"I think I'm beginning to see. You're wondering if it really was an accident, or if it was suicide. You people have the same attitude toward suicide that we have—I mean as far as burial as concerned?"

"Not quite. In a sense, our practice is similar to yours. The suicide is not publicly mourned, no eulogy is said, and he is supposed to be buried off to one side rather than in the main part of the cemetery. But your church is a large authoritarian organization—"

"And what difference would that make?"

"Just that there's a sort of hierarchy, a chain of command that tends to keep the rules of the church uniform."

"And you are your own boss. Is that it?"

70

"Something like that. At least no religious body passes on my decision."

"So if the rabbi is easygoing and soft-hearted—"

"He still has his own integrity to live up to," said the rabbi firmly. "But apart from that, the philosophical basis for our disapproval of suicide is somewhat different from yours, and that in itself permits greater flexibility."

"How so?"

"Well, the attitude of your church is that each and every one of us was put on this earth to fulfill some divine purpose, and life is essentially a test to determine an individual's eventual destination—Heaven or Hell or Purgatory. So the man who takes his own life is in a sense dodging the test and flouting God's will. For us, on the other hand, life on this earth is the sum total of man's destiny. But we hold that man was created in God's image, and hence to destroy himself is to commit a sort of sacrilege by destroying God's image.

"At the same time, we do not condemn the man who is driven to suicide by reason of insanity or by great pain, grief, or mental anguish. In the Old Testament, there are several suicides whose memories we still honor. Samson for one. He pulled down the pillars of the Philistine temple, you remember. That could be defended on the grounds that it not only killed him but large numbers of Philistines who were the enemy. In a sense, then, his could be regarded as death on the battlefield. King Saul is another example, a more clear-cut case perhaps. After the death of his sons in battle and realizing he was likely to be captured by the enemy, he asked his armor-bearer to run him through with his sword. When he refused, Saul thrust the sword into his bosom with his own hand. Here it has been argued that the suicide was justified on the ground that if he had been captured, the enemy would have made a mockery of him which would have brought great shame and dishonor to the Jewish nation. Then too, there was the certainty his men would have tried to recapture him and that many would have died as a result. So his death could be regarded as a sacrifice to save the lives of his people.

"Martyrdom is really a form of suicide even though the actual blow is not dealt by one's own hand. And starting with Hannah and her seven sons, all of whom died rather than bow down to Greek idols as recorded in Maccabees of the Apocrypha, we have had a long record of martyrdom. It is referred to, in fact, as *kiddush ha-Shem,* the sanctification of the Name. Not all the rabbis were in agreement on the matter. Maimonides, for example, held that it was justifiable to pay lip service to false gods to save one's life. But the general consensus was that there were worse things than suicide; that where a man had to choose between killing himself and killing another, suicide was preferable. So, too, with the woman forced to transgress the commandment 'Thou shalt not commit adultery'; rather than permit herself to be ravished, a woman should commit suicide.

"These attitudes still prevail today. Look at the enormous pride the modern State of Israel, an Orthodox theocracy if you please, takes in the reconstructed fortress of Masada, where, according to Josephus, some nine hundred Jewish defenders were besieged and withstood the might of the Roman armies for several years and then committed suicide en masse rather than be captured and enslaved."

"But if you condone suicide when a man is not in his right mind or when driven to it, what's left?" Lanigan asked. "It seems to me that that would include just about every suicide."

"Well, it certainly gives us a lot of leeway," the rabbi admitted. "But I don't think you'd find many rabbis who would approve of the Japanese practice of hara-kiri, where it is considered proper to take one's life because of some fancied dishonor to one's house or loss of face. Nor would we condone the old Indian practice of suttee where a wife to show her loyalty, throws herself on her husband's funeral pyre."

"How about those Buddhist monks who set fire to themselves in Viet Nam? We've even had a couple such cases here."

The rabbi nodded thoughtfully. "That *would* pose quite a problem. My guess is that most modern rabbis would dodge the issue by considering it a form of insanity; on the other hand, a stickler for the rules might treat it as a bona fide suicide on the grounds that it presumed a sound mind and was being done knowingly, out of philosophical conviction."

"Still, there are plenty of loopholes—enough certainly to include Hirsh."

"Then you *do* think it was suicide: Why did you call it accidental death?"

"To answer your second question first, Rabbi, because we couldn't prove it either way. So naturally we called it accidental death, which is kinder to his widow. Remember, suicide is a crime and we can't go labeling a man a criminal with no definite or positive proof."

"And my first question?"

"What was that?"

"I asked whether you thought it was suicide, setting proof aside."

"No, Rabbi, I don't. You tell someone that a man was found dead of carbon monoxide in his garage and the first thing that comes to mind is suicide. But actually, there are plenty of accidental deaths from carbon monoxide. It's pretty tricky stuff. A few years back, a couple of kids parked their car, a leaky old rattrap of a jalopy, right up here near Highland Park. They were just planning on a little fancy necking, but it was midwinter and cold so they kept the motor running to stay warm. The stuff seeped through the car and we found them both dead. It happens all the time. A man goes into the garage to tinker with his car. It's cold, so he keeps the garage closed and passes out. If he's not found in time, he's dead.

"Another thing. You wouldn't think so in a town of this size, but in my time I have seen quite a few suicides. Most of them, curiously enough, are apt to be young people. But there have been grown-ups too. The grown-ups almost always leave a note of some kind. The kids don't for some reason. Maybe they're just trying to make their folks feel sorry. You know that poem by Edwin Arlington Robinson, Rabbi? 'Richard Cory'? About this young fellow who had everything and then for some reason put a bullet through his brain? A bachelor might do that, but somebody who has a family, they usually leave a note."

"Is that your only reason? That Hirsh left no note?"

"There's another reason, although it wouldn't be much good in a court of law. This is a heavy drinking town. We've got a lot of pretty rich people with idle time on their hands, and they drink. Then we've got a lot of high-strung executive types who are busy raising ulcers—and they tend to drink more than is good for them. And finally, we have a bunch of fishermen, and they know what to do with a bottle. Well, I've never known a heavy drinker, what is apt to be called an alcoholic these days, I've never known one of them to commit suicide. I once asked a psychiatrist who was down here for the summer why that was. And do you know what he said? He said they don't commit suicide because they're already doing it. According to him, these alcoholics are really suicides who are doing it the long way. Does that make sense to you, Rabbi?"

"Why, yes, I can understand that. But how about legal proof? Anything?"

"Well, except for the absence of the note and the fact Hirsh was drunk, there's nothing definite. It's the drinking that tips the scales with me. A man taking his life usually does so with a clear head. My experience is that in that last final step he's not thinking about chickening out, because he has thought it through and made up his mind that this is the logical—the only—thing to do.

"Now you look at the facts leading up to his drunk, and they certainly don't seem the pattern of a man determined to commit suicide. In fact, it seems all a grotesque accident.

"When Mrs. Hirsh called in that her husband was missing, we notified the State Police as well as various police departments hereabouts to be on the lookout. A State Police cruising car remembered seeing a car matching the description parked on Route 128 at one of the turnouts not far from the Goddard Lab. So they drove over, and the car was gone. But they found a ball of rumpled paper and cardboard—the wrapper from a vodka bottle. It had a gift card enclosed and was addressed to a party who lives right across the street from Hirsh. A little routine police work showed that the bottle had been delivered after the Levensons— that was the party—had gone off to the temple. The driver asked Hirsh if he would sign for it and give it to the Levensons, and Hirsh agreed."

"I see."

"Now, he wouldn't have taken the wrapper off just to look at the bottle. He must have taken an experimental drink or two. In fact, why else would he have pulled up at the turnoff? He must have started for the lab, and stopped at the turnoff for a drink, then decided to go home and do a good job of it. As a matter of fact, it might explain his drinking in the first place. He wouldn't go out and buy a bottle—he was trying to keep off the stuff. But receiving a bottle out of the blue, you might say—getting it on the eve of the Holy Day, too—well, I can see where he might regard it as almost foreordained."

"I doubt if even a devout believer, and I don't suppose Hirsh was, would think of a bottle of vodka as having been sent by the Almighty," said the rabbi with a smile. "But, in any case, in your view, the weight of the evidence is on the side of accidental death."

"Well, that's the way it seemed to us. But keep in mind we naturally preferred that finding to suicide. Of course the

74

insurance company is likely to look at the picture a little differently."

"Oh? Have they made inquiries?"

"No, not yet," Lanigan said, "but they will, they will."

15

Pat Hirsh, accompanied by Liz Marcus, arrived home in the undertaker's limousine to find Dr. Sykes parked in the driveway. His small foreign roadster had made the trip from the cemetery much faster than the big limousine.

"Come in, Liz," said Pat. "I'll make some tea."

"Thanks, but I don't think I'd better. Joe is taking care of the kids, and he'll be wanting to get back to the office." Liz kissed her impulsively—she had been more emotional than Pat during the entire proceedings—and left, saying she'd try to get over that evening after putting the kids to bed.

Dr. Sykes held open the door for Mrs. Hirsh. "You didn't need to go to the expense of renting the limousine, Mrs. Hirsh. I could have driven you out and back."

"I know, but somehow it didn't seem right to go to the funeral in a sports car. Can I fix you something to drink?"

"No thanks, I've got to be getting back to the lab. I just stopped for a minute to see that everything was all right."

"Oh." She took off her coat. "It was a nice funeral, wasn't it?"

"I guess so. I couldn't tell much since it was all in Hebrew. I guess it was Hebrew—or Yiddish. No, Hebrew. Yiddish is a kind of German, and with all the scientific reading I do I would have caught a word here and there."

She fished in her purse. "The rabbi gave me this little booklet. It has the prayers with the English translation on the opposite page. So I could follow the service, you know. But I was kind of upset and just put it in my purse."

He looked over her shoulder as she leafed through the pages.

"It doesn't say much about death," she remarked, "Just praises God. Oh, here's a section—'O God, who art full of compassion . . . grant perfect rest beneath the shelter of Thy

75

divine Presence. . . . We beseech thee . . . shelter him evermore under the cover of Thy wings. . . .' It says *El Moley Rachamim*. What do you suppose it means?"

"That's just a transliteration of the Hebrew. That must have been what the cantor chanted. You remember in the middle he said Ike's name. Here, you see there's a dash where you supply the name of the deceased."

"Oh, yes. Didn't he have a lovely voice?"

"It was kind of eerie, all that twisting and turning—in a minor key."

"Yes, but it reminded me of Ike somehow. You know, he used to sing like that sometimes. Not sing exactly, but kind of hum. Sometimes when he was trying to work something out in his head, he would walk up and down the room and hum that way to himself. Poor Ike. He was alone so much of the time. He had no family, no friends. He had cut himself off from his own kind—"

He was afraid she was going to break down. "There were a lot more people there than I expected would be," he said to change the subject.

She brightened. "Yes, weren't there? Of course, I knew Liz Marcus was going to come. But the Levensons, and Aaron and Molly Drake, I wasn't sure they could make it. They've been good friends. That little thin man was Mr. Brown the insurance agent. I was surprised he came."

"He's also chairman of the Cemetery Committee. I guess he wanted to make sure everything went off all right."

"Who were those three people standing together behind the rabbi?"

"They were from Goddard. One is a general handyman we have and the other two were technicians. They were all friends of your husband."

"It was nice of them to come. And did you see Peter Dodge?"

He grinned. "I noticed he wasn't wearing his collar."

"Well, under the circumstances I think that's only natural," she said defensively. "Who was that tall, heavy man who kept pretty much to himself?"

He looked at her in surprise. "Didn't you know?"

She shook her head.

"That's the great Mr. Goralsky, Mr. Benjamin Goralsky, financial genius, president of Goraltronics."

"What a shame I didn't know," she said. "I would have thanked him for coming today, a busy man like that. He left right after it was over, though."

"Yes. His mother is buried there and I guess he wanted to visit her grave."

"It's a very nice cemetery, don't you think? Ike would have liked it, a big field on a hill out in the country and all."

"There were only about two or three graves."

"Well, I suppose that's because it's new. Probably in time they'll have to put in a road and replace that broken wire fence, but I like the way it is right now. And Ike's grave, right there near the entrance. Everyone will have to pass by—"

He sat down on the arm of the sofa.

"I meant to ask you, Dr. Sykes. Who was the little red-faced man?"

"No one I ever saw."

"He kept eyeing me all through the service. Every time I'd look up, he was looking at me."

"That's only natural. You were the principal mourner."

"No, everyone else looked at the rabbi or the cantor."

"Maybe it was a friend of Dodge's; they were standing next to each other. Here he comes now. We can ask him."

He opened the door for Peter Dodge and the two men shook hands ceremoniously. "You did a wonderful job," Dodge said. "Everything went off splendidly. I would have offered to help, but it might have proved a bit awkward, you understand—"

"Of course. And I really didn't have to do much, the people at the temple took care of most everything. Well, now that you're here and Mrs. Hirsh is in good hands I'd better be getting back to the lab."

"Oh, do you have to go now, Dr. Sykes?" She held out her hand. "I haven't really thanked you for all you've done. You've been just wonderful."

"Glad I could help. Your husband was a friend, a real friend. He'll be deeply missed. Oh, by the way," he said to Dodge, "who was the short little man standing beside you?"

The minister shook his head. "Don't know. Why?"

"We thought perhaps he was a friend of yours. Well, he must have been someone from the temple."

"You think so? He didn't look Jewish."

"How can you tell these days?"

Both men laughed. Dodge watched through the open door until Sykes had climbed into his car, then shut the door and turned to Pat. He took her hands in his, and holding them wide apart looked at her, his eyes shining with admiration. "You were magnificent, Pat," he said. "A couple of times, I thought you were going to break down, but you rallied splendidly. I can't tell you how proud I was of you."

16

The Goraltronics plant, set back from Route 128 by half an acre of carefully tended lawn, was a one-story building covering two and a half acres with a parking space in the rear for four hundred cars. Seated in his modern office with discreet gray carpeting, the president of the corporation, Mr. Benjamin Goralsky, glanced at the calling card and snapped the corner of it with his thumb. " 'Investigator,' " he read aloud. "That's a detective. I saw you at the funeral. You don't look much like a detective, Mr. Beam."

The figure in the visitor's chair on the other side of the curved slab of teak that comprised Goralsky's desk was short and fat with a round red face like an Edam cheese. His dark eyes all but disappeared when he laughed. He laughed easily.

"I don't suppose any detective that looked like one would be worth much," he said and smiled. "But I'm not a detective—at least, not the kind you read about. I don't carry a gun and go around rescuing beautiful blondes. I just ask questions."

"And you want to ask me some questions about Isaac Hirsh. Why me?"

"Well, for one thing, Mr. Goralsky, you were at the funeral. Everybody else I could account for: they were friends of the widow, or associates of the deceased, or officials of the temple. But I couldn't understand why a big, important businessman like you would be there. And in the middle of a working day too."

"It's what we call a *mitzvah,* a blessing or a good deed, to go to a funeral. The rabbi announced it at the minyan—that's our regular service—this morning. He asked as many as could to go. Strictly speaking, it's a service so you're supposed to have ten men there. The others couldn't get away—they've got jobs. I'm my own boss, so I went. Besides, my mother is buried there and it gave me a chance to visit her grave."

"I see."

"But what's all this about? Does your company always make this kind of investigation before settling a claim?"

"Only where there's a question, Mr. Goralsky."

"What sort of question?"

"Well, when a man drives into his garage, turns off the headlights, closes the garage door behind him, and then is found dead of carbon monoxide poisoning there's always a question."

"Suicide?"

"Isaac Hirsh took out an insurance policy of twenty-five thousand dollars less than a year ago. There's a two-year suicide clause on all our policies and double indemnity for accidental death. If his death was an accident, the company forks out fifty thousand dollars. If it was suicide, we don't pay a red cent. The company feels that fifty thousand dollars is worth a little investigation."

"Yeah, I guess it is. And now that you've done a little investigating, what do you think?"

Beam smiled, and his eyes seemed to vanish. "I'm not the front office, but I'm guessing that when they get my report they won't pay without the beneficiary going to court and making us. Look, this is a little narrow garage he's got. There's a trash barrel on the right. To get the car in far enough to close the door, Hirsh has to drive all the way to the back wall and in between the barrel on one side and the garage wall on the other. It's a tight squeeze—I measured it myself. As it was, he left himself just over a foot on the driver's side and about the same on the other. Get the picture?

"Now that's pretty good driving for a drunk. Then he douses the lights but leaves the motor running. He slides out from under the wheel on the passenger side. It's too tight a squeeze on the driver's side because he's kind of a fat little guy like me—and he pulls down the garage door. Then he comes back and gets in the front seat again, on the passenger side, where he was found.

"Now when you consider that most people shut off the motor almost automatically when they get into the garage, and that he didn't forget to turn off the car lights or shut the garage door, that's kind of hard to see as an accident. If he was so boozed up that he didn't remember to shut off the motor, how come he was able to drive so straight

79

and true, and how come he was able to remember to turn off the car lights and pull down the garage door behind him?"

"So why did the police call it accidental death?"

"The police! The guy is a citizen. He's got an important job with the Goddard Lab, which is kind of a big outfit around here. What are they going to do? Make trouble? I figure before they'd call it suicide they'd practically expect him to make out a written statement stating his intentions and then have it witnessed by a notary."

"I see. So what do you want from me?"

"Anything at all, Mr. Goralsky. Anything you can tell me."

The interoffice communicator buzzed. Goralsky pressed a button. "Yeah?"

"Mr. Stevenson of Halvordsen Enterprises is here to see you," came from the box on the desk.

"I'll be right out." He turned to Beam, visibly agitated. "Sorry, Mr. Beam, this is important. There's nothing I can tell you, nothing at all."

17

"Is something wrong?" Mrs. Hirsh asked Dr. Sykes. He had phoned from the lab to say he had important news she ought to know about at once. She led him into the living room, still unstraightened from the afternoon visitors.

"I wouldn't call it wrong, exactly, Mrs. Hirsh, but I thought you ought to know. That fat little red-faced man who was at the funeral—you remember you said he was eying you all through the ceremony."

"Yes, I remember."

"Well, his name is Beam, Charles Beam. He was at the lab when I got back. He's an investigator for the insurance company that sold your husband his policy."

"What was he doing at the funeral?"

"Good question. I guess he was investigating."

"What are you trying to tell me, Dr. Sykes? What is there to investigate?"

"That policy your husband took out, like all policies written these days, had a suicide clause. It also had an accidental death clause."

"I knew that."

"Very well. If it was suicide they pay nothing; if it was an accident they pay fifty thousand dollars. That's a lot of money, and naturally they want to make sure it wasn't suicide."

"Well, sure, I don't blame them, but it wasn't. The police did some investigating, too, and they decided officially it was accidental. I should think that would settle it."

"I'm afraid it isn't as easy as that. The police don't have to pay out any hard cash. They just have to come up with a cause of death for their records. Naturally, unless they have positive proof, they'll put down accidental death. It's kinder to the family."

"But why would Ike commit suicide? He'd have no reason. He liked living here. We were getting along fine."

Sykes said nothing.

"They've got to prove that it was suicide, don't they? They can't just say they think it was suicide and refuse to pay, can they?"

"No, of course not."

"Well?"

"Look, Mrs. Hirsh, the custom in such cases is to investigate and should they decide it's suicide they refuse to pay and it's up to you to bring suit to collect. If they don't have positive proof, they're apt to offer a settlement—seventy-five percent of the claim, say, or fifty percent—depending on how strong they feel their case is."

"But I don't have to take it."

"No, of course not, but you should have all the facts before you make up your mind one way or the other."

"What do you mean by that?"

"That's why I came over." Choosing his words carefully, he said, "I never was going to tell you this, Mrs. Hirsh, and I wouldn't now if you didn't need to know to help decide a very important question. But the fact is your husband was going to be fired and he knew it."

"Fired? But why? I thought he was doing well."

Sykes obviously was embarrassed. "I wish that were so," he said gently. "Especially since from all I've heard, your husband was quite a man when younger. When he was on the Manhattan Project his work was very well thought of by some mighty important people. But since coming to Goddard, and probably for a while before that, he just didn't have it. He made half a dozen mistakes in the—what is it, less than a year?—he'd been with us. I covered for him each time with the boss, but this last time he made a mistake that was pretty serious. It was on a job for one of our most important clients, and I did what I could but the boss was stubborn. Ike had an appointment with him for Monday morning."

"But what did he do?"

"I don't think I could explain it unless you were a mathematician. But in general, his research seemed to prove that a whole new process was possible, a much cheaper way of doing the thing—sorry, but I can't be any more explicit—and doing it better. The story leaked out and the company's stock went up. And then we found that your husband had made a mistake. Naturally the client was angry. What made it bad is that the company is involved in a merger, so it makes them look as though they were manipulating their stock."

"And Ike knew it?"

Dr. Sykes remained silent.

"Oh, Ike, you poor dear. He must have known and wanted to keep it from me. He was probably afraid we'd have to pick up and move along. We had moved so many times—because of the drinking, you know—and he knew I was beginning to think we had it pretty much licked and we'd be able to stay. He knew I liked it here—"

She broke off as a sudden thought occurred to her. "You don't think it was because he was afraid he didn't have it anymore, Dr. Sykes? I mean, you say he made mistakes—he never used to make mistakes. If he thought his mind wasn't as sharp—from the drinking perhaps— But I wouldn't have cared. He must have known that. No matter what happened, he'd still be plenty smart for me."

"I'm sure he did know, Mrs. Hirsh," Sykes said.

She sat up and squared her shoulders. "All right, then, what do I do now?"

"Nothing. You don't have to do anything. When you hear from the insurance company, you can decide then. If I can help—" He got up. "If there is anything I can do, Pat —anything at all—you have only to call."

She nodded. "Yes, I know. You've been a good friend to us."

18

   "Possel? What do you mean *possel?"*

"It's like *tref,* not kosher, it's unclean."

"What are you saying, Mr. Goralsky? How can our cemetery be unclean?"

"It's unclean because there's a suicide buried there. A suicide is supposed to be buried in a corner, near the wall, off to one side. You buried a suicide right in front and that makes the whole place *possel."*

"We didn't bury any suicide, Ben. Who are you talking about?"

"Look, Mr. Schwarz, don't pull that with me. Yesterday you people buried Isaac Hirsh in your cemetery. I was there. I saw it. Today, the insurance investigator comes to see me, and there's no doubt the guy committed suicide. So I mention it to my father and he gets terribly upset."

"Why should he be upset?"

"Why? Because, in case it's slipped your mind, my mother is also buried there. All her life, she was a good, pious woman. She kept a kosher house and observed every rule and regulation, and now she lies in ground that's been contaminated. And I shouldn't be concerned? And my father shouldn't be upset?"

"Look, Ben, Mr. Goralsky, I don't know anything about Isaac Hirsh. First I've heard of the name. This is a matter the Cemetery Committee takes care of. I'm sure there's some explanation. Did the rabbi officiate at the burial?"

"Of course he did. And he made a eulogy, and he made the blessings. Yet only a few days ago—on the eve of Yom Kippur—with my own ears I heard him threaten my father that if he didn't take his medicine and died, he would consider him a suicide and bury him in a corner without blessings or eulogy. Then along comes this Isaac Hirsh, who isn't even a member of the temple—and this is supposed to be a private cemetery for members only—and his wife isn't even Jewish, and the rabbi buries him with all the trimmings. You say there's an explanation. I guess there is. The explanation is that you guys wanted to sell a cemetery lot, and for the couple of hundred bucks or whatever it runs, you didn't care what happened to anybody else who was buried there."

"I assure you, Ben, it was nothing like that. Marvin Brown, the chairman of our committee, would never do a thing like that. And our rabbi wouldn't either. There must be some mistake."

"You think my father doesn't know what's kosher and what ain't?"

"Of course not, but that insurance investigator could be mistaken."

"How could he be mistaken? He laid it out for me plain as day. This Hirsh goes into his garage and closes the door. Then he sits in his car swigging booze with the motor running. So is it suicide, or isn't it?"

"Well, it certainly sounds that way, but— Look, if anything can be done—"

"If?"

"Well, tell me, what do you want us to do?"

"You can get him out of there."

"You mean exhume the body? Ben, we couldn't do that. You wouldn't want us to do that. It would create a scandal. We'd need the consent of the widow. The town would—"

"Look, Schwarz"—Goralsky's tone was cold and dispassionate—"you've been sweet-talking my father about building a chapel, and he's half committed himself to you. Personally, I think the congregation needs a new chapel about as much as they need a pogrom, but if the old man wants it it's all right by me. But I'm telling you right here and now that if you don't take care of this cemetery business, any money you get out of us wouldn't even build a pup tent."

"Mort, I'm not one of the rabbi's most ardent admirers any more than you are, but you've got to admit he knows his stuff. I mean, if he buried Hirsh then it must be okay."

"You don't understand, Marvin. You still don't get it," said Schwarz wearily. "The rabbi probably didn't go into the question of suicide at all. Maybe he suspected and maybe he didn't. Suppose he did, what would he do? He'd call his friend the police chief who would naturally give him the official finding, death by accident. So he went ahead. In his place I wouldn't have done any different. And if we ask him, I'm sure he'll say everything is right and kosher. He's not going to come right out and say he made a mistake."

"So what can we do about it now? We can't take the body out."

"Well— You know, if the widow wouldn't object—"

"Forget it, Mort. Even if she were willing, and if I'm any judge of character she wouldn't be, we'd have to get the approval of the Board of Health of Darbury where our cemetery is, and of the Board of Health of the place where he would be reburied. There'd be so much red tape and so much publicity—"

"Actually, it was Ben Goralsky's idea, Marve. I told him all that."

"So have you got any other ideas?"

"Well," Schwarz began cautiously, "it stands to reason this must happen fairly often, especially where we bury them as soon as we can. Then a couple of days later they find a note, and what they thought was a normal death now is a suicide. So I figure there must be some machinery for taking care of this kind of thing. Some ceremony of purification, say, that the rabbi can perform that would make the cemetery kosher again. The rabbi could dress it up, put on a real show— What's the matter?" as Marvin shook his head slowly.

"I don't think the rabbi would do it."

"Dammit, if the Board orders him to, he'll have to."

"I don't know. I'm not sure that's something the Board can order. It seems to me it would be up to the rabbi to decide. And I'll tell you something else: I'm not so sure I like the idea myself."

"Why not?"

"Because I don't think it would do the cemetery any good."

"Now what's that supposed to mean?"

"Look, Mort, you're an architect so maybe you don't understand the psychology of selling. It's hard enough to sell someone a cemetery lot—it's what we call an intangible, like insurance. The people in our congregation are all pretty young. Their minds aren't running to things like cemetery lots. But a good salesman can convince them. Sometimes, he appeals to their sense of loyalty to the temple; sometimes to their sense of responsibility to their wives and families. Sometimes you just shame them into it. But whatever your approach, you've got to make sure your product is perfect, without a flaw. The minute there's something wrong with your product and your prospect knows it, he grabs onto it and uses it against you. If we let on there is something wrong with the cemetery, that maybe it isn't a hundred percent kosher, I figure three quarters of those people I've got lined up right now I can kiss them goodby."

"So they'll buy a little later—"

"Mort, you talk as though you didn't realize what the cemetery can do for a congregation. Remember, the temple bought the land last year when Becker was president. And whatever you say against Becker, remember he was a businessman. He made me chairman of the committee because he figured that a guy who could sell insurance could sell cemetery lots. Like I say, they're both intangibles. He used to kid me about it. 'Marve,' he used to say, 'you sell them insurance which is like betting them that they're going to live, and they're betting they won't. So when you sell them a lot, you're hedging your bets. Son of a gun, you got them coming and going.' And I've used that on some of my prospects—it kind of makes a joke of it."

"I'll admit you're good, Marve. That's why I kept you on as chairman when I was making up my committees. So what are you getting at?"

"All I'm saying," said Marvin doggedly, "is you should appreciate what the cemetery can mean to the congregation."

"But if we don't do something right now, we stand to lose the Goralskys."

Marvin was not impressed. "I'll admit it's nice to have a first-class tycoon type like Ben Goralsky associated with the temple, but not if we have to kowtow to him every time he—"

"Look Marvin, if I tell you something, can you keep it under your hat? Suppose I said I practically have an ironclad promise from the old man, Ben's father, that he will ante up the money for a new chapel—not just a big donation, but the whole cost, maybe a hundred and fifty thousand dollars."

Marvin whistled. "A hundred and fifty grand!"

"Maybe more."

Marvin drew a pencil from his pocket. "Then in that case, I may just have an idea," he said. He fished around and brought forth from an inside pocket an advertising folder, which he discarded in annoyance.

"What are you looking for? Paper?" Schwarz slid a pad over to him.

"Thanks." He drew a rough square and in the bottom righthand corner made a small x. "This is the cemetery and here is where Hirsh is buried. All right. According to Goralsky, a suicide is supposed to be buried in a corner off to one side. So we make a corner." He drew an oval inside the perimeter of the square. It enclosed the entire area except for the four corners. "By building a circular road inside the cemetery, that leaves Hirsh's grave *outside*—and in a corner. What do you think?"

Schwarz looked at the drawing in amazement. "Marvin, you're a genius! You just thought that up?"

"Well, I've been playing with the idea in another connection. You remember a couple of Board meetings ago I said we had to have a road through the cemetery. The Board turned it down because they didn't want to go into that kind of money at the time. But I thought about it a lot, trying to figure out a pattern that would give access to all parts of the cemetery and still eat up the least possible land. This seemed to fill the bill."

"But isn't a circular road apt to be more expensive?"

"We don't have to do the whole road. Even keeping to our present budget—the money already voted that I have in hand—we can lay it out and do just one corner, Hirsh's corner to start with. We'll finish the rest when the Board votes more money."

"By God, Marve, I think that'll do it. I still say you're a genius."

Marvin looked dubious. "How about the rabbi?"

"What about him?"

"Do we tell him?"

Schwarz considered. "I guess we better, if only to make sure this will do the trick."

19

"Surely you must be joking," exclaimed the rabbi. "You're harking back to the Dark Ages. During the Nazi Terror, there must have been hundreds of suicides. Would you have denied them ritual burial?"

"But you yourself threatened old man Goralsky with just that, according to his son," said Schwarz.

"Threatened him? I was scaring an adult with the bogeyman. He could tell I wasn't really serious. I was just trying to get him to take his medicine. I told you all about it at the temple."

"Yes, but Ben Goralsky evidently took it seriously," said Schwarz.

"I doubt if he did at the time," said the rabbi. "But in any case, on what grounds can you assume Hirsh was a suicide? The police verdict was accidental death. And I went to the trouble of discussing it personally with the chief of police, and he feels the evidence overwhelmingly favors that finding. Are we to be more callous in our dealings with the dead and bereaved than the civil authorities?"

"Suppose it finally was decided that he was a suicide?" asked Marvin.

"Decided by whom?"

"Well, by a court of law."

"Even then, the chances are that he was either temporarily insane or suffering from a compulsion so extreme he was powerless to withstand it. So he wouldn't be accounted a suicide in the eyes of Jewish Law."

"Yes, but if he *was* a suicide, just suppose he was," Marvin persisted. "Then wouldn't it be up to us or to you to do something about it?"

"Why would anything have to be done about it? He was buried—that in itself is a cleansing action. 'The earth is the Lord's and the fullness thereof.' Burial itself cleanses. When a utensil becomes *tref*, the way you cleanse it is to bury it in the earth. Are you suggesting that the presence of this man's body pollutes God's earth? And if so, where does it stop? At the boundary of our cemetery, which is an artificial line recorded in the Registry of Deeds, or does it go on indefinitely until it reaches the ocean?"

"Well, maybe there's some prayer—"

"Some bit of hocus-pocus? That I can make a few magician's passes over the grave? Is that what you had in mind, Mr. Brown?"

"Now look here, Rabbi," said Schwarz. "We are all practical men, I hope, and we are up against a practical matter. I'm not worried about the cemetery being polluted and Marvin here isn't either. But this is something that Ben Goralsky, and evidently his father, take seriously. Call it superstition, if you will. Call it ignorance, but it bothers them.

"Now we're practical men, Rabbi, Marvin and I. As chairman of the Cemetery Committee, Marvin is concerned with the effect on sales of cemetery lots if this story gets around, and I am concerned with keeping the Goralskys in the temple organization. We've worked out what I consider a practical solution to a sticky little problem, and what we want from you is just some information. What we have in mind is to build a circular road inside the cemetery. Like this—" And he took out the sketch. "Now here is where Hirsh is buried. If we keep him outside the road and from now on sell lots only on the inside, will that satisfy the regulations? Actually, Hirsh stands to gain. Since we can't use the corner land naturally we'd want to beautify it—put in some shrubbery, trees. What we want to know is whether that would do it."

The rabbi rose from his chair. He looked at each of them in turn, as though unable to believe they were serious. "Is a man a dog?" he demanded, his fury all the more intense because he kept it controlled, "that you presume to toss his body from one place to another as suits you? Is the service I conducted at his grave just a bit of mumbo jumbo of no significance and no meaning? Last week I joined with other rabbis in submitting a petition to our State Department asking them to protest the Russian government's desecration of Jewish graves. And now you would have me party to a plan to desecrate a grave in our own cemetery to satisfy the superstitions of a foolish and ignorant old man and his equally foolish and ignorant son? Are our ceremonies to have a price to be sold to the highest bidder?"

"Just a minute, Rabbi, we're not desecrating any grave. We have no intention of molesting Hirsh's grave."

The rabbi lowered his voice even further. "A woman not of our faith comes to us and asks us to bury her dead husband in our cemetery because he was Jewish. She regards it as her last act of loyalty and love to lay him to rest among his own people, and you propose to differentiate his grave from all the rest? And you don't consider this desecration? In good faith, she paid her money—three or four times the price of a lot in the public cemetery, mind you—only to have her husband separated, markedly separated from the rest of the cemetery, as—as a thing unclean?"

"I'll bet I could get her to agree," said Marvin.

"It's purely an administrative matter," said Schwarz.

"You are a salesman, Mr. Brown, and a successful one," said the rabbi. "It's quite possible you could persuade a widow in her bereavement to consent to your plan. But you can't persuade me. And I consider it something more than just an administrative matter, Mr. Schwarz. I will not be a party to it."

"Well, I'm sorry you feel this way, Rabbi," said Schwarz.

"I consider it a practical solution to a practical problem. I am concerned with the living rather than the dead. I am concerned with the effect on our congregation of having the Goralskys as members rather than whether the grave of Isaac Hirsh who was not even a member of our organization is on one side of a road or another."

"I cannot approve and I will so tell the Board when the matter comes up."

Schwarz smiled. "I'm sorry we don't have your approval, Rabbi, but I'm afraid we'll have to go ahead without it. And it won't come up before the Board. This is a matter in which the Cemetery Committee has full authority."

"Of course, we'll take a vote of the committee," Marvin observed.

"Vote or no vote, I forbid it."

"Look, Rabbi, we didn't have to come to you in the first place. We just wanted everything aboveboard."

"But you did come, and I forbid it."

Schwarz shrugged his shoulders. He rose and the two men left. The rabbi stood by his desk, angry and baffled.

"What did he mean he forbids it?" asked Marvin. "Can he do something?"

"Like what?"

"I don't know, call some board of rabbis—"

"Don't be silly. Our temple is a completely autonomous body, and the rabbi is just an employee. He's told us that often enough himself. The only thing he can do if he doesn't like it is resign."

"After what I just heard, that might not be such a bad idea," said Marvin.

"You don't like him?"

"I think we can do better," said Marvin evenly.

"Yeah? How do you mean?"

"Well, I'm a businessman. Over the past few years I've had a lot of people working for me—salesmen and office help. I've got a rule about help. I don't care how good they are, I don't care how much of a world-beater a salesman is; if he can't take orders, he goes."

"That's the way I feel, Marve. Say, who's on your committee?"

"Summer Pomeranz, Bucky Lefkowitz, and Ira Dorfman. Why? Not one of them has done a damn thing, but they're on the committee."

"That's three and you make four. Didn't I appoint another so as to have an odd number?"

"You're on it ex officio. That makes five."

"Good. So all we need is one more for a majority. Look, Marve, why don't you get hold of them. Tell them as much as you think they have to know and get their vote for this new road. Just in case the rabbi gets cute."

"No sweat. They know I do all the work, and they don't ever go against my decisions."

"Right. When you get it nailed down, why don't you call the rabbi and tell him you've taken a vote, and your committee is one hundred percent in favor of the new road."

"That is a good idea, Mort. It will keep him from getting any fancy ideas."

"Let me know how you make out. But act fast. I don't want to give the rabbi a chance to block us."

20

Marvin was elated when he called Schwarz Friday morning. "I just got through talking to the rabbi. I didn't crow, but told him I thought he'd like to know that the committee vote was unanimous."

"What did he say?"

"He didn't say anything."

"Dammit, Marvin, he must have said something."

"I'm telling you he didn't say anything. Just, 'I see,' or something like that. No, come to think of it, that's all he said, 'I see.' "

"Was he sore?"

"I couldn't tell, but since he didn't say anything, I figure he knows he's beaten. So the thing for us to do is go ahead full steam."

"I'm not so sure, Marve. I've had some second thoughts on the matter."

"How do you mean?"

"A thing like this—it could backfire on us. If he were to bring the matter before the Board Sunday—"

"And Wasserman and maybe Becker side with him and

between them they'd pull over a few more—yeah, you got a point there. What do you think we ought to do?"

"What we need, Marve, is a consensus. Maybe I ought to talk to some of the members before the Board meeting. What are you doing tomorrow night?"

"Well, Mitzi suggested we take in this foreign film at the Strand—"

"Strictly a dud. Ethel and I saw it last week in town. Why don't you come over, and I'll contact some of the boys—"

"I get it. You're going to show them the model."

"Right."

The group returned from the study to the living-room where Ethel Schwarz had prepared coffee and ice cream and delicious little French cookies. "You know, Mort," Hal Berkowitz said, "what I can't get through my noggin is why the rabbi, of all people, should want to do anything to keep that building of yours from going up. I mean, your chapel has class, and what's more, it's his—"

"That's right," chimed in Abner Sussman. "It's his place of business, you might say. I was visiting my brother in Richmond Friday night and the rabbi was over. Most of the time we were talking business, and I had been telling them how I remodeled my store. After dinner we all started out for services, and when we got to the temple the rabbi says, "How do you like *my* store? "

"What gets me," Berkowitz said, "our rabbi is supposed to be so traditional and the building we got now looks like anything but a synagogue. Now Mort's scheme here makes it look like a real synagogue—"

"Seems to me you're both missing the point," said Nelson Bloomberg. "Here we've got a chance to make a giant step forward. We can make our temple a real showplace on the North Shore. I don't claim to have any great aesthetic appreciation—although in the dress business, let me tell you, you better develop a sense of style or you're in trouble—but to me, Mort's is the kind of building that would get talked about. The kind of building you might expect to see pictured in some magazine. To me, it represents progress. And what's standing in the way? A ghost. No, not even a ghost, a corpse—the dead body of this guy Hirsh who wasn't even a member of the congregation. Here we have something that means progress for an entire community—something wholesome and alive—and the rabbi throws in a monkey wrench with a lot of ghoulish technicalities about graves and burials and death. It's just plain gruesome, when you come right down to it."

"Nel's put the whole thing in a nutshell," said Nate Shatz. "We had a pretty awkward situation here. This idea of having the driveway so everybody is satisfied, Goralsky, the widow, the temple—that's the kind of thing the rabbi is supposed to dope out. And what happens? Marve and Mort figure it out, and the rabbi instead of being grateful says he forbids it. Either we like it or lump it. Well, I say the fat's in the fire and we go ahead with the road. He can resign, for all I care."

"What's he ever done to you?" asked Jerry Feldman. "You sound angry."

"I am. He acts as though he's too good for the likes of us. I see him at the Board meetings and sometimes he says hello and sometimes he doesn't. My wife gave a bridge and invited his wife, but when she got there all she would take was tea. If he's too good to eat with us, he's too good to rabbi for us."

"Well, I wouldn't condemn a man because he sticks to his principles," said Feldman. "If a man wants to eat kosher, especially if he's a rabbi, I see no harm in it. My mother always kept a kosher house with two sets of dishes and everything. When she'd come to my house, she wouldn't eat with us either. At the same time—I say maybe we can do better. Personally I'd like to see a man who was a leader and looked like a leader. A man who would take hold and build this place up."

"A lot of people come into your store, Abner, and you must have heard them talking," said Schwarz. "How do you think people feel about him?"

Sussman rotated his hand. *"Comme ci, comme ça.* Some people say he keeps to himself a lot and they don't like a rabbi to be so standoffish. Some say when they go to the temple on a Friday night they like to hear a sermon—not just a casual talk like he thought it up on his way over. But don't think he hasn't friends; he has. A lot of people like the way he talks—common sense and no bull. Like Jerry here, some object to the way he dresses—more like a bookkeeper making seventy-five a week. But that works for him too—brings out the motherly instincts, if you know what I mean.

"Of course, I see mostly women in my place, and they're always complaining about something. He's not interested in their work. Half the time when he's supposed to go to a Sisterhood meeting, they're not even sure he'll show up. But you know women; if he were a big handsome guy he could do anything he liked and they'd love it. On the other hand, there's no doubt they've got a lot of influence with their menfolk."

"How about those who are strong for him?"

"Well, like I say, he's got his friends but they're scattered, so I wouldn't say he has what you might call a following. I mean he's not the kind of guy that goes out of his way to get a group behind him. And he hasn't exactly got what you'd call a magnetic personality like some of these glad-handers. You know, my father was president of one temple and a big shot in another, so I know a little about rabbis. You take a smart rabbi, the first thing he does when he comes to a new place he sort of gets the lay of the land—who's important and who isn't. Then he develops a party, a clique. Everybody knows they're the rabbi's friends, see? Then any time the rabbi wants something, he doesn't ask the Board of Directors himself personally. He whispers to one of his buddies who is damn important, some guy with plenty of dough who has kicked in to the building fund or who can be tapped for a big contribution when you need it. Then this guy, he talks to the other friends of the rabbi and when one of them gets up in the Board meeting and says, I think we should do thus and so, why somebody else seconds it quick as a wink and before you can say *Gut Shabbes* it's passed. A rabbi like that, he runs the organization."

"I see."

"Now our rabbi—he don't have any organization behind him."

"How about Wasserman and Becker and Doc Carter?"

Sussman shook his head. "They're not an organization. Wasserman backs him because he picked him, and Becker because he helped out his partner when he got into that trouble a couple of years ago so he feels obligated. You know how a rabbi goes about setting up an organization? He visits with them, he invites them to his house. He's nice to their wives and he's helpful to their kids. One I knew who used to help his friends' kids with their school lessons when he'd come to visit—not their Hebrew school lessons but their public school lessons. Another one would play baseball with some of the kids, and this one even had a beard. Can you imagine our rabbi playing ball?"

Everyone laughed.

"All right," said Schwarz, "so the consensus of the meeting is. . . ."

Marvin Brown held back after the others left. "You know, Mort, if this doesn't go through we'll be left with egg all over our faces."

"Marve, old boy, it's in the bag. Nel Bloomberg gave it to us when he said the rabbi was fighting progress. That's our new theme song—the rabbi is against progress."

"I didn't mean the rabbi, I was thinking of Goralsky. How much of a commitment do you have from the old man?"

"It's pretty firm. Ben was the stumbling block, but now with this, he's sure to be on our side."

"How do you mean?"

"Well, when he called to tell me about the cemetery, he mentioned his father's interest in the chapel and said we wouldn't get it if the situation wasn't taken care of. Well, if we do clean it up, and we point out that to do it we had a regular hassle with the rabbi, will he have the nerve to say he changed his mind?"

"Maybe, but you know how these things work. Goralsky can stall. The old man can say he put it in his will—why not?" as Schwarz shook his head.

"Because, Marve old boy, I just decided this is going to be called the Hannah Goralsky Memorial Chapel. Get it? We'll make this a memorial to his wife, Ben's mother. So isn't the old man going to want to see it? Isn't he going to want to be there to lay the cornerstone, and be at the ceremony when it's completed, and to be the first one called up for the Reading on the first service that's held there?"

Marvin Brown began to chuckle. "You know, Mort, you're pretty cute yourself. I think we pulled a fast one on the rabbi."

21

Saturday morning at morning services the rabbi's throat felt dry and scratchy. When he got home he was tired and had little appetite for lunch. He intended to return and spend the afternoon in the temple study, but his bones ached so he lay down on the living-room couch and dozed off. After his nap he felt better and went to the temple for the evening service, and by the time he got home he had a chill; his head felt warm.

The rush of warm air as Miriam opened the door struck him like a blow. His nose twitched and he exploded in a loud sneeze.

"Are you catching cold, David?"

"I don't think so," he said, but she stood on tiptoe and kissed him on the forehead. "You're warm. You've probably got a temperature."

"Oh, I'm all right." But he sneezed again. Paying no attention she marched into the bathroom and appeared a moment later shaking the thermometer with a professional snap of the wrist, inserting it over his mumbled protest.

"101.4. You've got a fever," she announced. "You get undressed right now, David Small, and get into bed."

"You're making too much of it," he said. "I caught cold. I'll be fine in the morning."

"Not if you don't take care of yourself." She forced water and orange juice on him and aspirin, but when she took his temperature later on in the evening it had risen to 102.

"I'm calling Dr. Sigman," she said.

"Oh, what's the sense. It's just a cold, there's nothing he can do about it. I'd rather you wouldn't call."

"Why not?"

"Because he won't charge me but he'll feel it necessary to come out anyway."

"I can ask him if he wants to see you." From her tone of voice he knew it was useless to argue.

"He had it himself last week," she said when she returned to the bedroom. "He says there's a lot of it going around. It's a virus infection but doesn't last long, a couple of days. Just as I said, you are to stay in bed, take aspirin and liquids, and you're not to venture out until you've had a normal temperature for twenty-four hours."

"A couple of days! But I've got a Board meeting tomorrow."

"Not any longer. You're staying in bed, at least until Monday. The Board will manage for once without the wisdom of your counsel, I'm sure."

"But tomorrow is particularly important. I've just *got* to be there."

"We'll talk about it tomorrow. And don't count on it."

The Board meeting began at ten; but a number of members arrived earlier, since they had children in the religious school which began at nine. Before that, at eight-thirty, was the morning minyan when the rabbi normally arrived on Sundays. After the service, he would go visit the classrooms, and at ten join the Board of Directors at their meeting. Since it was a special privilege, he tried to attend as often as possible; of all the rabbis in the area, he alone was permitted at Board meetings.

But this Sunday he did not appear at the minyan or at religious school classes. Instead he was at his own breakfast table in bathrobe and slippers having eggs and toast, the diet Miriam considered proper for a sick man.

At the temple, no one commented particularly on his absence; several times before he had been unable to attend. But Mortimer Schwarz and Marvin Brown felt it had special significance.

"It's obvious, isn't it?" said Schwarz. "He's thought it over and found he hasn't a leg to stand on. If he were to make a fight of it—and he'd have to—and were beaten, he'd either have to resign or back down. He doesn't want to do either one so he just stayed away."

"So what do we do now?"

"Well, you know, Marve, I think this kind of changes things. With the rabbi not here, maybe you should give a committee report. This might be a good time to ask for an increase in your budget. You don't have to mention Hirsh. You could just talk of the need to build a road."

Just then Arnold Green, the corresponding secretary, signaled Schwarz to come over.

"What's up, Arnie?"

Green drew the president to a corner and held out a letter. "Read this. It was in the Board mailbox when I came in. According to the postmark, we must have got it Saturday. It's from the rabbi. I thought I better speak to you before I read it to the Board."

Schwarz read the letter quickly, then folded it and put it back in the envelope. When he spoke his voice was intense. "Look, Arnie, I don't want this read at the meeting today. I want you to forget you ever received it, understand?"

"But I'm supposed to read all communications received."

"Well, you weren't supposed to receive this one. It was addressed to me, and I want you to promise you won't say a word about it."

"What's it all about?"

"I don't know a hell of a lot more than you do, but unless I get a chance to find out, this organization can be split

97

wide open. You remember what happened when his contract came up for renewal. You wouldn't want that again, would you?"

"Of course not. But when the rabbi sends a letter to the Board, he's going to wonder why it wasn't read."

"But he's not here today. Don't worry—it'll get read. But it'll keep for a week."

"If that's the way you want it."

"That's the way I want it. Now let's get the meeting going."

"The rabbi's got a touch of the grippe," Dr. Sigman explained when the Board members had settled into their places. "Had it myself last week. He should be up and around by the middle of the week."

"I just got over it a couple of days ago," remarked Bob Fine. "And I was going to call you, Doc, but when your Shirley told Myra you'd had it, too, I figured you wouldn't have anything to prescribe so why not save myself a few bucks?"

Dr. Sigman laughed. "I'll have to talk to Shirley about giving away my secrets."

Sitting well to the back in the room, Marvin Brown managed to catch the president's eye. Schwarz nodded briefly and called the meeting to order. The secretary read the minutes, then he called for the reports of the committee. Marvin Brown did not offer a report, but when the New Business was announced he raised his hand and was recognized.

"I don't know if I should have given this during committee reports, but I'm planning to make a motion so I thought I'd hold it until now. Before I make my motion, I'd like to give a few words of explanation."

"You're supposed to make your motion, then if it's seconded and the president calls for discussion you can make your explanation." Al Becker, last year's president, was a stickler for parliamentary rules.

"Well, that's all right, Al, but suppose nobody seconds my motion. Then I don't get a chance to explain."

"So it means the explanation isn't necessary."

"Yeah, well then if I quit as chairman of the Cemetery Committee, and you ask me why, I'll tell you the reason was in the explanation you didn't let me give."

"Look, fellows, there's no sense getting sore about this," Schwarz interposed. "You're absolutely right about the correct procedure, Al, but it sounds as though Marve has a beef and I think we ought to hear it. I can rule him out of order if in my opinion he's not talking to the point."

"That's just the point," Becker objected. "How can you tell if he's talking to the point when he hasn't made a point yet?"

"Aw, let him talk."

"I'm not trying to keep him from talking. I just say we ought to operate according to the rules. But you guys want to do it this way, go ahead."

"All right, Marvin."

"Well, it's like this. I'm damn sick and tired of trying to sell what can't be sold. It's a thankless job. Now I'm a salesman by profession and a salesman depends on his confidence. And this assignment of the Cemetery Committee—I tell you, fellows, I'm losing my confidence. It seems to me that most of you don't have the slightest idea of how important the cemetery is to the congregation. Most of you take the attitude that it's some kind of joke. Oh, I don't mind you whistling a funeral march when I get up to give my report. I can take a joke as well as the next guy, but what bothers me is that you're not serious about the thing itself. All these wisecracks about my getting you coming and going, insurance while you're living, and a plot in the cemetery when you're not—that's well and good; but sometime we've got to look at this realistically, and as far as I'm concerned the sometime is now."

"So what do you want, Marve?"

"I want you to think about what this cemetery can mean for a progressive organization like ours. This community is growing. Someday, and it's not far off, there's going to be another temple in Barnard's Crossing, maybe a couple of them. And their membership won't be made up entirely of newcomers to the area. Maybe one of the temples will be Reform and I'll bet there'll be a lot of our members who will feel like switching. But if they own a family plot with us, or if a member of their family is buried there—a husband, a wife, a father, a child—wouldn't that make them think twice before they leave us? And then think of the money. A cemetery can be a gold mine. We charge about four times what the town charges for a lot in the public cemetery. In ten or fifteen years, it could cut our dues, or if it's operated right enable us to expand.

"Now, what are the problems I'm faced with? First off, most of our members are young people. They haven't even started to think about maybe God forbid they'll need a plot someday. And let's face it, when you ask someone to plank down a hundred and fifty-odd bucks for a lot which he doesn't think he's going to need—and I for one hope he doesn't—it's a lot of dough. What's more, a lot of our members work for some of the big corporations and they don't know when they might be transferred to another city. So are they going to come back here to be buried? Well, I got some ideas on the subject. I think we ought to sell lots on the installment plan. I'd like to see members pay as little as ten bucks a year, which could be billed with their membership dues. And I'm in favor of having a clause in the contract to the effect that they can sell the lot back to us anytime they want without losing money. In that way, if they're transferred, they can always get their money back. I'm even toying with the idea of maybe selling lots like a kind of insurance policy, where if the member dies before he has paid in full the widow doesn't have to pay any more."

"Is this the motion you're making, Marve?"

"No, that isn't my motion. I just mentioned all this to show that your committee is thinking about their job all the time. I've had prospects make the kind of objections I've mentioned. But," and here he looked around to make sure he had their attention, "the biggest argument my prospects give me is, 'See me when you get a cemetery. All you've got now is an abandoned hayfield.' And that's the truth. That's all we've got there right now. A hayfield with a saggy wire fence running along the main road and a tumbled-down stone fence running along one side. We don't have a chapel. We don't have flowers and shrubbery to make the place look halfway decent. We don't have the place properly fenced off. We don't have a road to give us full access to the cemetery, the back plots especially. That's the main trouble right now."

"We're planning all those things, but wasn't it decided we would make all the improvements out of income?"

"Sure, but you've got to spend a little money to make some money. Remember, it's the packaging that sells the product."

"Well, you've got a budget of two thousand dollars."

"Yeah, and how far will that take you? Just keeping the grass cut and paying for a part-time caretaker eats that up."

"So what do you want, twenty-five thousand dollars for a regular Forest Lawn so you can sell a couple of lots for a hundred and fifty bucks?"

"I don't think that's fair to Marve," said Schwarz.

"I'll tell you what I want: I want enough money to build a decent road. Then I can sell lots in any part of the cemetery, not just near the corner where there's a hole in the fence. To take care of that we've worked out a scheme that's both practical and economical. What we're planning is a circular road. That will give us access to all parts of the cemetery. What I want is for our budget to be increased to at least five thousand dollars so we can go ahead. We could lay out the whole road and get bids on what it would cost to pave it. Then if the low bid goes above the five grand, and I don't think it will, I'd expect the Board to pick up the tab. And that's my motion."

The secretary looked up from hastily scribbled notes. "A motion was made—did anybody second it?"

"Second the motion."

"Sure, I'll second it."

"All right. A motion was made and seconded that the Cemetery Committee budget be increased to five thousand dollars for the purpose of building a road—"

"Make that a circular road."

"All right—a circular road within the boundaries of the cemetery, any excess monies that are necessary to be . . ."

Morton Schwarz sought out Marvin Brown after the meeting. "I've got to hand it to you, Marve, you certainly put that over. I thought you were all set to hand in your resignation."

Marve grinned. "It's just a selling job as I see it."

"Well, you certainly got the technique. And you sure worked in our theme song." He chuckled. "I'd like to see the rabbi buck this setup."

22

As the founder and first president of the congregation, Jacob Wasserman was considered the elder statesman of the temple. In his sixties, he was quite a bit older than most of the members. He had worked almost single-handed to get the organization started, spending his evenings going to see each of the fifty or so Jewish families that comprised the

Jewish community in Barnard's Crossing shortly after the end of World War II. The first High Holy Day services had been held in the basement of his house with a Torah Scroll borrowed from one of the Lynn synagogues, and he had led the prayers and chanted the portions from the Torah.

Al Becker, who succeeded him as president, accompanied him on his visit to the rabbi. Becker was a short, stocky man with a deep gravelly voice and a belligerent way of using it. Although he had none of Wasserman's learning, to say nothing of his understanding of Jewish tradition, he followed him faithfully and usually voted with him on most Board matters.

"It's lucky Becker and I decided to drop in on you, Rabbi, to see how you were getting along," said Wasserman. "I knew old man Goralsky was an ignoramus, but that his son, a boy born and brought up in America, should be such a superstitious idiot, too—this I wouldn't have believed."

"Just a minute, Jacob," said Becker. "Right is right. How can you say the old man is an ignoramus? A man like that with a beard—he says the prayers faster than anyone in the congregation and most of the time he doesn't even bother to look at the book."

"Please, Becker, stick to things you know about. Goralsky may pray faster than anybody in the congregation and he knows the prayers by heart. Why not? He's been saying them every day morning and night for almost eighty years. But he doesn't know the meaning of them."

"You mean he doesn't understand what he's saying?"

"Do you, when you recite the prayers in Hebrew?"

"To tell the truth, most of the time I use the English side."

"So that's an advantage that you have over him. But the question is what are we going to do now?"

Becker shook his head dolefully. "Too bad you had to get sick, Rabbi. If you had been at the meeting yesterday when the discussion came up, you could have explained what the real issue was—"

"I'm not sure I could have, from the way you report it," said Rabbi Small. "As I gather, the motion was a general one—to give the Cemetery Committee a budget to improve the grounds. In general I think that's a good idea, so under the circumstances I'd be unlikely to rise and accuse Marvin Brown and your president of ulterior motives."

"Of course not," said Wasserman. "It would have been unseemly for the rabbi. It would be like calling Schwarz a liar. And even if he had, and the whole business had come out into the open, what good would it have done? After Schwarz got through explaining, do you doubt that the majority of the Board would have voted with him? Building a road which might affect the grave of an outsider against a building worth a hundred thousand dollars or more?"

"I cannot permit the desecration of the grave of a Jew by fellow Jews," said the rabbi quietly.

"But what can you do about it, Rabbi?" said Becker. "You've got to be reasonable. The road has already been voted, so it's no longer a simple question of being fair to this guy Hirsh. Now it's a question of who is to set policy for the congregation, you or the Board."

"Not quite, Mr. Becker," said the rabbi. "In this matter, my authority is supreme."

"I'm afraid I don't follow you there, Rabbi."

"It's simple enough. Although it is customary to speak of the rabbi as an employee of the congregation, it is a mistake to equate him with other employees. My position here is more like that of the CPA who is engaged to audit the books than that of Stanley Doble who is hired to maintain the building and grounds. I am not a tool of the congregation to be used any way they see fit. I cannot be asked to do something that runs counter to the principles of my profession any more than you can ask a CPA to cover up some discrepancy in the books. The CPA has loyalties to the entire business community that transcend his loyalties to the person who engages him. In the same manner my loyalties cannot be commanded completely. Transcending my loyalties to this congregation are my loyalties to the Jewish tradition, to the Jews of the past, and to Jews as yet unborn. In certain areas, and this is one, my authority is supreme and not subject to question by the congregation."

"But—"

"A widow comes to me," the rabbi went on impatiently, "and asks to have her late husband buried in a Jewish cemetery according to Jewish custom. It is for me to determine if he is a Jew, and I decided he was. Again, it is for me, and only for me, to determine if his manner of death warrants burial according to Jewish rites. If there is the suspicion of suicide it is for me, and only for me, to decide how much weight to give the evidence, how much to allow for mitigating circumstances, and then to decide how rigidly to apply the regulations that govern burial of a suicide. These are not congregational matters; these are purely rabbinic."

"Well, if you put it that way—"

"Now, having made my decision, I referred the widow, or her representative, to the chairman of the Cemetery Committee. Mr. Brown, as the voice of the congregation in this matter, sold the widow a lot in good faith and accepted her money. If the congregation had a regulation limiting the cemetery only to members, and on those grounds had refused to bury Hirsh, I might have considered the regulation harsh or ill-advised but there I would have no authority —only what influence I could bring to bear. But the regulations made special provisions for a case like this. It called for the payment of a fee which conferred nominal membership. And this fee was paid and accepted."

"No question."

"Once having made Hirsh a nominal member of the congregation in accordance with the regulations they themselves made up, they then have to treat his burial exactly as they would any other member's."

"That's not only in the bylaws, but it's in accordance with our tradition," said Wasserman.

"Now, suppose sometime later evidence is adduced, incontrovertible evidence, that Hirsh had actually committed suicide—and such is not the case—then once again it becomes a decision entirely for me, and me alone, whether his presence compromises the cemetery. And if I were to decide that it did, it would be up to me, and me alone, to decide what measures of purification were necessary. But the Board chooses to follow Mr. Goralsky in this matter. Why? Is his *smicha* greater than mine? Did he perhaps receive his from the Vilna Gaon?"

The rabbi's voice had risen, and his normally pale face showed the heat of his indignation. He sat back in his chair and smiled, a small, deprecatory smile. "I told Mr. Schwarz and Mr. Brown that I would forbid this desecration of Hirsh's grave. Of course, in the present congregation-rabbi relationship, my ban has no force behind it. So when Mr. Brown called to say that the committee was going ahead anyway, I did the only thing I could do: I sent in my resignation."

"You resigned!" Wasserman was aghast.

"You mean already, you've already sent it in?" said Becker.

The rabbi nodded. "When Brown hung up, I wrote out my resignation and dropped it in the mailbox."

"But why, Rabbi, why?" Becker pleaded.

"I've just explained that."

Wasserman was upset. "You could have called me. You could have discussed it with me, explained your position. I could have talked to Schwarz. I could have brought the matter up before the Board. I could——"

"How could I do that? This was between Brown and Schwarz and me. Could I come running to you to help me exercise my authority? Besides, what good would it have done? You would have split the congregation, and in the end the Board would have voted with Schwarz. As you yourself said, given the choice between an unknown's corpse and a hundred-thousand-dollar building, is there any question which way the Board would vote?"

"And how does Mrs. Small feel about this?" asked Wasserman.

"Just a minute, Jacob," interrupted Becker. "You say you sent this letter out Friday morning? So it must have been received no later than Saturday. If it was addressed to the president of the temple it would have been put in with the rest of the temple mail, and the corresponding secretary would have got it and showed it to Mort Schwarz. So why didn't Schwarz have it read at the meeting?"

"That's a good question, Becker."

"It must mean that Schwarz just isn't accepting it."

"That could be," said Wasserman slowly, "but I don't think so."

"You think he wanted to discuss it with the rabbi first?"

"That could also be, but I doubt it."

"So how do you figure it?"

"I think he wants to talk it over with his group on the Board first, and get them all to agree. Then when he brings up the matter in the meeting, they'll railroad it through just like that." He snapped his fingers.

"But why, Jacob? You think he wants the rabbi out?"

"I don't think he'll let anything interfere with his new building."

"Why is the building so important to him? We don't really need it."

"Because it's a building, that's why. It's that progress they were talking about. It's something he can point to, something solid and substantial. It's a hundred- to a hundred-and-fifty-thousand-dollar property. It's a value that he can say he brought into the temple organization. Now the present building came in during my administration."

"I didn't put up any buildings," said Becker.

"The cemetery—that you bought. When they put up the central gate, your name will be on it. Schwarz wants something he can say, 'This is what I did.' What do you say, Rabbi?"

The rabbi, who had promised to say nothing about Schwarz's personal involvement, nodded slowly. "Yes, I think it might be something like that."

"Well, Rabbi," said Wasserman, "it's not going to be easy, but we'll try our best."

Outside, Becker said, "What really gets me is why he didn't get in touch with us. We're his friends, and we're not the only ones. And he sure went out of his way to help me that time my partner Mel Bronstein was in all that bad trouble. So I, for one, sure owe him one mighty big favor.

"You know, the rabbi has changed in the few years he's been here. I remember when he first came, he was so shy you could hardly hear him when he spoke. Now he lays it on the line like he's in complete control of the situation."

"That's because he's grown; he's matured," Wasserman said. "When he came here, he was fresh out of the seminary, a boy. He had ideas, and he was firm about them, but he said them so quietly no one really paid attention. But in these few years he's got confidence, and he doesn't mind asserting himself. I tell you, Becker, he's got like a radar beam in his head."

"What do you mean, radar beam?"

"It's like the way an airplane flies at night. He's got an instrument, the pilot, and it's as if he's flying an invisible line. The minute he goes off to one side or the other, the instrument gives out a beep. It's like that with the rabbi. He's got in his head the principles of the Jewish tradition. When the congregation goes off to one side or the other, the rabbi gets a warning, like a beep, and he knows we're making a mistake."

"Yeah, well, this time that beep may cause a crash landing."

"Why?"

"Because the poor bugger is apt to lose his job. And his wife's going to have a baby soon."

"You might at least have told me," said Miriam. "It was all I could do to restrain myself from coming in when I heard you tell Mr. Wasserman and Mr. Becker. I noticed when one of them asked how I felt about it, you were careful not to answer. Evidently they thought it was my concern."

"I'm sorry, Miriam dear. It was foolish of me; I was wrong, but I didn't want to distress you at this time. I thought that by today, by this morning, the whole affair would have been properly settled. It didn't occur to me that Schwarz would suppress my letter."

"And suppose he had read your letter and the Board had gone along with him?"

"I didn't think they would have—not with me there to explain it." He had been talking apologetically, but now his tone changed. "If they did, then I would have no choice but to resign. I could not remain here. The issue, as far as I'm concerned, is basic and fundamental. Either we are a religious group, a congregation, or we are nothing and I have no job here."

"So what are you going to do now?"

He shrugged. "What can I do now? The matter is out of my hands. We can only hope that Wasserman and Becker can rally enough support—"

"You mean you're going to sit with your hands folded and wait until the matter is resolved one way or the other?"

"What do you suggest?" He was nettled.

"You called this desecrating a grave. Very well, then you can appeal to the town authorities. You could talk to Mrs. Hirsh."

He shook his head. "I could never do that. I am still an employee of the congregation, and if their elected representatives want to do something I disapprove of, I can't protest to authorities outside."

"It seems to me," she said tartly, "that you're a lot more concerned with your struggle with the Board than you are with Hirsh. You've dissociated yourself from their action, but if as you say it's the desecration that really concerns you, what are you doing to prevent it?"

"Well—"

"The least you could do is prove what really happened."

"Yes? And how would I go about that?"

"Well, if you found a note, that would prove that it was a suicide, wouldn't it?"

"Yes, but not finding it proves nothing. It's negative evidence."

"It seems to me that if you can prove something took place, you ought to be able to prove it didn't."

He realized that her fine scorn for logic was because she was hurt he had not confided in her. "But don't you see," he said patiently, "that simply because you can prove one thing doesn't mean—"

"All I know is that if someone has done something, someone else ought to be able to find out what it was. Besides, there's the widow to think of. There's been a man around town, an investigator for the insurance company, and Mrs. Marcus—you remember she called—was saying that her friend Mrs. Hirsh was worried about losing the insurance money if he proves it's suicide."

"He can't prove it's suicide any more than we can prove it was an accident."

"Yes, but he could make her a lot of trouble—hold up the money indefinitely. David, you've *got* to do something."

"But how, woman, how?"

"I don't know. You're the rabbi. That's your department. At least, you could try."

He looked at her for a moment. Her face was intense. "All right, Miriam, I'll try. I'll call Lanigan and see if he'll go over the facts with me. It's just possible we can come up with something."

"I'll do better than that," said the police chief when the rabbi got him on the phone. "I hear you've been under the weather, so instead of your coming down to my office tomorrow, I'll get the files on the case and bring them over to your house tonight."

"Oh, I don't want to put you to that bother."

"Look, Rabbi, you'll be doing me a favor. Gladys is having some friends over, and I don't want to be caught in a hen party."

"Well, if you put it that way—"

"I do. Say, I've got another idea: has Charlie Beam got around to talking to you yet?"

"Beam?"

"He's the man who's been investigating for the insurance company. How about if I bring him along?"

"Fine."

"Beauty," said Lanigan. He chuckled. "You know, I'm really going to enjoy this little get-together."

"How do you mean?"

"Well, you're hoping to prove that it's a case of death by accident, and Beam naturally would like to prove that it's suicide so his company won't have to pay. And here I am, in the middle, and for once in the clear. I'll just let you boys fight it out and I'll sit back and enjoy it."

23

Out of respect for his guests, the rabbi had shed his bathrobe and was dressed in slacks and a sport shirt. After the introductions, Miriam, feeling this was not part of her husband's official function and that she had a stake in the proceedings, remained in the room.

"Maybe I'd better run through the facts as we know them," said Lanigan, "and then we can talk about it afterward." He opened a Manila folder. "All right. Isaac Hirsh, 4 Bradford Lane, married, white, fifty-one years old. He was five foot three or four and weighed one hundred and ninety pounds. Did you know him, Rabbi? Had you ever met him?"

The rabbi shook his head.

"He was built along the lines of Charlie here. Maybe a little shorter—"

"I'm five feet five," said Beam.

"I would have said so. I make a point of this because it's important, as you'll see. All right, it's Friday evening, September 18, the eve of your Yom Kippur. Hirsh gets home from the Goddard Lab where he works, his regular time—a little after six. In this case, that's unusual because all other Jewish employees left a bit early. But although Hirsh was Jewish he did not attend services, so he worked a full day. He got home and left his car in front of the house instead of putting it in the garage—"

"He didn't want to trouble himself getting out to open the garage door, is that it?" remarked Beam.

"No, the garage door was up. It's common around here; we don't have much pilfering. A man will leave the door up all day and close it only when he locks up for the night."

"You know this in the Hirsh case?" asked Beam.

"Yeah. It also figures in the story, as you'll see. Now there are a number of Jewish families in this section of Colonial Village; in fact, all his immediate neighbors are Jewish. I understand it's sometimes called the Ghetto." He smiled apologetically at the rabbi. "That's a little joke among them."

"I understand."

"Patricia Hirsh, that's Isaac Hirsh's wife, was going to baby-sit for the Marcuses who live across the street. She agreed to be there early, so she served Hirsh his dinner and left at six-thirty. Hirsh finished and left around seven."

"You're sure of the time?" asked the rabbi.

"Pretty sure. We got that from the deliveryman I told you about. Anyway, after the deliveryman left, Hirsh headed for the laboratory. He was next sighted by the State Police at a siding on Route 128 about four hundred yards from the lab. You remember, they went back and found the wrapper from the bottle."

"Did they indicate when they saw him?"

The chief shook his head. "They had no reason to note the time. They just remembered having seen the car during the evening; they didn't even remember the exact place. They had to check each of the sidings along the section they patrol until they found the right one. All we know is that Hirsh was there sometime during the evening. And that was the last time he was seen alive."

"But you yourself said they didn't really see him. They just saw the car. Isn't that right?" asked the rabbi.

"Well, they saw a figure in the car. We assume it was Hirsh. Is it important?"

"Probably not. Go on."

"Mrs. Hirsh came home around eleven or a little after."

"As late as that?" asked the rabbi. "Our services ended at a quarter past ten."

"The Marcuses didn't return directly. They stopped off to visit some friends," explained Beam. "I got that from Mrs. Marcus."

"And I suppose they talked with Mrs. Hirsh for a few minutes when they did get back," said Lanigan. "Around midnight, she called the lab to find out when her husband was coming home."

"How did she know he was there?" asked the rabbi.

"He frequently returns at night, and at supper he mentioned he was going. But the janitor-night watchman reported he never signed in that evening, which is when she called us." He went on to explain how they put out an alert, and how when the cruising car stopped by to get more information, the patrolman noticed the garage door was down and remembered it had been up when he passed earlier.

"So he investigated and found the car inside, right close to the side of the garage, about a foot and a half. He squeezed by, opened the front door on the driver's side, and found Hirsh dead on the passenger side. About half the bottle was gone. The ignition was on but the motor was not running—out of gas. He radioed in to the station and we sent down the doctor and a photographer—the usual."

He opened the folder and took out a large glossy photograph. "This picture shows the situation best. It was taken from the driveway when the garage door was first raised. You'll notice how close the car is to the side of the garage on the driver's side, about a foot and a half. And on the other side, you'll notice this trash barrel about a foot from the car. That's important to Charlie's case. The picture doesn't show it, of course, but the bumper of the car was just touching the rear wall of the garage. Since the car had no gas, we took out the body and left the car where it was. The following morning, we poured some gas into the tank and drove it down to the station where we've had it ever since. Mrs. Hirsh doesn't drive, at least she doesn't have a license, so we haven't got around to bringing it back yet. And that's about all."

"Oh, yes, we did an autopsy on the body that confirmed the presence of alcohol in quantity commensurate with the amount missing from the bottle. It also gave us the time of death, roughly eight-thirty, give or take twenty minutes. That would be pretty accurate since it was based on stomach content."

All four were silent for a moment as if out of respect for the deceased. Then the rabbi said, "There was much that you didn't mention, Chief, I suppose because you assumed we knew it. One was that the man was an alcoholic, and you yourself indicated that alcoholics don't generally commit suicide."

Beam smiled. "That's one of those generalizations, Rabbi, that are used to bolster a pet theory. And since there are almost as many theories about alcoholism as there are doctors studying the subject, it's easy to theorize. There's one to the effect that all alcoholics are sexually deficient. If something runs counter to your theory, you just say it proves the man wasn't a true alcoholic. It's arguing in circles."

"All right. How about this? From all I can gather, Hirsh was very fond of his wife. He took out a sizable insurance policy—that alone indicates he cared about her welfare and well-being. Would he take his own life without leaving a note of explanation?"

"They do it all the time. Sometimes the note turns up later, sometimes it's found and suppressed by the interested parties, if you know what I mean. Sometimes, too, they purposely don't leave one in hopes it won't be thought suicide, and the beneficiary can collect."

"But nothing in his general attitude would indicate that he might commit suicide."

"How do we know? How do we know what sets a man off? Maybe the fact it was your Yom Kippur, the Day of Judgment as I understand it, had something to do with it."

"What is that supposed to mean?" asked the rabbi.

"Merely that he may have been thinking about suicide for a long time, and the bottle of vodka coming on the Day of Judgment the way it did—well, it could be kind of an omen."

"More likely it served as an excuse to satisfy the thirst that was always with him," the rabbi retorted. "We know he discarded the wrapper on the siding, and if he started drinking then, he must have been pretty far gone by the time he got home."

"And yet was able to drive a car for some distance, a good ten miles, and steer it into the garage so nice and true that he doesn't hit the wall on the one side or the trash barrel on the other?"

"That's your case, is it?" asked the rabbi. "That he was able to drive into the garage without bumping into anything?"

"That," said Beam, "and the fact that he had sufficient command of his reasoning faculties to shut off the car lights but not shut off the motor, get out of the car and pull down the garage door, and then get back into the front seat. If he were drunk and didn't know what he was doing, why would he have gone back to the car? Why wouldn't he go directly into his own house? He knew he'd be alone and alone for some time. He may not have gone to the temple regularly, but I guess he'd know that on your Yom Kippur the services wouldn't be over much before ten."

"Alcoholics frequently have special feelings about where they can drink and where they can't," interposed Lanigan mildly. "I suppose his house was one place he considered off limits. For that matter, after he pulled down the garage door, why get into the front seat at all? If you say he was planning to commit suicide—and may have wanted to

112

anesthetize himself with alcohol, since carbon monoxide takes a little time—why not get into the back seat, which is not only more comfortable but nearer the garage door?"

Beam shrugged. "Matter of habit, probably. The important thing is that he was sober enough to do all these things: to steer within the narrow space between the trash barrel and the garage wall—"

"Just a minute. What kind of trash barrel is that, Chief? It looks like one of those new plastic types."

"That's right, Rabbi. It's a red plastic twenty-gallon barrel with a cover."

"Full or empty?"

"Oh, it must have been empty, David," said his wife. "It was Friday." She explained to Beam that the trash on even-numbered houses is collected Friday morning. "The husbands usually put out the barrels Thursday night and the wives bring in the empties the next morning."

"The lady is right," said Lanigan. "The barrel was empty."

"So what?"

"So there is a difference," the rabbi began, his voice taking on the impersonal tone of a lecturer. "There is a difference between a full barrel and an empty one, and an even greater difference between a galvanized iron barrel and one made of plastic."

"Are you going to pull one of those Talmudic tricks of yours, Rabbi? What do you call it, a pil—something?"

"You mean a pilpul? And why not, if it helps us to get at the truth."

Lanigan grinned. "The Talmud," he said to Beam, "is the Jewish book of Law. They have a special way of arguing that the rabbi has used on me on occasion. This pilpul, it's a kind of hair-splitting that—"

"Rather it's the tracing of a fine distinction," said the rabbi reprovingly.

"Well, I don't mind fine distinctions," said Beam patronizingly. "But what difference does it make whether the barrel is full or empty, or made of galvanized iron or plastic or anything else for that matter?"

"Actually, there are four possibilities." The rabbi rose from his chair and, thrusting his hands deep in his trouser pockets, began to pace the floor. "The barrel can be of iron and full or empty, and it can be of plastic and full or empty. The first point to consider is the difference between the full one and the empty one. The full barrel is normally heavy and relatively immovable. The empty barrel is light. That is, of

113

course, why men usually take it out onto the sidewalk; while bringing it back empty is something a woman can do because it does not tax her strength. Now, if the barrel were full, then it could indeed be considered a fixed obstruction. A sober man would no more think of driving his car into it than of driving into the wall. But what if the barrel were empty? Then it is comparatively light, and if he struck it with his car no great damage would be done beyond a scratch or two. And the barrel? Even if it were toppled over nothing would spill out. But—" and he held up an admonishing forefinger, "the sober driver would have no problem in either case. He has more than a foot on either side—plenty of room, even for a driver of my caliber. How about the drunken driver, though? Let us admit that he would have trouble"—he paused—"*if* it were a full barrel. But he knows it is empty—"

"Just a minute," Beam interrupted, "how does he know that the barrel is empty?"

"Because it was inside the garage, of course. If it were full, it would be outside on the sidewalk where he'd left it the night before. So here we have a man parking his car in a narrow garage. He knows he has to be careful on one side, but on the other there's only an empty barrel. Even half sober he'd know that subconsciously, and know it really would not constitute an obstruction. Still, he would probably try to avoid it, and his capacity to steer between the two might be some indication of his relative sobriety. But"—and again he held up a forefinger—"this is not a galvanized iron barrel that could be dented if struck by the car fender and that in turn could damage the car. It is a plastic barrel, an empty plastic barrel. When struck, it yields or skitters away."

Then, as his voice took on a Talmudic singsong, his forefinger made circles in the air in time to the rhythm of his discourse. "Now if a man would not mind hitting a galvanized barrel because he knew it was empty, then *al achas cammo v'cammo*"—he broke off and smiled. "I'm sorry, I got carried away. That Hebrew phrase, a common one in Talmudic argument means—er—'how much more.' How much more, then, would he be likely to disregard an empty plastic barrel." Turning to Lanigan, he said, "Because you have expressed an interest, that line of reasoning is very common in the Talmud. It is called *cal v'chomar*, which means 'light and heavy,' and consists of showing that if one argument applies, then a stronger argument of the same sort is even more applicable and can be considered proof. Now from our point of view, the empty plastic barrel is no more obstruction than a beach ball. Hirsh could in fact have struck it, and it could very well have caromed off the fender and come to rest in its present position."

The chief shook his head in admiration. "He's got you fair and square, Charlie. The fact that it is an empty plastic barrel just about kills your case."

"Well, I'm a city boy myself and I don't know about plastic barrels. But that's not all there is to my argument by a long shot. How about bringing the car right up against the rear wall of the garage? That's a mighty neat trick for a guy too soused to know enough not to turn off the ignition."

The chief looked at the rabbi for an answer but he seemed not to have heard. In fact, he seemed to have forgot they were there, for he was leaning back in his chair, his eyes focused on the ceiling.

"What do you say to that, Rabbi?" asked Beam.

The rabbi disregarded the question.

"There is another facet of Talmudic reasoning," he said, and his voice was withdrawn as though he were talking to himself. "It is the *im kain* argument. The words mean 'if so,' and it is essentially a sort of *reductio ad absurdum*. In the present case, it would go like this: if the car was so near the side of the garage, how could he get out on the driver's side? And if it were so near the barrel, how could he get out on the other side?"

Lanigan looked at the rabbi in surprise. "But you've already answered that. You proved that the barrel was no obstruction."

"It was no obstruction to the car, but it was an obstruction to Hirsh."

Lanigan was exasperated. "Dammit, Rabbi, you can't have it both ways. You pointed out that an empty plastic barrel was no obstruction, and now you say it is."

The rabbi nodded. "Precisely. It was no obstruction to a man driving a car, but it was an obstruction to Hirsh going to lower the garage door."

"Why? He had only to nudge it aside with his foot."

"But he didn't, because it was still there when you found him and took your picture."

"I'm not sure I understand what you're driving at," said Lanigan.

"Include me," said Beam.

"Very well. Hirsh brings the car to a stop. He can't get out on the driver's side. No room. So he gets out on the

115

passenger side. He nudges the barrel out of the way, walks to the front of the garage and pulls the door down. Very good! Now he comes back to the front seat of the car. He passes the barrel. What does he do? Pull it back in position again? Why would he do that?"

"Why—why he must have," exclaimed Lanigan. "Or maybe when he pushed it away the first time, he pushed it so hard he sent it spinning and—no, that doesn't make sense either." He glared at the rabbi. "Dammit, we know he couldn't get out on the driver's side. We know that. It was physically impossible. And now it seems he didn't get out on the other side. But those are the only two ways of getting out of the car, so—"

"Go on, say it. If he didn't get out on either side, then he didn't get out of the car. But the garage door was down, so it must have been pulled down by someone else. And that person, in all likelihood, was the driver. And Hirsh was sitting on the passenger side, because he was indeed the passenger. And that in turn could explain how a man could consume a pint of liquor and yet travel by automobile ten miles or more and park his car in his garage. There was no problem because he was not driving; he was being driven. And when they got to the garage, the driver, a much thinner person than Hirsh, got out of the car on the driver's side, pulled down the garage door and walked away. And Hirsh did nothing about it because he was either too drunk to know what was happening, or more likely, had passed out completely."

Lanigan stared at the rabbi. "But that's murder!"

The rabbi nodded. . . .

An hour later, they were still at it.

"It's crazy, Rabbi."

"But it fits all the facts. There are obvious objections to suicide, and similar strong arguments against accidental death, but there are no logical arguments against murder. On the contrary, murder explains everything."

"And I thought I was in the clear," said Lanigan ruefully.

"Are you going to report it to the district attorney?" asked the rabbi.

"I can't right now. First I've got to check it out."

"Check it out how?"

"I've got to talk to my boys. Maybe they didn't shoot that picture as soon as they raised the garage door. Maybe they circled the car first, I don't know, but I've got a lot of questions."

The chief was unhappy. "Hell, I'll need some kind of legal proof. I can't go to the D.A. and he can't go to a jury with this—this chop logic of yours, Rabbi. I'm not even sure I could repeat it. I need something definite. I've got to be able to prove beyond a doubt that the barrel wasn't moved. I've got to prove beyond a doubt that Hirsh couldn't have got by that barrel. I've got to have accurate measurements."

"You said Hirsh was short, five feet three. The chances are the driver was taller," said the rabbi. "Wouldn't the position of the car seat—if it were pushed back, that is—indicate that someone else was driving?"

"You would bring that up," said Lanigan morosely. "Trouble is, the police officer who found the body could have changed the position. If not, we probably would have done so to get the body out. In any case, Sergeant Jeffers, who is close to six feet, would have pushed it back to drive the car to the station, and even if he remembered doing it I couldn't accept that as evidence. No, we flubbed it all right." He threw up his hands. "But how could we know it was anything except a straightforward case of suicide or accident?"

"Fingerprints?" suggested Beam.

Lanigan shook his head dolefully. "We didn't take any. Why should we? The patrolman who found him opened the car door, and later we were all over the car getting him out. Any fingerprints would be on the door handles, the steering wheel, and the gear shift, and they would be obliterated."

"How about the light control?" asked the rabbi.

"You mean for the headlights?"

"Someone turned them off that night."

"So?"

"Well, if the car was driven to the police garage by day, there'd be no need to put them on again."

"By God, you're right, Rabbi! They would have no reason to touch the button. It's a chance. The car has been under seal ever since."

He reached for the phone and dialed. "I'll get Lieutenant Jennings—he's our fingerprint expert." Then into the phone, he said, "Eban, Lanigan. Meet me at the station house in five minutes. No, I'm not there yet but I'll be there by the time you are. Come along, Rabbi?"

"I think he'd better stay right here," said Miriam.

"Maybe you're right. I'll call you."

"Mind if I go along, Chief?" asked Beam.

"Come on, if you're sure you're all through here."

Beam's eyes all but vanished as he smiled. "The rabbi has convinced me it's murder. But I'll be staying in town a little while. There are a few points I want to clear up. When I talked to Mrs. Marcus, she said they called home to say they'd be late and there was no answer. They tried again when they arrived at their friends' house, and the phone rang for the longest time before Mrs. Hirsh answered. She said she'd been napping."

"So?"

"So maybe the reason she didn't answer was not because she was asleep but because she wasn't there."

"Mrs. Hirsh?" Lanigan exclaimed. "But how could she be involved? She doesn't know how to drive."

"She doesn't have to—only how to pull down the garage door."

"You mean she might have done it? Mrs. Hirsh?"

"Done it, or helped to do it."

"Why do you want to pin it on her?"

Beam smiled. "Because the law says a murderer can't benefit from his crime."

"Rabbi?" It was Chief Lanigan calling from the station.

"Yes?" He had been pacing the floor impatiently, waiting for the call. The moment the phone rang he snatched it up.

"There were no prints on the light button."

"No prints? But there had to be. The car was driven at night, so somebody had to turn them off."

"Wiped clean," said Lanigan grimly. "You know what that means?"

"I—I think so."

"No chance of the driver saying he walked away and forgot to turn off the motor. He knew what he was doing, all right, which makes it first-degree murder."

118

24

The Reverend Peter Dodge stood framed in the doorway, one hand resting on either doorjamb like Samson about to collapse the temple.

"Why, look who's here, David," Miriam said. "Come in."

His handsome head instinctively lowered to enter. "I heard you were a bit under the weather, David, and decided to include you in my pastoral calls."

"That was thoughtful of you, but it was just a touch of the virus. I'll be going to services tomorrow."

"Your trouble, David, is you don't get enough exercise. I wouldn't recommend anything strenuous, but you ought at least to arrange time for a nice long walk every day. It will firm up your muscle tone. Now every evening without fail I take a regular walk over a regular route. It's exactly four and six-tenths miles, and I do it in just over an hour, depending on whether I meet anyone. And most afternoons when I can manage it I get in a couple of sets of tennis."

"Where do you play?"

"We have a court back of the Parish House. Any time you want, just give me a ring and we can volley for a while. It would do you good."

The rabbi laughed. "How do you think my congregation would feel if their rabbi went to the Episcopal Church to play tennis?"

"About the same way my people would feel if I came down to your temple." He hesitated. "I hear you have been having a spot of trouble with them lately."

The rabbi and his wife both showed their surprise. Dodge chuckled. "You're from New York, aren't you? And I'm from South Bend. We're city folks, so I don't suppose we'll ever get used to how fast news travels in a small town like Barnard's Crossing. I was chaplain in a federal prison for a little while, and the grapevine there is the only thing comparable—"

"What did you hear, Peter?" asked Miriam.

Dodge became vague. "Oh, something to the effect that poor Ike Hirsh had committed suicide and you weren't supposed to have buried him. It didn't seem to make much sense to me, because how could David know he was a suicide, especially when the official police finding was death by accident? Surely your congregation can't expect you to play detective every time someone passes away."

"You knew Hirsh?" asked the rabbi. "Of course you did —you were at the funeral, weren't you?"

"Hirsh? Oh, yes. He was in the movement."

"What movement?"

"The Civil Rights movement. He made a small contribution and I went to see him. I try to make a personal visit to anyone like that—you'd be surprised how often they kick in with more. Besides, I pass by the Hirshes' street on my regular walk, so I took a chance and just rang the bell. Well, talk about a small world, who should come to the door but Mrs. Hirsh who turns out to be Pat Maguire. We went to school together in South Bend. After that, I made it a habit to pop in from time to time, and had dinner there once."

"What sort of man was Hirsh?"

"Oh, a very decent sort. I thought at first he was motivated more by his dislike of the South and Southerners— he had lived there for a while. But later, when I got to know him better, I felt he had a genuine sympathy for the oppressed. Once he even said something about going down to Alabama to join the demonstrators, but I don't think he was really serious. It's the sort of thing well-intentioned people say."

"Were you recruiting demonstrators for Alabama?" asked Miriam.

"Oh, that goes on all the time. But right now, Miriam, I'm really involved. I am in charge of MOGRE for the entire North Shore."

"Mogah?"

"M-O-G-R-E, Rabbi—Men of God for Racial Equality. It's made up of ministers of all faiths. Although mostly Protestant, there's a Greek Orthodox priest, and we're negotiating with the Archdiocese for a contingent of Catholic priests and we've got several rabbis." He said casually, "Interested, David?"

The rabbi smiled.

"Think it over." He hitched his chair closer. "I'll bet it might even solve your little problem here with your congregation."

"How would it do that?"

"Well, as I heard it, you have forbidden them to build a

120

special road, and they're going ahead anyway. If you stand by and do nothing it's going to be pretty embarrassing. But if you're down there, obviously you can't do anything. Then when you come back, you'll have got a lot of prestige which ought to give you more bargaining power with your congregation."

"*If* he comes back."

"What's that, Miriam? Oh, I see what you mean. You're thinking of the danger. Actually, there's less than you might think, for our group at least. All of us will be clearly identified as ministers, men of God, my bunch and the Catholics and the Lutherans—we'll have our clerical collars, and, as I understand it, the rabbis are planning to wear the skullcap—what do you call it?"

"*Kipoh.*"

"That's right, the rabbis will be wearing the *kipoh* and, I believe, the prayer shawl."

"The *tallis?*"

"That's it. Even if they don't recognize the regalia they'll sense it has something to do with religion. Oh, there'll be incidents, I suppose. But compared to the opportunity to demonstrate for the sake of the Lord—"

"I thought it was for the sake of the Negro."

He smiled to show he was aware that he was being twitted and that he could take a joke. "Same thing, David. For the glory of God manifested in man, in all men, black as well as white. What do you say?"

The rabbi shook his head.

"You're not feeling up to it yet? The group is not leaving for a couple of days."

Again the rabbi declined.

"Oh, you're thinking of Miriam. It should be pretty soon now, shouldn't it?"

"It's not so much that either," said the rabbi. "You see, Peter, I'm not really a man of God, at least no more so than any other man. And what would I say? We don't go in much for petitionary prayer. If I prayed in Hebrew, who would understand? And if I recited any of our regular prayers in English, the Shema or the Kaddish or the Shimonesra, they don't really apply. No, I'm afraid I couldn't go down there as a rabbi. I could as an individual, of course, like the college students; but you don't want that."

"Well, of course we want you as a rabbi. There are rabbis who are coming down with us, and many have already been down and borne witness."

The rabbi shrugged. "We have no hierarchy to promulgate belief. This is my view of the situation; other rabbis see it differently, I suppose. Some feel it their duty as spiritual leaders of their congregations—a habit of mind they picked up from you people, incidentally, or perhaps it was the congregations who then forced it on them. And others are so moved by the plight of the Negro that they don't care to balance their attitudes as men and citizens against their attitudes as rabbis. Frankly, that may be just as well."

"Now you've lost me completely."

"People differ: there are the quiet ones and those who storm barricades. I'm afraid I'm one of the quiet ones, but I must admit that the other, the aggressive ones, are probably the ones who bring about changes in the world. I respect you for what you are doing, Peter, and I respect the others; but I don't feel an urgency to thrust myself personally and physically into the battle any more than I feel an urgency to go to South Africa to help the Negro there. So if I did, it would be for some secondary reason like the one you suggested—to give me prestige in the eyes of my congregation—and that would be hypocritical."

"But this is more than just helping the southern Negro, David. It's a new feeling, a new spirit that's developing in the church, your church as well as mine, and we mustn't let it die out. The church is coming out of its traditional shell. It's burgeoning with new life. It's giving up its self-satisfied praying and smug psalm singing to go out into the highways and byways of men to serve them, to help them to fulfill themselves. The Civil Rights movement is not for the Negro alone; it's also for the church itself. And that's why her ministers, priest and rabbi and pastor, are all involved."

"It's not new to us, Peter," the rabbi said softly. "We've been doing that for several thousand years, in fact, ever since we accepted Deuteronomy and the commandment, 'Six days shalt thou labor . . . but the seventh day is the Sabbath in honor of the Lord; on it thou shalt not do any work, neither thou, nor thy son, nor servant, nor thy ox, nor thy ass, nor any of thy cattle, nor the stranger that is within thy gates; in order that thy man-servant and thy maid-servant may rest as well as thou.' You people parted company with us a couple of thousand years ago when you fixed your eyes on Heaven. A little suffering here on this earth didn't matter much to you, because compared to the infinite time in the next world, life here was a snap of the fingers, a blink of the eye. But we've always been involved with life on this earth and its many injustices. So I suppose you could say that we've been in the Civil Rights movement from the beginning."

"But haven't you missed something in the process, David?"

"Such as?"

"Such as the inspiration of the blessed saints. Such as the inspiration of lives devoted to Heaven and God. Such as the handful of people who by their example brought mankind a little closer to the angels."

"Yes, I suppose we have, but we thought it was worth it. And now, it seems as though you people are beginning to think so, too."

25

"The district attorney is not happy with me," said Lanigan. He had stopped by the Smalls on his way home. "And I don't think he's happy with you either, Rabbi."

"What have I done?"

"A district attorney doesn't mind going into court with a clear case and winning it. Just as a ballplayer doesn't mind hitting a home run. But to dump a murder case in his lap, with no suspects and a good chance that the murderer may never be found, that he doesn't like. And that's why he's not happy with you. And he's not happy with me because he thinks I bungled it. It never occurred to me that it might be murder, so I didn't take the normal precautions on fingerprints and—"

"But the fingerprints were wiped off."

"On the light button, yes, but what about the steering wheel and door handles and handles on the garage door? You might assume that if the murderer took the trouble to wipe the light button he'd wipe off the rest, but it doesn't necessarily follow. You'd be amazed how often they slip up. And they can slip up on the most obvious thing while being scrupulously careful on the least likely. If I had thought there was a possibility of murder, I would have handled it differently. And I should have considered the possibility. No, I'm afraid I don't look good in this case so far."

"That will make you look all the better when you find the culprit," said Miriam.

"That's not going to be easy. This isn't like any other case."

"How do you mean?" asked the rabbi.

"Well, in any crime there are three basic questions, three lines of investigation you might say, and where they meet, that's your answer. There's opportunity, there's weapon, and there's motive." The chief ticked them off on his fingers. "Here, what was the weapon? The car. That means that anyone who can drive can be said to have access to the weapon. If you wanted to stretch it, he wouldn't even have to know how to drive a car."

"I'm afraid I don't follow you there."

"Well, say Hirsh had made it back to the garage and then passed out. Anyone passing, seeing him, could just pull down the garage door and that would do it."

"But then Hirsh would have been behind the wheel—not on the passenger seat," the rabbi objected.

"Yeah, that's right. All right, so the murderer—or at least an accomplice—is anyone who can drive a car. That still leaves an awful lot of people. So we come to opportunity. Well, considering how accessible or available the weapon was, it means it could be anyone who might have been at the Hirsh house or was passing by sometime around eight o'clock in the evening." He grinned. "That kind of eliminates your people, Rabbi. Just their luck it was Yom Kippur and they were all in temple. It gives them a collective alibi."

The rabbi smiled faintly.

"And so we come to motive. And that's what makes the case particularly hard, because you see you don't need much of a motive for this killing."

"Why is that?"

"Because it doesn't involve much doing—not much planning and not much nerve either. Look here, suppose you see a man drowning and although you're a good swimmer and could easily reach him you just turn away. See what I mean? Deliberately to plan on drowning a man takes resolution and nerve; you wouldn't do it unless you hated him or had good reason for wishing him dead. But to just turn away—that you might do if you happened only to dislike him. Why should I go to the trouble, you'd say, especially if life would be easier with him gone.

"Take me, for example. I'm considered a pretty decent, law-abiding citizen. I'm considered a good husband and a good father, and even the people I deal with professionally—criminals and lawbreakers—speak of me as fair and honest. But every now and then thoughts go through my head—"

"This is common to all men."

"Of course. It isn't what you think but what you do that matters. But what if the opportunity came to do one of these things just when it happened to occur to me, and it involved no great risk on my part, no real action—just a turning away— failing to do something rather than doing it. Do you see what I mean, Rabbi?"

"All right, I see the point you're trying to make. You mean that in this kind of killing, almost accidental and so easy, no great animus is required."

"That's it."

"So where does that leave you?"

The chief shrugged. "With damn little to go on."

"Suppose you ran the story in the newspapers. That might turn up something."

Lanigan shook his head. "It will have to wait for a few days, I'm afraid. The D.A. thinks we may be able to come up with an answer if the story is kept secret."

"Then you do have a lead."

"Not really," the chief said. "Beam's idea, but the D.A. thinks it's worth checking. And, mind you, from a straight, logical basis, it's possible. He's got it in his head that the widow did it. Why? Because then his company won't have to pay off. His argument is that as far as we know she's the only one who profits. She becomes richer by fifty thousand dollars for one thing, and for another she gets rid of a husband who was not only old enough to be her father but was no bargain in a lot of other respects, too."

"She married him when he was an alcoholic. Does Beam think that now that he at least partially reformed, he was a less desirable husband?"

"I'm just giving you his idea, Rabbi. There's a little more to it. He feels that business about having him buried in a Jewish cemetery with the Jewish rites was just a big act to show how devoted she was, like another woman might pretend to faint or weep whenever she thought someone was watching. That if all this had been on the up and up, she wouldn't have bothered to bury him in the Jewish cemetery since he had no feelings about it when he was alive."

"Such involved psychological analysis," said the rabbi. "I wouldn't have thought our friend Beam capable of it."

"Well, of course, he's seen a lot of this kind of thing," said Lanigan apologetically. "I can understand where he might be suspicious of any unusual manifestation of grief on the part of the widow. And when you add the fact that she didn't answer the phone when the Marcuses rang—"

"But that happened after ten o'clock, and according to the autopsy Hirsh was already dead sometime before nine."

"According to Beam, the fact that she didn't answer shows she left the house. If she left then, she could have left earlier. Suppose she sees him drive into the garage but doesn't see him get out. So she goes across the street. Maybe she tries to rouse him. Maybe she gets a kind of revulsion and says, all right, stay there. It crosses her mind that it might be easier without him. Then later after ten, just before the Marcuses called, she runs out to see what the situation is. Is the motor still running? Is he still alive? She finds him dead and runs back in time to get the second call. Then she plans what she's got to do after that. She goes home, makes believe she hasn't noticed the garage door is down, and calls the police so that they can discover the body for her."

"You keep referring to Beam. How do you like it?"

"Mrs. Hirsh doesn't seem that kind of person to me, but I've had enough experience to know my feelings about people don't mean a darn thing. On the other hand, what else have I got? It's a logical starting point—she's the only one we know who profits from his death."

"I see."

"So we're keeping it quiet for a few days—at least until we can check Mrs. Hirsh out."

"And if it's not Mrs. Hirsh, do you have any other leads?"

"We're checking into anyone who might have had any contact with Hirsh. It's all we can do. I went over to the Goddard Laboratories yesterday to see the big boss himself."

"Goddard?"

"No, Lemuel Goddard has been dead for several years. He was local—a Crosser in fact. He started the lab when he retired from G.E. They retire them at sixty-five there, whether they're ready or not. Lem Goddard wasn't ready, so he started a lab of his own. He had a place—an old warehouse in Lynn. Then he went public and sold stock. They expanded and built this place on Route 128. When he died, the Board of Directors decided that the man they wanted to head up the organization was not a scientist but an administrative expert, so they got this army general, Amos Quint. One of these desk generals from the Quartermaster Corps. Iron-arse Quint, I understand he used to be called in Washington." He glanced at Miriam. "I'm sorry, Mrs. Small, that just came out."

She smiled faintly. "I've heard the word."

"There's nothing so army as one of those desk generals," the chief went on. "His secretary who brought me into his office didn't actually salute but she kind of stood at attention." He laughed. "When I asked him how well he knew Hirsh, the general says, 'I make it a point not to know my men well.' How do you like that?"

"Wasn't it Caesar, or Napoleon, who knew every man in his army by his first name?"

"I guess that's old-fashioned. Quint explained to me that if you're going to run an efficient organization and not get bogged down in a mass of trivia—that's the word he used and with a flick of the hand as though brushing something away—you've got to operate strictly through channels. 'I see them when I hire them and when I fire them and that's all.' From then on, everything goes through channels. He tells them that when he hires them, and when he fires them, he tells them why. So as far as Hirsh was concerned, anything he wanted to bring to the notice of old Iron—of Quint—had to go through his superior, Dr. Sykes."

"I see. The Lowells talk only to Cabots and the Cabots talk only to God."

"That's about it, Rabbi. But, of course, Quint had a dossier on Hirsh and knew quite a bit about him. I gather that Hirsh was not too hot lately. Maybe he was at one time, but certainly not while he was at Goddard. In fact, I gathered he made a number of rather bad mistakes—the last one, just a few days before his death."

"Why didn't they fire him?"

"I asked the same question. I gather Quint was going to this last time because this time it was real serious, or perhaps the general had come to the end of his patience. You know, Rabbi, that could have been another argument in favor of suicide, if I had known about it at the time."

"I wonder why Quint didn't fire him earlier. From what you say, he doesn't sound like the type to stand for more than one error on the part of an employee, especially one so far down the ladder as I gather Hirsh was."

"That was Sykes. I asked the same question, and Quint said Dr. Sykes went to bat for him each time and so he played along. Even the time Hirsh got drunk Sykes managed to get him off. It started right there in the lab as a matter of fact. They were working on a special method for aging whiskey quickly by shooting an electric current through it somehow. The chemist who was working on the project mixed up a batch and brought it around for the boys to sample and give their opinions. Hirsh was one of those offered a taste and it set him off. The chemist, by the way, was fired."

"Why?"

Lanigan laughed. "That's another thing about this lab. You'd think they'd all be working together, sketching diagrams and circuits and formulae and whatnot on the tablecloths at lunch. Nothing like it. You see, most of their work is done for industry, and if news leaks out their clients' stocks can be affected. I gather that in the past some of the scientists weren't above taking a little flyer on this inside information. So the rule was laid down that everyone is to keep his nose firmly set against his own little grindstone. The men in any given section will confer with each other but they don't contact the other sections except when absolutely necessary—and then it's done through the department heads."

"Interesting. So you didn't get much from Quint. Did you question any of the other employees?"

"I did, but I got nothing that helped. As I said, everyone there tends to keep to himself. And Hirsh was a quiet sort, even withdrawn."

"It doesn't leave you with much."

"No, it doesn't." He looked eagerly at the rabbi. "Any ideas, Rabbi? Anything strike you?"

The rabbi shook his head slowly.

"Well, it helps just to talk it over, I suppose." But it was obvious that he was disappointed. He looked directly at the rabbi. "By the way, did you know that Ben Goralsky knew Hirsh?"

"No, I didn't, although I saw him at the funeral."

"S'truth. In fact, it was Goralsky who got Hirsh the job at Goddard."

26

The door was opened by a maid in uniform. She escorted him into the library and said she would tell Mr. Goralsky he was here.

Ben Goralsky appeared almost immediately, and showed him to a chair. "I'm glad you could come, Rabbi. My father

128

was pleased when I told him you said you'd be over to see how he was."

"I would have made it earlier, but I was laid up myself for a few days."

"Yes, I know." He hesitated. "I heard some rumors—I may have made a little trouble for you about this business with Hirsh."

"There has been a little trouble," the rabbi admitted.

"Well, I just want you to know I'm sorry."

The rabbi was curious. "Your father feels strongly about the matter?"

"I haven't talked about it with him—except that once. When this fellow Beam told me it was probably suicide, I mentioned it to my father and he was awfully upset. It was a day when he wasn't feeling so good. I guess he thought it was near the end. He said it wasn't according to the regulations, and he started to worry maybe you folks weren't going to keep the cemetery on a strict Orthodox basis. You know, this being a Conservative temple, instead of Orthodox like we're used to, you're apt to take a lot of shortcuts and make a lot of changes. So he was worried about being buried there."

"I see."

"According to him, Hirsh should have been buried on the side somewhere with no ceremony or anything. He told me about one that he had seen in the old country when he was a young man. There was this girl who took her own life. She was going to have a baby, and she was still a girl—I mean, she was unmarried. They just put her in the ground, and the next day her father went to work as though nothing happened. I mean, they didn't even mourn her for the seven days. It must have made a terrible impression on him, because he was terribly upset about Hirsh getting a regular funeral. He said if she was buried that way then Hirsh should be, too. Of course, he was confused because there's no connection."

The rabbi made to rise, now that the amenities were over, but Ben Goralsky waved him back. "My father's dozing right now. I told the nurse to let me know when he wakes up. Are you in a hurry?"

"No. As a matter of fact, I wanted an opportunity to talk to you. I understand you knew Isaac Hirsh."

"Yeah, I knew him. I knew his whole family. They lived next door to us in Chelsea, years ago. I knew his father and mother, and I knew him."

"And that's why you recommended him for that job at Goddard's?"

His thick lips parted and his heavy face relaxed in a grin. He shook his head slowly. "I recommended him for that job, and I put enough muscle behind it to make sure he got it. We're good customers of Goddard Lab, and I can talk turkey to Quint who runs the place. I got Hirsh that job because I hated his guts." He laughed aloud at the look of surprise on the rabbi's face.

"Like I said, they lived next door to us, the Hirshes. Both our families were mighty poor. We had this chicken business, his father had a little tailor shop. Mrs. Hirsh was all right. She was a good woman, and when she died I went to the funeral. We all did. My father closed the store so we could all go. Mr. Hirsh, he was something else again. A lazy good-for-nothing, always bragging about his precious son. We were four kids. I got two brothers and a sister, and every one of us worked in the store, after school, Sundays, nights. You had to in those days to make a living. I didn't even finish high school. I quit at the end of my first year and went to work in the store full time. But Ike Hirsh, he finished high and then went on to college and then went on after that to become a doctor—not a regular doctor, a doctor of philosophy. He didn't play with the other kids in the street. He was a little fat, roly-poly kid, the kind the other kids make fun of. So most of the time, he stayed inside reading books. And his father would come over to our house and brag about him. You know how Jews feel about education, so you can imagine how my father felt about us, especially in comparison with him. And old man Hirsh never let him forget it. But let me tell you something, Rabbi, my father never threw it up to us.

"Then Mrs. Hirsh died, and Mr. Hirsh waited just one year, practically to the day, to remarry. Now you know, you don't meet a woman and ask her to marry you and get married in a day or two. Not at that age, you don't. That means he was making arrangements during the year of mourning, while his wife was hardly cold in her grave. Ike had got himself a government job—big deal, after all that build-up—and didn't even come to the wedding. And he didn't go to his father's funeral a year later. My father went. He wanted me to go, but I wouldn't.

"Well, things had been getting better for us right along. The war helped. We had gone on living in the same little old house in Chelsea, in the same old neighborhood even though at that time we could have afforded a lot better. By the time the war was over, we were pretty comfortable. My father had done a little speculating in real estate. He had bought some good stocks. And still he went to work every morning in the store. We had expanded there too, doing a big wholesale business, but my father was down there every morning in his apron and straw hat. That's the kind of man my father is."

"And in all this time, I take it you hadn't heard from Hirsh?"

"That's right. Then one day he comes to visit us. He's got an idea for manufacturing transistors. Nothing revolutionary, you understand, but it can cut costs anywhere from ten to twenty percent. I hardly knew what a transistor was, let alone my father, but he was convincing and my father had great faith in him. I guess without realizing it, my father had been sort of sold on the idea that he was a genius. Hirsh had it all worked out, and it looked good. He had contacts with all kinds of government agencies and we'd be sure to get government contracts. Well, to make a long story short, my father agreed to invest ten thousand dollars. Hirsh didn't have to put up a dime and he was a full fifty percent partner.

"We got a warehouse and we set up our plant and started to operate. He was the big idea man, and I was the dumb slob that knew just enough to check in supplies, check shipments, see that the employees worked. And in a year we had lost ten thousand dollars on top of our original investment. Then we got a contract. It wouldn't show us much of a profit, but it would carry us for a while. I went out and bought a bottle to celebrate. We had a couple of drinks, drank each other's health and success to the business. In the middle I got called away and had to be gone the whole afternoon. When I got back, I found Hirsh still in the office— dead drunk."

His face portrayed his shock of the memory. "Imagine, Rabbi, an educated Jewish boy—a drunkard. I didn't tell my father. I was afraid to. I was afraid to admit it to myself. I kept telling myself it was an accident, that he had got a little high and didn't realize how much he was taking. The next day he didn't come in. But the day after, he was there right on time as if nothing happened. And the next day, he was drunk again. I stood it for a couple of weeks, and then I told my father. 'Get rid of him'—that's what my father said. 'Get rid of him before he ruins us.'"

"I take it you did."

Goralsky nodded his head in grim satisfaction. "I put it up to him to buy us out or let us buy him out. Of course he couldn't raise the money, and it wouldn't have done him any good if he could. Could a man like that run a business? We paid him fifteen thousand in cold cash, and said goodby. And you know, Rabbi, it was like pulling up an anchor. A couple of months later we got a really good government contract and we were on our way."

"Did you know about the contract when you made him the proposition?"

"As God's my witness, Rabbi. We had filed our bid months before, but we hadn't heard a word about it."

"All right. Then when did you see him next?"

"I never saw him again. We went public and sold stock and we got to be a big operation. We moved to this house. And then one day I got a letter from Hirsh telling me he's applied for a job at Goddard Lab and figures that perhaps I can help him because they must know me. So I called Quint and put it to him as strong as I could, and made sure that in his letter to Hirsh he'd say they were giving him the job largely on my say-so."

"But I don't understand. You say you did it because you hated him."

"That's right. There he was with his Ph.D. from Tech and I hadn't gone beyond the first year high. I wanted him to know that with all his education, he had to come to me for a job, and that I could deliver."

"But didn't you see him after he came?"

Goralsky shook his head. "He called a couple of times, and each time I told the girl to say I was out. I'm like superstitious, Rabbi. You had trouble with some hard-luck guy, I'm afraid it can rub off. And you want to know something: I was right. Twenty years ago, this Hirsh almost ruined us. He comes back to town and, sure enough, the son of a bitch almost ruins me again."

"How do you mean?"

"We had a little problem here and I gave it to Goddard to chew on to see what they can come up with. So after a while, we get a preliminary report and it says they think they've found a way to lick it and then some—a kind of breakthrough. At this time we're sort of playing with the idea of merging with another outfit—on a stock transfer basis. You understand?"

The rabbi nodded.

"This is confidential, Rabbi."

"Of course."

He laughed. "Confidential! Every brokerage house in Boston knows about it, but all they've got is rumors. You can't keep this sort of thing secret. Still, I wouldn't want it known that it came straight from me. See?"

The rabbi nodded again.

"So our stock starts going up. It's normal whenever there's news of a merger. It goes up for a couple of days and then slides back, sometimes even below where it was originally. But it doesn't work that way with us. It keeps climbing, and after a couple of weeks it's almost double. And I know damn well it isn't the rumor of the merger that did it. It was something else—a rumor that we had something special in the works. I guess you can't keep that kind of secret either. Maybe I'm a little sore about it. Maybe I got some idea that those double-domes over at the lab are playing the market, but I'm not hurting. After all, I'm in a merger situation on a stock transfer basis. Where I planned to give two of my shares for one of theirs, it looks now that I'll be swapping even, so what harm is done? And it's perfectly legit, you understand, because if I've got a new process coming through then my stock is worth that much more. Get it?"

"Yes."

"And then I get a call from Quint at Goddard Friday afternoon, just as I was leaving. It was Kol Nidre night, and I was leaving early. And he tells me he's very sorry, the preliminary report was premature—premature, hell, they'd flubbed the dub. You understand?"

"I think so," said the rabbi doubtfully. "They had made a mistake."

"That's right. So where does it leave me? Here I am involved in a merger with a high-class outfit, and it looks like I've been manipulating my stock to get a better deal."

"I see."

"What can I do? It's Yom Kippur, and when I get home I find my father is really sick. And the next day, he's no better—maybe even a little worse. And the next day, Sunday, I get a call from these people, and they're sore—and suspicious. Well, Monday I went down to Goddard to have it out with Quint. Maybe you never had any experience with these army types. He used to be a general, very dignified, very efficient, very businesslike. Bip, bip, bip. But I can see he's uncomfortable, and he's squirming. And finally, you know what he says? 'Well, it's your man who was at fault,

Mr. Goralsky. You put him here. You practically forced us to take him—Isaac Hirsh!' How do you like that? The first time I ever did business with him, he almost ruins me. Then for twenty years I don't see or hear from him. When he comes here I'm careful to have nothing to do with him. And again he almost ruins me. See what I mean when I say you've got to keep away from guys like that? You want to know something, Rabbi? I'll bet you're wondering why I went to his funeral."

"Well, to go to a funeral is traditionally considered a blessing, a mitzvah."

"Mitzvah nothing! I wanted to make damn sure he got buried. . . ."

The maid put her head in the door. "Your father is awake now, Mr. Goralsky."

As they started up the staircase, Goralsky said, "Not a word about the cemetery business, Rabbi. I don't want my father upset."

"Of course not."

The old man was out of bed and sitting in a chair when his son and the rabbi entered. He extended a thin, blue-veined hand in greeting.

"See, Rabbi, I fasted and now I'm getting better."

The rabbi smiled at him. "I'm happy to see you looking so well, Mr. Goralsky."

"So well, I'm not yet." He glared at his son. "Benjamin, are you going to let the rabbi stand? Get him a chair."

"Oh, really you don't have to trouble." But Ben had already left the room. He came back carrying a chair, and set it down for the rabbi. He himself sat on the edge of the bed.

"I missed Kol Nidre," the old man went on, "for the first time in my life. Not once, since I was maybe five years old, did I stay away from the Kol Nidre service. My Ben tells me you gave a fine sermon."

The rabbi glanced covertly at Ben, who pursed his lips in a mute plea not to give him away. The rabbi grinned. "You know how it is, Mr. Goralsky, for Yom Kippur one tries a little harder. Next year, you'll be able to judge for yourself."

"Who knows if there'll be a next year. I'm an old man and I've worked hard all my life."

"Well, that's what gives you your vitality. Hard work—"

"He's been saying that for as long as I can remember," said Ben.

The old man looked at his son reproachfully. "Benjamin, you interrupted the rabbi."

"I was only going to say that hard work never hurt any-one, Mr. Goralsky. But you mustn't worry about what will happen a year from now. You must concentrate on getting well."

"That's true. One never knows whose turn will come next. Once, a few years ago, I had a sore on my face like a wart. I read the Jewish papers, Rabbi, and they have there every day a column from a doctor. Once it said that a sore like this could become, God forbid, a cancer. So I went to the hospital. The young doctor who examined me thought maybe I was worried the sore would spoil my looks. Maybe he thought I was an actor and wanted to look pretty. He asked me how old I was. Then I was maybe seventy-five. So when I told him, he laughed. He said if you were younger maybe we'd operate, like with a man my age it was a waste of time. So he gave me a salve, I should put it on and come back the next week. The next week when I come back, is already a different doctor. So I asked where's the doctor from last week, and they told me he had been killed in an automobile accident."

"Serves him right," said Ben.

"Idiot! You think I was complaining he was making fun of me? He was a fine young man, a doctor. What I mean is you can't tell who God will pick first. I understand the Hirsh boy died, right on the night of Kol Nidre. He was a good boy, too, and educated."

"He was a drunkard," said Ben.

The old man shrugged his shoulders. "Used to be, Rabbi, a drunkard was a terrible thing. But only a couple days ago I was reading in the Jewish paper, in this same column from the doctor, how a drunkard he's like a sick person—it's not his fault."

"He took his own life, Papa."

The old man nodded sadly. "That's a terrible thing. He must have suffered a lot. Maybe he couldn't stand it to be a drunkard. He was an educated boy. So maybe for him to be a drunkard was like for another person to have a cancer."

"You knew him well?" asked the rabbi.

"Isaac Hirsh? Sure, I knew him when he was born. I knew his father and mother. She was a fine woman, but the husband, the father, he was a nothing." He canted his head on one side in reflection. "It's hard to know what to do, what's right. Here was Hirsh who never did an honest day's work in his life. Even while his wife was alive, he used to be interested in the ladies. They used to say that a decent woman didn't want to go into his shop for a fitting. He made with the hands

—you know what I mean. And when she died, he could hardly wait to get married again. Yet his son was an educated boy who went through college on scholarship and even became a doctor, a Ph.D. doctor. And I, what I worked hard all my life and I observed all the regulations, not one of my four children went to college."

"Well—"

"And yet, Rabbi, on the other side, all my children, they're in good health, they're well off, and they're all good to me. And Isaac Hirsh didn't even come to his father's funeral, and now he too is dead. So you can't tell."

"Then you feel differently now about Hirsh's burial," suggested the rabbi.

The old man's mouth set in a hard line. "No, Rabbi," he said. "A rule is a rule."

27

No formal announcement was made by the district attorney; only a short notice appeared in the inside pages of the *Lynn Examiner* stating that the district attorney's office was looking into the circumstances surrounding the death September 18 of Isaac Hirsh of 4 Bradford Lane, Barnard's Crossing, and that a petition might be filed for an order to exhume the body.

Marvin Brown caught the item as he glanced through the paper during his morning coffee break and called Mortimer Schwarz immediately.

"I'll bet the rabbi had something to do with that, Mort. It's a trick—it's one of the rabbi's little tricks, I tell you." He sounded excited.

"But how could the rabbi get to the district attorney? And what does he gain by it?"

"He's thick as thieves with Chief Lanigan and Lanigan goes to the D.A. As for what he stands to gain—why, he stops us from going ahead."

"You mean with the road? What's that got to do with the D.A.'s investigation?"

"Well, wouldn't it look kind of funny if we start building a road to set off the very grave they're interested in? The paper said they were going to exhume the body. Wouldn't that look nice while they're digging up the body for us to be laying out the road? You don't think there'd be questions?"

"I still don't see anything for us to get excited about, Marve. Obviously there's no connection between our work and theirs. And frankly, I can't imagine the rabbi going to all that trouble, especially where it doesn't change things the least bit. You know what I think? This guy Beam, the investigator for the insurance company, he must have got the ball rolling on this. After all, he represents a big insurance company that has a lot at stake. My guess is that they'd have a lot more influence with the district attorney than the rabbi would."

"Well, as far as I'm concerned, Mort, I'm not going ahead with the road business until after the district attorney is out of there."

"Personally, I don't see it. But if you feel that way, okay, so we'll wait a week."

"But what about the Board meeting Sunday? It's not safe to go ahead with the rabbi's resignation while this business with Hirsh is still hanging fire."

"Yeah, you've got a point there, Marve. You sure you don't want to go ahead with our plans—"

"No."

"All right, I'll tell you what we'll do: we'll call off the Board meeting."

"Isn't that kind of high-handed?"

"I don't think so. As president I can call a special meeting, can't I?"

"Sure, but—"

"So why can't I call off a meeting? Matter of fact, I could just call up our friends and tell them not to show. Then we wouldn't have a quorum."

"Maybe that would be better."

"Well, I'll see. In the meantime, keep your eye on the situation."

Brown was aware that the door of his office had opened and that his secretary was standing on the threshold. He wondered uneasily how much she had heard. He looked up at her inquiringly.

"There are two men to see you, Mr. Brown—from the police."

Since the death of her husband, Patricia Hirsh had not been left alone for a single evening by her friends and neighbors. She had been invited to dinner, and even when she was too tired and had to beg off, someone would drop in to spend part of the long evening with her. So she was not surprised one evening when Peter Dodge dropped in on her, although she had not seen him since the funeral.

"I'm afraid I've been neglecting you, Pat. But I've been so busy with details of the MOGRE trip."

"Oh, I understand," she said. "And you've had to give up your walks, I suppose."

He seemed embarrassed. "No, I've passed here several times and thought of stopping, but there always seemed to be company—"

"They were just neighbors, friends from around here."

"I suppose it was foolish of me. I—I didn't want them to think I might be calling for—well, for professional reasons."

"Professional reasons?"

"Well, you see your friends and neighbors are mostly Jewish, and I was afraid they might think I was trying to win you back, now that your husband was gone."

"But I was never converted," she said. "Ike and I were married by a justice of the peace."

"I know, I know. It was silly of me. Please forgive me."

"There's nothing to forgive, Peter."

"Oh, but there is. You were all alone, and I should have been by your side, as your oldest friend here, as someone from your hometown—"

She smiled. "Well, all right, Peter, I forgive you."

She patted his hand, and immediately he capped it with his own. "Tell me, how are you really? I know it was a terrible shock, but are you all right now?"

Gently she withdrew her hand. "Yes, Peter. It's lonely, of course, but everyone has been very nice."

"And what are you planning to do? Go back to South Bend?"

"Oh, I don't think so, not to South Bend. I left there some time before I met Ike, and I have no one there, or anywhere else, for that matter. I haven't thought about it much, but I suppose I will stay on here for a while and try to get a job of some sort. I'd like to keep this house as long as I can, but I might have to give it up and take a small flat in Lynn or Salem—"

"A job is a good idea; it will keep your mind occupied."

"I suppose it will do that too, but it will mean I can eat regularly." She smiled. "I sort of got into the habit."

He was shocked. "I didn't realize. Didn't Ike—"

"Leave me provided? There's a small checking account, less than three thousand dollars, and a savings account of a little over a thousand. We paid down four thousand dollars on the house, and I'm sure I won't have any trouble selling the house for what we paid for it. And there's the car which I plan to sell. After what happened I never want to see it again."

"But wasn't there insurance?"

"Yes, there was insurance. But there also was a suicide clause, and there's a man around, a Mr. Beam, who is working for the insurance company, an investigator. If the insurance company decides it was suicide, then they'll just return the premiums we paid in and that's all."

"But they have to prove it, Pat. They can't just decide on their own."

"That's true, they can't. But they can refuse to pay, and then I would have to sue them for the money. It could drag on for years. Dr. Sykes said they might offer me a settlement, but it would be a lot less than the policy calls for. Still I think I'd probably take it if it were anything within reason."

"But why? You don't think he committed suicide, do you?"

She nodded slowly. "I think perhaps he may have." And she told him what happened at Goddard, how he was going downhill. When she finished, Dodge was silent a moment. Then: "I can't believe it. I didn't know your husband for long, and I didn't know him very well, but his mind—well, he was still one of the smartest men I ever met." He rose. "Look, Pat, I've got to go now. I've got to pack. I'm taking a plane south on this Civil Rights business tonight and just came to say goodby. I'll be gone a week or two—three at the most. You can't tell what's likely to happen once you get down there."

She held out her hand and he took it in both of his. "Promise me you won't do anything—you won't come to any decision on the insurance or anything else—until I get back. There are people in my parish, important people, businessmen, and I will consult with them. If you should need a job, I'm sure one of them will help. I want you to stay on here."

She smiled at him. "All right, Peter. I'm not likely to do anything for the next few weeks." She went to the door with him.

"Good. Believe me, dear, we'll work something out."

"Look here, Rabbi, we're on opposite sides of this cemetery

business. Maybe I'm wrong and maybe I'm right. To me, it's a matter of what's best for the temple. I don't like the idea of selling a man something and then taking it back from him, even if he pulled a fast one on me in the transaction. If someone puts something over on me, all right, I'll know better the next time. Let the buyer beware—that's law, isn't it? And even though I sold Mrs. Hirsh that lot for her husband and it turns out maybe I shouldn't have, his death not being strictly kosher, I'd be the last one to crybaby on it, even though you're supposed to come to a deal with clean hands. But Mort Schwarz tells me that it isn't kosher, and that it might lose the temple a lot of money, enough to build a whole new chapel. So I come up with this idea, and it was all for the good of the temple. All right, maybe you don't agree with us, and maybe you're right, but what I say is fight fair."

"Would you mind telling me what you're talking about, Mr. Brown?"

"Oh, come on, Rabbi. Everybody in town knows that the chief of police and you are buddy-buddy."

"So?"

"So, I don't think an outsider, who isn't even a member of our faith, should interfere in a matter that is strictly a temple matter."

"Are you trying to tell me that Chief Lanigan came and tried to get you to change your stand on Hirsh?"

"He didn't come himself. But he sent a Lieutenant Jennings down with another officer. They're both in plain clothes and they come in and ask to see me. So my secretary —secretary?—she's the bookkeeper, general officer worker, errand girl—she tells them I'm busy and can she help. So they say, no, they got to see me personal. So she says I'm busy and can't be disturbed. And then they flash their badges and say they guess I got to be disturbed. Now you know what that can mean in an office. There were a couple of my salesmen around, and they were talking to some customers. And the girl herself."

"Anyone is subject to police inquiry, I suppose, Mr. Brown. Are you suggesting that I sent them?"

"Well, they came to talk about Hirsh. They wanted to know what connection I had with him. What connection would I have with him? I hardly knew the man. When he first moved into town, I sent him an announcement. I send them out to all new residents, that's business. A little later, I sent him another announcement. It's a special kind of letter that offers a special free premium if you fill out the enclosed card. I think at that time we were using a kind of wallet that you carry in your breast pocket and it has a little pad of paper and a ball-point pen, twenty-eight fifty a gross. So when he or his wife signed the card and sent it in, I called him on the phone and made an appointment, just like I would with anyone else. Maybe you got one when you first came to town. Then I went over there and sold him some insurance. And that's all there was to it. I didn't even deliver the policy. I was busy at the time and sent one of my salesmen down. I never saw him again, I'm not even sure if I would remember him if I did see him again. That was my connection with Hirsh.

"But the way they acted and the questions they asked, like I had done something criminal. Why was I so interested in changing the layout of the road? Didn't I realize that it would cut Hirsh's grave off from the others? What did I have against Hirsh? I couldn't tell them about the Goralsky business. That's all hush-hush, and as far as I know Ben Goralsky hasn't even agreed to give the chapel. So I told them about our law against burying suicides. And then they tell me that they understand according to you it isn't against the law, and couldn't it be I had some other reason. Then they begin asking me what I was doing the night Hirsh died."

"Well, that should have been easy. It was Kol Nidre."

"None of it was hard. They were just giving me the business. And don't tell me, Rabbi, that they can't touch me if I haven't done anything wrong. Aside from taking up my time, they can do me lots of harm just by coming to see me. A man in business, especially the insurance business, has to be above suspicion. What if word gets around that the police are coming down to the office to question me? Do you think that would improve my business?"

The rabbi was spared the necessity of answering by the ringing phone. It was Lanigan.

He sounded jubilant. "Rabbi, remember I told you that Goralsky, Mr. Ben Goralsky, was the one who recommended Hirsh for the job at Goddard?"

"Yes."

"Well, did you know that Hirsh and Goralsky were originally partners, and that the process the Goralskys now use by which they made a fortune, I might add, was Hirsh's idea? They backed him with money and then bought him out."

"Yes, I knew that."

There was a pause, then—and the voice was cold, "You never mentioned it to me."

"I didn't think it was significant."

"I think you and I should have a little talk, Rabbi. Maybe tonight?"

"That will be all right. Right now, Mr. Marvin Brown is here with me. He tells me that a couple of your men were down to see him."

"And I might say that he wasn't what I would call overly cooperative."

"That may be, but what I'm concerned with right now is that he seems to think it was done at my instigation. Did your men say anything to give him that idea?"

"You know better than that, Rabbi."

"Of course. But then how can you possibly be interested in him?"

"Well now, Rabbi, on that point I received a bit of intelligence not twenty minutes ago. Since he's there with you, you might just ask him a question for me. Ask him, why did he leave the temple before the service was over?"

"Are you sure?"

"I'm sure, Rabbi." With a laugh Lanigan hung up.

The rabbi turned to Marvin Brown. "That was Chief Lanigan."

Brown's smirk seemed to say, I told you so.

"Tell me, Mr. Brown, Friday night, the Kol Nidre service, did you leave the temple early?"

Marvin Brown reddened.

"So that was why you did not respond when you were called for your honor. Why, Mr. Brown, why?"

"I—I don't think I have to answer. I—I don't care to—that is, I'm not on any witness stand, and I don't have to answer as to my whereabouts to anyone."

28

"I'm a cop first and foremost, Rabbi," said Lanigan, "and I don't take kindly to your withholding information that might be of value to our investigation."

"I don't see how the fact that Goralsky recommended Hirsh

142

for a job should make me think he wanted to kill him," said the rabbi. He was matching the chief's reserve and his tone was coldly polite.

"Rabbi, Rabbi, I explained all that. We've got a weapon that practically anybody could have used, and a motive that can be almost anything. The only line we can take is to check opportunity. I told you the Jews of Barnard's Crossing had practically a communal alibi because they were all in the temple at the time, so for that very reason anyone who wasn't has some explaining to do. Now who wasn't? Your friend Marvin Brown, for one. I understand he's some kind of big shot in your temple, a vestryman or something like that."

"He's on the Board of Directors."

"Okay, so if anyone should have been there, he should. And we know he was at the temple but left early—why, he wouldn't say. Now on top of that, we find he sold Hirsh his insurance. It isn't much, but for a guy like Hirsh who kept to himself pretty much, it's a connection. So we question him. If it upsets him, that's too bad. It's one of the burdens of citizenship."

"Aren't you supposed to tell a man what he's being questioned for? And in a murder case, aren't you supposed to warn him that what he says may be used against him?"

"We haven't accused him of anything. We were just looking for information. Maybe when we go see him again, I'll take just that line. Right now, I'm letting him stew a little. And remember, no one is supposed to know that Hirsh was murdered."

"How long are you going to keep that up?"

The chief grinned, for the first time since he arrived. "It's actually not much of a secret right now. Once I reported the matter to the D.A., it was bound to get around town. You can't keep those things dark. The chances are that your friend Brown has already figured out that we wouldn't send two men to question him at his office and check on his whereabouts unless something like murder was involved. In tonight's *Examiner* there was a little item in Fred Stahl's Roundabout column. Didn't you see it?"

"I don't read gossip columns."

"Well, sometimes it pays. The Roundabout asks: Are the police hiding something? Why should the office of the District Attorney be investigating the death of a well-known scientist in a town not many miles from here? Could the death possibly be more mysterious than it appeared? Did the police goof and are they covering up?"

"And this is how the most important business of the community is conducted?" asked the rabbi sadly. "Hints in gossip columns, rumor, speculation? And if Marvin Brown's secretary and the other people in the office see that item and jump to the conclusion that he's a suspect in a murder case, that's just one of the burdens of citizenship, is it? And all because he sold the dead man an insurance policy."

"It wasn't just the insurance policy. There was also the matter of selling the widow a grave site. And trying to shunt the body aside in the cemetery. And in this crazy case where we have so little to go on, we check any two facts that happen to coincide."

"And Ben Goralsky—he is suspect because he got Hirsh a job and because years ago they were partners for a short time?"

"And because he wasn't at the synagogue either. And according to what I hear, the Goralskys are very Orthodox and very devout. It seems funny that he shouldn't have gone."

"You also heard, I suppose, that his father was very sick and that he was afraid he might die?"

"Not from you, Rabbi." And once again, the atmosphere which had warmed somewhat, cooled.

"You said you were first and foremost a policeman. Well, first and foremost I am a rabbi. Mr. Goralsky is a member of my congregation, and I cannot see myself inviting his confidence in order to transmit it to the police."

"You mean that if you found a member of your congregation had committed murder you would not inform the police?"

"I am bound by the duties of citizenship just as is everyone else," said the rabbi stiffly.

"But you won't help us find him."

"I will not cast suspicion on innocent people so that the police can harass them—"

"Harass them? Do you think we grill them for the pleasure of seeing them squirm?"

"The effect is the same. Marvin Brown was upset—even frightened. I'm sure it wasn't because he had committed murder and was afraid he might be discovered. He was afraid of the effect on his business and his friends, on his wife and children."

"But he did leave the temple early and he wouldn't tell you why."

"What of it? There were probably lots of people who left the temple at one time or another. It's a long service, and

144

people get tired. They go out for a breath of air, or to stretch their legs—"

"And would they be ashamed to say so?"

"Of course not. But Marvin Brown might have left for any number of reasons he would hesitate to admit to me. Maybe he went home for a bite, and he wouldn't like it known that he had broken his fast."

"And he might have gone to kill Hirsh."

"Why? Because he sold him an insurance policy? You might as well question anyone else who had the slightest contact with Hirsh—the baker who sold him bread, the butcher who sold him meat, the mechanic who fixed his car, a hundred others. And since most of them probably are not Jews, they would not have been in the temple and a good many probably would be unable to prove their whereabouts."

"I'm not saying Brown's guilty of murder because he left the synagogue early. I'm just saying that in a case like this where the weapon was so accessible, and the motive could be almost anything—"

"Aren't you, perhaps, riding that idea a little too hard?"

"How do you mean?"

"Because there was ample opportunity for the killing you have proceeded on the theory that no strong motive was involved. That may very well be true, but it doesn't have to be. The killer may have been planning to kill Hirsh for months, but either didn't quite have the nerve or the opportunity never arose. Perhaps he may have planned to kill him in some conventional manner and taken advantage of this situation merely because it presented itself."

"I don't see how that gets us any further."

"It suggests other lines of investigation."

"Such as?"

The rabbi shrugged his shoulders. "We know Hirsh worked on the Manhattan Project. Perhaps his background there might be worth investigation. I don't want to sound melodramatic, but conceivably he had information someone might want, or even might *not* want him to tell."

"But that was almost twenty years ago. It's unlikely such information would have much significance today. Besides, why wait all this time before acting?"

"There may be nothing to it, but can you rule it out for certain? Up till now, he's been in another part of the country. Now he comes back East—where there is the greatest concentration of scientists. Who's to say he didn't run into someone—maybe at Goddard?"

"I suppose we could check the personnel files to see if anyone else there worked on the Manhattan Project," the chief said doubtfully.

"What about the fact that Mrs. Hirsh is a rather attractive young woman?"

Lanigan looked at the rabbi. "As a rabbi, I wouldn't think you'd notice such things."

"Even your priests who are celibate can, I'm sure, distinguish between an attractive woman and a plain one."

Lanigan smiled reminiscently. "Yeah, I guess Father O'Keefe could, although I have my doubts about Father Chisholm. Are you suggesting that the widow might have a lover—"

"From what I have seen of her I would doubt it, but it's not impossible. Rather I was thinking that some man, a man younger than her husband, might have been attracted to her and think he'd have a better chance with Hirsh out of the way."

"It's worth checking into, I suppose." He turned to his host with sudden suspicion. "You wouldn't be trying to tout me off Marvin Brown and Goralsky, would you now, Rabbi?"

"I am merely suggesting that there are other lines of investigation than members of my congregation who happened for one reason or another to have missed the Kol Nidre service."

"Yeah? Well, that's as may be. But we're going to continue to check into the movements and whereabouts of your friends that Friday night regardless of whatever other approaches we make. I'll bid you good night now, Rabbi, but I don't mind saying I'm a little disappointed. I don't suppose I have to warn you that if you tip off Goralsky or anyone else I've mentioned, I could consider you an accessory after the fact."

29

In a small town there are no secrets; a secret is not something unknown, only something not talked about openly.

By Thursday, when the district attorney finally met with the press, it was generally known that there was some mystery connected with the death of Hirsh. Nor did the district attorney clarify matters much in his press conference. In spite of sharp questioning he would admit only that evidence had come to the attention of the police of Barnard's Crossing that suggested Isaac Hirsh had not met with death by accident.

"Are you suggesting that his death was suicide?"

"That's certainly one of the possibilities."

"Are you perhaps suggesting that he might have been murdered?" asked another reporter.

"We are not ruling out that possibility."

"Can you give us some idea of the nature of the new evidence that was brought to your attention?"

"I do not think it would be in the public interest at this time."

"Isaac Hirsh was at one time connected with the Manhattan Project. Is there any connection between his death and his government work on the atom bomb?"

"We are not ruling out that possibility."

"Can you tell us what steps you plan to take—"

"The investigation is at present being conducted largely by the Barnard's Crossing police in cooperation with state detectives."

"If there is any connection with the federal government, or for that matter if it is murder, isn't it unusual to leave this to a small town police force?"

"We have every confidence in Chief Lanigan, and since he is intimately acquainted with the people of the town we feel he is the best man to work on the case at this stage. Of course —through this office—he can call on every facility of the commonwealth, or of the federal government if it should turn out to be involved."

"Are you planning to exhume the body of Isaac Hirsh?"

"That is a distinct possibility."

And that was as far as he would go. To all other questions he answered, "I don't think I care to go into that at this time."

Lieutenant Eban Jennings was a tall, thin man with sparse grayish hair. He had watery blue eyes which he dabbed frequently with a folded handkerchief, and his Adam's apple bobbed in his scrawny neck as he talked.

"I went over to see the widow like you said. You know, Hugh. She's really something."

"How do you mean?"

"Well, she's a big woman and right handsome, with a head of flaming red hair, white skin, and tits like a pair of silver cups—"

"My, aren't we getting poetic!"

"It's just that she's a fine figure of a woman with a lovely round arse your hands just itch to pat—"

"You're a horny bastard."

"I'm just telling you how she struck me," said Jennings reproachfully. "My point is, there she is—a woman like that, not more than thirty-five I'll bet, and she's married to a little shrimp of a guy old enough to be her father. And what a guy. Bald, pot-bellied, a rummy, and a Jew at that. So why would a woman like her want to marry somebody like him? All right, maybe she'd had tough times and wanted someone who'd treat her decent. But, dammit, it couldn't last. After a while, she'd stop feeling grateful and start looking around, and there'd be plenty of men willing to start making up to her."

"Hear anything—rumors, gossip, to that effect?"

"No-o, but then I haven't really asked around. I just questioned the widow about whether anything unusual had happened that day. You know: any unusual letters, phone calls, visits. She couldn't think of anything but did happen to mention that the young curate, whatsisname, Peter Dodge over at St. Andrews, had said he might drop in on Hirsh that evening."

"The Reverend Peter Dodge?" Suddenly Lanigan had a thought. "Say, that's right. That time he came down to complain about some fracas at Bill's Cafe he mentioned he was from South Bend. And that's where she's from."

"Yeah? Then listen to this. After what she told me, I figured maybe he did drop in that night. Maybe Hirsh said something that could help. So I went on over to this place where Dodge boards, with Milly Oliphant—just routine follow-up—and he was gone."

"Gone?"

"Not for good. According to Milly, Dodge packed a bag and flew to Alabama. He's head of some bunch of clergymen who are going down there to picket. But now, get this—the group isn't supposed to leave for a couple of days. I got that from Dr. Sturgis, the rector, who is his boss. He said Dodge decided to go down a little earlier to take care of some administrative details."

"Peter Dodge. A clergyman."

"Well, that's where we don't agree, Hugh. You can't think of a clergyman in connection with a woman, but to me, they're men just like anyone else. I don't care whether he's a priest or a minister or a rabbi. The right kind of woman comes along, and he's going to feel his pants tighten. And this Dodge fellow—he's pretty new at the game. Before this, I understand he was a professional football player. And he's a big man—which would appeal to a woman her size. And he's young, her age. And he's not married. And he left town."

"Are you trying to suggest that he ran away?"

"All I'm saying is look at the facts, Hugh. This group he's connected with, they aren't scheduled to leave for a couple of days yet. He had planned to go with them but instead he went early."

"So what do you have in mind?"

"Isn't it funny that he left right after that item appeared in the *Examiner*? The one that hinted at new developments about Hirsh's death?"

30

On Friday there were two evening services at the temple: the regular minyan at sunset primarily for mourners that lasted about fifteen minutes; and a more comprehensive family service that began at eight, ran for about an hour, and was followed by a collation in the vestry. Miriam always attended the later service, not only because it was expected of her as the rabbi's wife, but because she felt he appreciated the encouragement of her presence as he delivered his sermon.

But this Friday had been one of her few bad days during a comparatively easy and uneventful pregnancy. She was tired and her feet were swollen from the extra housework required to prepare the house for the Sabbath. Rather than upset him by suggesting she stay home, she asked if he'd mind if she rode to temple.

Immediately he was solicitous. "Aren't you well, dear? It isn't—"

"No, it isn't time yet." She smiled. "It's just that I've been on my feet all day and I'm not up to walking. I'll call the Margolises to pick me up."

"Nonsense, I'll drive you."

"But David, you don't ride on the Sabbath—"

"It's not really a religious scruple, Miriam. That would be hypocritical of me as rabbi of a Conservative congregation where the whole congregation rides. No, it's just a matter of habit really; I'll take you."

"But when they see you drive up, won't they possibly connect it with the rumors of your resignation—"

He laughed. "You mean they'll think I've been a hypocrite all along, and now that I'm resigning I'm showing my true colors? Well, if they want to think that, let them. Come on." He took her by the arm and marched her out to the car. Flinging open the car door, he waved her in.

It would have been a grand gesture if the car had started immediately. But five minutes later, he was still jabbing his toe at the starter—and producing nothing more than an angry whir. He muttered under his breath, and she had just about decided to remark brightly that she was no longer tired and would now like to walk when the motor caught.

He drove to the end of the street and slowed down to make the turn.

"Turn left," Miriam said.

"But the temple is right," he protested.

"We're driving, so we've got plenty of time."

He shrugged as if to say, who can argue with a pregnant woman, but did as he was told.

They went a couple of blocks and she said, "Pull up here." He realized he was abreast of the office of the local cab company, and at last understood.

"My husband has been having some trouble with his car," she said when the proprietor came over, "and one of these days he may have to get me to the hospital in a hurry. Are you available all the time?"

"Twenty-four hours a day, Mrs. Small."

"What happens if all your cabs are busy?" the rabbi asked.

"Don't worry, Rabbi. We've got four cabs, and in the last couple of months the only time I've had them all out at one time was that Friday night you had your important holiday. They were shuttling back and forth to your temple until half-past seven or quarter to eight. And then we didn't have another call until around midnight. Guess everyone drove home with friends." He seemed somewhat aggrieved.

"Then we can depend on you if my husband can't get his car started?"

"Nothing to worry about, believe me, Mrs. Small. With

150

business the way it is these days, I could guarantee to get you there if you was to have twins." He laughed uproariously at his own joke.

When once again the rabbi had difficulty in starting, the taxi man showed professional interest. "Sounds like the carburetor," he said. "Better attend to it right away."

Just then the motor caught and the rabbi raced it for the sheer pleasure of hearing the motor roar. "I'll do that," he called out as he drove off.

"I'm glad you thought to ask about the cab service. It's extra insurance."

"It isn't because you don't want to be indebted to Chief Lanigan, is it?"

"Of course not."

The temple parking lot seemed fuller than usual for a Friday night service.

"Do you think it's because they've heard of your resignation?" asked Miriam. "And they want to show they're behind you?"

"More likely it's curiosity. They may want to find out what's happening with me, and they've probably heard conflicting stories about Hirsh's death."

"You're being bitter and cynical, David."

He looked at her in surprise. "Not at all. Actually, it's an indication that the temple is fulfilling one of its principal and traditional functions—as a center for the community. In the ghettos of Europe, or for that matter in the voluntary ghettos of America, the moment something happened news traveled with the speed of a telegram from house to house. But here, where there is no real Jewish section, where every Jew has Gentiles on either side, if something happens that is of particular interest to Jews they come to the temple to get the lowdown. I don't feel hurt. Quite the contrary, I'm pleased."

But those who thought the rabbi might speak of his rumored resignation and the reasons for it were disappointed; by no word did he suggest that this Friday evening was different from any other. After the service, when he joined the congregation in the vestry for the tea and cake the Sisterhood regularly provided, his ear caught snatches of conversation; for the most part it seemed concerned with the death of Isaac Hirsh. Once he heard someone say, "I'll bet the rabbi knows what it's all about. I wouldn't be surprised if his resignation had something to do with it."

"But how?"

"Don't ask me, but happening at the same time the way they both did—"

Yet to those few who came up and asked him what he thought about the Hirsh business, in each case he replied, "I don't know. I didn't know the man."

He was pleased to see that Miriam, who would normally have remained standing at his side, had shown sense enough to take one of the folding chairs against the wall. A small group of women had gathered around her and were being solicitous.

"Above all, my dear, you mustn't worry. That's the worst thing you can do. When I was having my third, my Alvin, the doctor said to me, 'Whatever you do, don't worry; it tightens the muscles.' I shouldn't worry when my Joe was being transferred here from Schenectady, and we didn't know if we were going to be able to get a house or have to live in a hotel, and what would I do with Marjorie and Elaine, with their school in the meantime. But I made up my mind that the baby comes first, and I told Joe to go ahead and make any arrangements he wanted and I'd live with them."

"That's right," said Mrs. Green. "Mental attitude is important. I know it's old-fashioned to think that you have to think beautiful thoughts during your pregnancy, but when I was having Pat I had the phonograph going all day long, and didn't she get to be the first drum majorette of the high school band? The instructor said she had an innate sense of rhythm, whereas Fred who had trumpet lessons for years could never even keep in step, let alone keep time to the music."

"It didn't work with me," said Gladys Moreland flippantly. "My mother went to the museum every Sunday right up to her seventh month, and I can't draw a straight line."

"Oh, but you've got artistic temperament," insisted Mrs. Green. "Anyone who sets foot in your living room can see that you've got exquisite taste."

"Well, I am interested in interior decorating."

Mrs. Wasserman, wife of the first president of the temple, pulled up a chair alongside Miriam. She was a motherly woman of sixty and had been friendly from the day the Smalls first arrived in Barnard's Crossing.

"You feel tired these days, huh?"—her way of noting that Miriam was sitting down instead of standing by her husband's side.

"A little," Miriam admitted.

152

She patted her hand. "Pretty soon now. Nothing to worry about. And I'll bet it will be a boy."

"David and his mother; especially his mother, won't accept anything else."

Mrs. Wasserman laughed. "If it's a girl, they'll accept. And after two or three days, you couldn't get them to swap for a boy. He's nervous, the rabbi?"

"Who can tell?"

"Oh, they all try to be like that, like it's not important, but you can tell. Before my first one was born, Jacob, he was so cool and calm. But he had the whole steam system checked over, he thought maybe the house was a little chilly. He had a carpenter come in and make a chute from the baby's room to the laundry in the basement. In those days we didn't have a diaper service. He hired a man to shovel the snow off the steps and the walk for the whole season. He took out extra insurance, God forbid anything should happen to him there would be plenty for me and the baby. I'll bet your husband is the same way."

Miriam smiled faintly. "You don't know my David."

"Well, he's so busy—"

"It was all I could do to make him stop at the taxicab office to arrange for transportation in case our car wouldn't start. But for the rest"—she smiled—"he thinks it's enough to examine his conscience and make sure he isn't doing anything he thinks wrong."

"Maybe that's the best way," suggested Mrs. Wasserman gently.

"Maybe. Though sometimes—"

"You'd like him to be a little more—excited?"

Miriam nodded.

"It doesn't mean anything, my dear. Some men, they keep their tenderness all inside. My father, may he rest in peace, he was like that. When I was born—my mother used to tell about it, it was like a family joke—she felt the pains coming so she sent a neighbor's boy for my father who was in the House of Study. It was in the old country, you understand. He was in the middle of a discussion, and maybe being a young man he was a little embarrassed before the older men, so he told the boy to go back and tell her to cover herself up good and that it would probably pass. But a minute later, he excused himself and ran so fast that he reached home the same time as the neighbor's boy."

Miriam laughed. "My David wouldn't be embarrassed, but

153

if he were really involved in a discussion he might forget to come. . . ."

Morris Goldman who owned a garage drifted toward where the rabbi was standing, talking loudly: "—a little shrimp of a guy, bald-headed with a potbelly, and he turns out to be married to a big gorgeous redhead, a *shicksa* yet, who is half his age. Oh, *Gut Shabbes*, Rabbi. I was talking about this guy Hirsh."

"You knew him?"

"I knew him like I know any customer. You know how it is, they're waiting around for their car, you pass the time of day. Him I guess I knew a little better than most because he had an old car so he brought it in more often—brakes, flat tire. Once I put a new muffler on."

"How'd he come to go to you?" asked one of the bystanders. "Your garage is way out of town."

"He worked at the Goddard Lab and I get all the cars from there. My place is off Route 128, maybe five hundred yards from the Lab. You know, right at the foot of the cutoff just before you get to the Lab. They leave their cars with me for a lube job, a tune-up, and then walk to work from there."

"You do all kinds of work?" asked the rabbi.

"You bet, and if I say so myself I've got as good a crew of mechanics as any place on the North Shore. I've got one man, an ignition specialist, I've had people come from as far away as Gloucester just so he can service them. Why, your car acting up on you, Rabbi?"

"I've been having a bit of trouble," he said. "She's hard starting. And sometimes when I come to a stop, she dies."

"Well, it could be almost anything, Rabbi. Why don't you ride out someday and let me take a look at it?"

"Maybe I will." He thought he saw Miriam sending out distress signals, and excused himself. "Are you tired, dear? Would you like to go home now?"

"I think I should," she said. "I'll get my coat."

He was waiting for her to find her things in the cloakroom when he saw a jubilant Jacob Wasserman and Al Becker bearing down on him.

"Well, Rabbi! Things certainly look a lot different now, don't they?"

"How do you mean?"

"This announcement by the police, by the district attorney," exclaimed Becker. "Of course, the D.A. was pussyfooting. He's a politician and all politicians have to double-talk,

154

but there's no doubt in anyone's mind that Hirsh was murdered. He as much as admitted it. So you're vindicated! He got you off the hook. You're in the clear."

"If you're referring to the burial service I conducted, Mr. Becker, I needed no vindication from the district attorney. And if I had, I would hardly consider it good news to be let off the hook as you put it, at the cost of a man's murder."

"Sure, sure, nobody likes to hear someone has been murdered. I'm sorry about it. Who wouldn't be? But don't you see —it knocks the pins out from under Mort Schwarz and his gang. You heard that he called off the regular Board meeting Sunday?"

"No, I didn't."

"You'll probably get a card in the mail tomorrow."

"And what significance do you attach to the cancellation?"

Wasserman rubbed his hands gleefully. "We think perhaps under the circumstances they want to see how the Hirsh business comes out before they bring up the matter of your resignation. I have it from a very reliable source that Marvin Brown refused to go ahead with laying out the road."

"Refused? Why?"

"Because the district attorney may exhume the body."

The rabbi gave a wan smile. "It comes to the same thing in the end, doesn't it, Mr. Wasserman?"

"Oh, but Rabbi, there's a difference. This is the civil authority, engaged in bringing a criminal to justice."

"Of course."

"What we've got to think about now is what steps to take. As far as Hirsh is concerned—" He shrugged his shoulders. "Well, it makes no difference to him what caused his death. He's dead; we've got to concern ourselves about the living. Now, the business about your resignation. You don't really want to resign, do you?"

"I wouldn't have if this matter hadn't come up."

"Good. So we have to figure out a way to keep Schwarz from reading your letter to the Board. I've discussed it with Becker here, and we both decided the easiest and best way would be if you wrote Schwarz recalling your resignation." As the rabbi was about to interpose, he hurried on. "You could say that in the light of recent events there is no longer any difference between you and the administration, and for that reason you are revoking your previous letter."

"No."

"But don't you see, Rabbi, without that there's just your

155

letter of resignation. All he has to do is to read it and call for a vote. Strictly speaking, he doesn't even have to call for a vote. He just announces it. But if there are two letters, he's bound to read them both and then he'll have to explain the issue between you. Even then, you're not out of the woods but at least we'll have the advantage."

The rabbi shook his head. "I'm sorry, gentlemen, but—"

"Now look here, Rabbi," said Becker sternly. "Jake and I have gone all out for you. We're trying to help you the best way we can, but there's a certain amount you've got to do for yourself. You can't expect us to work our heads off, calling up people, going to see them, explaining, when you won't do your part."

"I expect nothing." He turned to Miriam, who was emerging from the cloakroom. "You'll have to excuse me. My wife is very tired."

Becker watched his retreating figure, then turned to Wasserman. "That's what you get for trying to help a guy."

Wasserman shook his head. "He's been hurt, Becker. He's a young man, practically a boy. And he's been hurt. . . ."

As they walked through the parking lot to their car, Miriam said, "Mr. Becker and even Mr. Wasserman seemed rather cool, David. Was it something you said to them?"

He reported the conversation, and she smiled wistfully. "So now you have no one behind you—not Mr. Wasserman, not Chief Lanigan, not Mr. Schwarz. Do you have to quarrel with everyone, David?"

"I didn't quarrel with them. I just refused to ask Schwarz to disregard my letter. In effect, it's begging him to keep me on."

"But you do want to stay, don't you?"

"Of course, but I can't ask. Don't you see I can't ask? The relationship between the rabbi and the Board of Directors requires maintaining a delicate balance. If I have to beg them to let me stay when I'm only doing my job, how can I ever have any influence on them? How can I guide them? I would be just a rubber stamp for anything they wanted to do. Once they realized they made me knuckle under while exercising my official function as rabbi, what could I do? And what could they not do?"

"I suppose so," she said softly. "And I know you're right, but—"

"But what?"

"But I'm just a young married woman, a couple of hundred miles from my mother and my family, and I'm going to have a baby any day now."

"So?"

"So I wish I were sure my husband had a job."

31

"I never interfere, Hugh. You know that. I'm no policeman and I'd be the last one to try to tell you your job, but the police department does come under the administrative supervision of the selectmen, and it's the broader aspects"— he made a wide sweep with his arm—"that I think it's our duty to go into."

Alford Braddock was not the typical Barnard's Crossing selectman. He was a native, to be sure—it was unthinkable that anyone not a Crosser born would be elected to the Board —but whereas the rest of the members were small businessmen with a taste for town politics, he was a man of considerable wealth, inherited wealth, which included a stock brokerage firm in Boston. Where others had to campaign personally, calling on voters, appearing at meetings of fraternal orders, speaking before the League of Women Voters, he blitzed the electorate with campaign posters and door-to-door house calls by a group of paid "volunteers." He outpolled all the other candidates easily and consequently was elected chairman of the board. He was tall and distinguished with snow-white hair and the ruddy complexion of the yachtsman. His clear blue eyes were candid and without guile and yet could look hurt—hurt, but determined to bear up and not show it—when you disagreed with him.

"What is it that's bothering you, Alford?" asked Lanigan quietly.

"Bothering me? Bothering me? Well, yes, I suppose you could put it that way. Something Dr. Sturgis mentioned. Said you were inquiring about Peter Dodge. Now he got it into his head that it had something to do with this Hirsh business. Of course, I assured him it was unlikely, most unlikely. After all, what connection would Peter Dodge have with Isaac Hirsh?"

"He might have been trying to convert him," suggested Lanigan with a smile.

"Think so? Yes, it's possible. A very enthusiastic fellow, this Dodge, from the Midwest I believe," he added as though that explained everything.

"As a matter of fact, we know he was planning to see Hirsh the night he was killed," said Lanigan. "About this Civil Rights business, perhaps."

"Yes, that must be it. That must be the connection. He was terribly enthusiastic about Civil Rights. Now I know that for a fact, Hugh. I mean I know that personally."

"There's another connection, Alford. He happens to know Mrs. Hirsh. They come from the same hometown—South Bend."

"Whatsat? Knew Mrs. Hirsh? What are you trying to say, Hugh?"

"Not a thing. I'm not suggesting anything. It's just that we'd like to ask Mr. Dodge a few questions. We sent him a wire down in Alabama asking him to get in touch with us. But he didn't. We called the hotel in Birmingham where he was supposed to be staying, and he wasn't there. I don't mean that he checked out, I mean he wasn't there. In fact, he hadn't been there since checking in a couple of days ago. I spoke to the hotel people and they said it wasn't unusual, not too unusual where these Civil Rights people are concerned. They register at a hotel, but then they contact the local headquarters of their organization down there and that's usually the last the hotel sees of them. Usually, they check out though. So we called the Alabama authorities to contact him for us, but so far we haven't heard."

"You're trying to say something, Hugh. Dammit, why don't you come right out with it? You're trying to say that this man Dodge, an Anglican priest, got involved with the wife of this Jew, and as a result became mixed up in this murder business and ran off—flew the coop, beat it."

Lanigan grinned. "You mean, he took a powder?"

"Dammit, Hugh, it's no laughing matter. That what you're trying to say?"

"It's possible."

"But dammit, a man of the cloth, and from my own church."

"But he's young, unmarried, and—to use your own word—enthusiastic."

"Hugh, do you realize what this could mean?"

"Yeah, but I honestly don't think it will. We don't really

have anything on him, we just want to question him. Find out if he saw Hirsh, and if he did, what time he left him."

Braddock was obviously relieved. "You'll probably find there's nothing to his absence from the hotel. I mean, as far as I can gather from news stories, these people who go down to march and picket and whatnot make a point of living with the —er—with the people. You'll probably find he has been staying in some colored sharecropper's shack out of reach of a telephone." Braddock smiled broadly. "You know, Hugh, you really had me going there for a minute."

Lanigan grinned.

"You've got a real suspect now, haven't you? This insurance fellow?"

"Brown? Marvin Brown? We're interested in him. At least we'd like to know where he was at the time."

"No alibi, eh?"

"We haven't asked him yet."

"Why not?"

"Well, there's no hurry. We have nothing on him except a couple of points of contact with Hirsh. He'll keep. It won't do any harm to let him stew for a while. These quick, nervy types—they get bothered and start worrying if you leave them alone, and after a while they're apt to do something just a little foolish."

Braddock rubbed his hands. Police business was fascinating, and as chairman of the Board of Selectmen he was in on the ground floor. "I get it, I get it," he said.

"Actually, we find Mr. Benjamin Goralsky a lot more interesting."

Braddock sat up straight. "Goralsky? Ben Goralsky of Goraltronics? Hold on a minute, Hugh, now you're barking up the wrong tree. I know the man. He's one of the finest specimens of his race. His plant employs over a thousand people from around here. When they went public, our firm helped float the initial stock issue, and we've been close to them ever since. No, nothing there, I assure you."

"Well, maybe not, but we plan to have Ben Goralsky down and ask him a lot of questions."

"I won't have it, Hugh. You're planning some kind of psychological third degree and I won't permit it. You haven't got anything on him, and you're just going on a fishing expedition. Well, I won't allow it. There are things in the wind that you don't know about and this could have repercussions that would affect the whole community."

"You mean the merger?"

"Who said anything about a merger? What do you know about a merger?"

"Oh, come now, Alf, everybody knows there's talk of Goraltronics being involved in a merger."

"Well, maybe, maybe. I suppose there are rumors floating around. Well, I'll admit it, but you keep this under your hat, understand? It's true—there is a merger in the offing. And it could be a tremendous thing for this whole area. I don't mind admitting that my firm is a little interested, and right now things are very touchy. Understand? So I'm telling you to keep your hands off Ben Goralsky."

"And let him get away with murder?"

"Dammit, he's not getting away with murder. You prove that he did it, and he's all yours. But until you have something definite on him, you leave him alone. And that's an order, Hugh. Because if you badger him and come up with nothing, I'll personally have your head."

32

Sergeant Whitaker was a young man, and ambitious. Three nights a week he went into Boston to attend law school. If all went well, he would be able to stand for his bar examination in another four years. It would be a tough grind, but at least Chief Lanigan was understanding and tried not to schedule him for night duty on those evenings when he had school. Tonight he was working late, but since it was Friday and his class did not meet, he did not mind. True, he hadn't had dinner and Aggie was always upset when he couldn't eat with her and the children, but Lieutenant Jennings had made it plain he wanted all his assignments covered before he went off duty, no matter what time that was. Whitaker's sergeant's stripes were quite new, and he had no intention of letting the lieutenant down.

He was seated now in the Goralsky kitchen across the table from Mrs. Chambers, the housekeeper. His notebook was spread out before him, and though he tried hard to be the dignified, impersonal police officer conducting an important investigation, it was difficult. Mrs. Chambers was from the Old Town and knew him from the time he was a grubby little school urchin.

"Now what is it you want to know? You're not planning to cause Mr. Goralsky any trouble, I hope. Because if you are, I'll have no part of it. Mr. Ben is a fine, decent gentleman, and his father is an old dear, for all he's a foreigner and talks funny."

"As I explained, Mrs. Chambers, this is just a routine investigation that I'm conducting—"

"Well, aren't we grand, conducting investigations. And what is it you're investigating?"

"We're just checking anyone and everyone who had any connection whatsoever with the late Isaac Hirsh, the man whose picture I showed you. It's just routine." He flipped the pages of his notebook. "I've been at it all day and I must have questioned twenty people or more."

"Well, I never laid eyes on the man."

"Did he never come here at any time? Think now."

"Who you telling to think, Henry Whitaker? I told you I never laid eyes on him, didn't I?"

"Well, did Mr. Goralsky, Mr. Ben Goralsky, did he ever mention the name Hirsh?"

"Not to me, he didn't."

"And the old man?"

"Not that I remember."

"Well now, think back to the evening of September 18. That was a Friday night. It was the night of the big Jewish holiday—"

"That was the night the old gentleman took sick."

"And Mr. Ben got home early I suppose. At least, all the rest of them, the Jews, I mean, worked a short day, so I suppose he did too."

"That's right. And all the servants were dismissed early too, so it wasn't that they were taking any special privileges that they weren't passing on to others."

"But you stayed on."

"Well of course. Who else was there to take care of the old gentleman, and him burning up with fever?"

"So Mr. Ben got home around three? four?"

"Around four it was, as near as I can remember."

"And he remained here at home until it was time to go to the temple, I suppose."

"He didn't go to the temple. At least he didn't go to pray. He just drove the rabbi and his wife there and came right back."

"So while he was gone, you were here alone with the old man."

"That's right. I was right up there in his room sitting by his bed."

"And when Mr. Ben got back from driving the rabbi to the temple, he came up to the room to see how his father was getting along, I suppose."

"No." She shook her head decisively. "He didn't come up because he didn't want his father to see him. You see, his father assumed that he had gone to the temple and would have been upset if he knew he hadn't. So Mr. Ben stayed out of sight."

"Then how do you know he came right back?"

"Because he told me, of course."

"The next morning, you mean?"

"Oh, no, I saw him later in the evening. The old gentleman dozed off and I came down here to the kitchen to get a bite. That's when I saw Mr. Ben in the living room."

"And that was what time?"

"Nine, half-past."

"So you didn't see him from around seven when he took the rabbi to the temple until about nine." He frowned at his notebook. "But I suppose you heard him moving around downstairs earlier."

"No, can't say that I did," she said tartly. "The door of Mr. Goralsky's room—I kept it closed because there's a draft from the hallway. And the living room is on the other side of the house."

"But you heard the car coming up the driveway?" he persisted.

"I did not."

"No? That's a little funny—"

"It's not funny at all, Henry Whitaker. Do you think Mr. Goralsky drives one of those jalopies that you can hear through the walls of a building like this over the sound of the surf, and me watching the old man and worrying every minute of the time?"

"No, I guess you wouldn't," he said meekly.

"Well now, if you have no more questions, I'll be getting about my work. Mr. Ben will be coming back from the temple soon and will be wanting a late snack."

33

"Got it all wrapped up, have you?" asked Lanigan. "Know exactly how she did it? Why don't you stick around till we get a confession from her, and then we might give you a copy to frame and stick up on the wall of your office?"

But Beam refused to be drawn. "Look, Chief, I've got a job to do same as you. It isn't up to me to solve crimes. I just inquire around and then make a report to the home office. I spoke to them yesterday, and they decided there was sufficient question here to withhold payment to the widow for the present. If it turns out that she's guilty, she wouldn't collect anyway. As a matter of fact, without any other beneficiary the whole amount may escheat to the State. Of course, you may come up with someone else, in which case we'll be happy to pay her."

"And if we don't come up with someone else, your company sits tight and tells the widow to sue if she wants her money. And God help her if she does, because you'll dredge up every bit of scandal, any little tidbit of gossip, so that even if she wins she'll be unable to go on living in the community."

"No, Hugh," said Jennings, "they just threaten to do that and then offer her ten cents on the dollar to settle."

"That's normal business procedure," said Beam.

"I suppose next you'll be off for South Bend to start smelling around."

"Cops are always sore at private investigators," said Beam philosophically. "And everybody has it in for the insurance company. We're the big bad wolf when we come up before a jury, especially if there's a good-looking dame involved. But I didn't come here to fight with you boys. I just came to tell you I was being called back and to say goodby."

"All right, goodby." Morosely, Lanigan watched him leave the room.

"What do you think?" asked Jennings.

"I think he'd accuse his mother if he thought it would help the company."

"It's nice business. The widow practically has to prove she didn't do it."

"That's right. And about the only way she can do so is for us to prove someone else did. And right now, we don't have a thing."

"Well, my money's on Peter Dodge. I think it's funny he left right after Fred Stahl's Roundabout column. His landlady was under the impression he wasn't planning to leave till the end of the week."

"That could be coincidence. I'd be very much surprised if he read Stahl's column."

"Yeah? Then why hasn't he been heard from since?"

"The chances are he's been so involved with the Civil Rights business, running around attending meetings, that the police haven't been able to locate him. Besides, I can't see the police down there exactly knocking themselves out to find some Northern agitator for us. They've probably got their hands so full breaking up picket lines they haven't the time to do their regular work."

"A man like Dodge," Jennings ruminated. "A big, tall, powerful, good-looking guy like that, you wouldn't think he'd be too hard to spot."

"For some reason, Eban, you're always trying to tie in the clergy with some scandal. But the fact is, we don't have a damn thing on him—"

"Except that · he had the opportunity—he comes around that way every night at about the right time. He knew Mrs. Hirsh from way back, and she's a nice-looking woman. He's single and her age. You know, Hugh, the trouble with you Catholics is that your priests got you buffaloed so, you can't even imagine a clergyman doing something wrong."

"All right, all right. I didn't say I wasn't considering him. But I haven't got him, and all I can do is wait until the Alabama police pick him up. When we get hold of him we can shake him up and turn him inside out to see what makes him tick, but I can't just sit and twiddle my thumbs until he shows up."

"So there's this Marvin Brown."

"We don't really have anything on him."

"Except that he was pretty damn uncooperative and evasive when I questioned him."

"Yes—"

"And he has no alibi, and he refused to tell the rabbi why he left the services before the rest—"

"Sure, but that's nothing I could go to the D.A. with."

"All right, then how about Goralsky?"

"Now *he* interests me."

164

"Why? You haven't got any more on him than you do on Brown."

"No? How about this?" He ticked the points off on his fingers. "One, he was not at the temple. Two, he had some special interest in getting Hirsh out of the cemetery. Three, he knew Hirsh from way back, and he's the only man in town who did. Four, he was also in business with him and got rich from him. Finally, he got him the job at Goddard."

"Yeah, but he never saw him after he got here."

"That's what he says."

"It's also what Mrs. Hirsh says."

"He might have been in touch with him by phone—or secretly so she wouldn't know."

"Yeah, but that's just a lot of maybes—he might have, he could've—"

"All right, let's stick with what we do know. Goralsky and Hirsh were partners. Goralsky forced him out, and then right afterward built up the business to a multimillion-dollar concern. There at least we have a motive for the killing."

"But godammit, Hugh, you've got it arse-backwards. In the business dealings between Hirsh and Goralsky, it wasn't Goralsky that got screwed. It was the other way around. You'd have a motive for Hirsh killing Goralsky, but not—"

"How do we know what the relations were between them? Look, way back there was some trouble between them on a business deal. Right?"

"Right."

"Then twenty years later, Hirsh asks Goralsky to recommend him for a job at the Goddard Lab, and he not only gives him an excellent recommendation, he practically rams him down their throats."

"Right."

"But then he refuses to see him after he gets here. Now those three things don't jibe. If there was trouble between them, he wouldn't have given him the recommendation and Hirsh wouldn't have asked him for it. If he gave it and got him the job, he wouldn't have refused to see him afterward. Now all that suggests just one thing to me."

"Blackmail!"

"Right. And if you want to let your mind play a little, doesn't it seem mighty funny that it was Hirsh who was responsible for throwing a monkey wrench into this merger business?"

"Hey—and that could be a good reason for Goralsky wanting to kill him."

165

Lanigan considered. "That's a little weak. For one thing, it isn't a killing matter. And besides, the deal hasn't fallen through—not yet. And since Hirsh was going to be fired anyway he wouldn't be in a position to do any more damage."

"But that's just the point, Hugh." Jennings was excited. "It's like you've been saying all along—that this is the kind of killing where the motive could be weak."

"Yeah," said Lanigan, "and there's nobody I'd rather pin it on."

"I didn't know you knew Goralsky."

"I don't."

"Then why him?"

"Because I'm only human. The rabbi tried to tout me off, and Alf Braddock warned me that if I touched him he'd have my head. Well, I'd like to show the whole lot of them. Besides, if it should be the way we've figured—a weak motive —I'd get a lot of personal satisfaction telling it to the rabbi."

"So let's pick him up."

Lanigan shook his head. "What's the use? He's got an alibi. His pa and the housekeeper would swear he was there all evening. And the rabbi and his wife could account for what little time he wasn't at home."

"We've been able to break alibis before, Hugh. I say, let's pick him up."

"Yeah, but your head isn't on the block. Mine is."

The desk sergeant thrust his head through the door. "There's a guy here, Chief, a Marvin Brown. He wants to make a statement."

Lanigan shuffled the freshly typed pages. "Who's your lawyer, Mr. Brown?"

"Oscar Kahn of Kahn, Kahn, Channing, and Spirofsky. Why?"

"I want to be completely fair. This is a serious matter. It's a murder case and I'd like everything to be correct. I'm going to ask you to sign this. I told you that when we started. Well, I think it would be a good idea if you had your lawyer look it over before you swear to it."

"I don't get it," said Marvin. He was trying very hard to be jaunty and at ease. "You send a couple of guys to my office to ask me all kinds of questions. You don't bother to hide the fact that you're from the police. So I get to thinking maybe you'll come down again; maybe you'll come to the house and question my wife; maybe you'll shadow me." He laughed nervously. "I guess that's what you guys call using psychology. So I decide to save you the trouble and come down myself and make a statement. And now you say I should get a lawyer."

"I'm merely interested in protecting your rights, Mr. Brown. All I'm suggesting—"

There was a knock on the door and Lanigan shouted, "Come in."

Sergeant Whitaker opened the door. "Can I talk to you for a minute, Chief?"

34

The rabbi watched the car drive into the parking lot and pull up to a stop near the temple door. A uniformed chauffeur opened the rear door and helped out the elderly Goralsky. Although it was early in October, the morning was unseasonably warm, Indian summer. Nevertheless, Mr. Goralsky wore a coat and muffler. He leaned on the arm of the chauffeur. The rabbi hurried over.

"Why, Mr. Goralsky, how nice to see you up and about—and to have you join us at services. But is it wise? Does the doctor approve?"

"Thank you, Rabbi, but when I know what I have to do I don't ask the doctor. Today, I decided I had to come to pray. They came this morning and took my Benjamin." There was a quaver in his voice and his eyes filled with tears.

"Who came? What do you mean they took him? What happened?"

"This morning. We had just barely finished breakfast. I was not even dressed. These days, since I been sick, I wear my pajamas and a bathrobe all day long. I am in and out of bed. The police came. They were very nice, very polite. They were dressed like me and you, without uniforms. One shows his badge. He keeps it in his pocket. The other one shows a card, a business card, like a salesman. He's the chief of police. 'What do you want, gentlemen?' my Benjamin asks them. I thought maybe something happened at the plant, or maybe Gamison, the gardener, got drunk again. He likes to drink, but he's a good worker and always when he has too much he goes to his room and stays there till it's over. No trouble, no loud talk. He hides, I shouldn't see him. But then he works twice as hard afterwards. And he has troubles with a daughter with a couple of children yet and her husband can never hold a job. So I keep him. It's a pity. So I thought maybe this time he didn't hide and the police arrested him. But no, it's my Benjamin they wanted. They want to ask him some questions about this Isaac Hirsh who everybody thought committed suicide, but now it seems it's not suicide.

"So you want to ask questions, so ask. Sit down, have a cup of coffee; make yourselves comfortable and ask your questions. But no, in my house they can't ask my son questions. It isn't big enough? Somebody will maybe disturb them? They got to have my Benjamin should come to the station house with them. There, they'll ask him the questions. What kind of questions can they ask him there that they can't ask him in the house? And they're in a hurry yet. My Benjamin likes to sit with me, especially these last few days when I could come down to breakfast, he likes to sit with me and have another cup of coffee. And we talk—about the business, about problems, what we should do about this customer or that customer. After all, we worked so hard all our lives and there never seemed to be enough time to sit down and have a decent meal, always a bite here and a bite there when there was a minute. And now, when things are better and we can take it easy and Benjamin can go to work a little later, is it wrong, Rabbi? But no, they couldn't wait. They could barely wait until my Benjamin put on his tie and his coat, so much they were in a hurry."

"Do you mean that they arrested him? On what charge?"

"The same question I asked them, and my Benjamin too. And they said they weren't arresting—they were just taking him in for questioning. So if they weren't arresting why did they make him go? What would they do different if they were arresting? Carry him maybe? I said to them, 'Gentlemen, you want to ask my son some questions, ask. You don't want to ask here, only in the station house? All right, he'll come to the station house. But does it have to be now? It's Saturday which it is by us the Sabbath. Let him go now to the temple, and later he'll come to the station house. I'll guarantee it.' But no, it had to be right away. So they took him away. So what could I do? I dressed myself and I came here."

The rabbi took his arm. To the chauffeur he said, "I'll take him from here." Then turning to the old man, "Do you feel strong enough to lead the prayers, Mr. Goralsky?"

168

"If you want me to, I've got the strength."

"Good," said the rabbi. "Later we can talk."

The dozen or so men who had come to the service were impatient to begin, but when Goralsky entered on the arm of the rabbi those who knew him shook his hand and congratulated him on his recovery. The rabbi helped him off with his coat and scarf and then, draping a prayer shawl around his thin shoulders, led him to the table before the Ark. The old man prayed in a high, quavery voice which cracked occasionally on the higher notes of the chant; but he made no effort to hurry the service along, waiting each time for the rest to finish their recitations before chanting the line or two preceding the next prayer. At the Reading, the rabbi called him up for one of the portions. He seemed to gain strength as he prayed, and when he began the final prayer, the *Olenu*, his voice was strong and the thin little old man seemed to the rabbi to be standing straight and tall. He was as proud of him as though he were his own father.

At the end of the service all came up to wish him a *Gut Shabbes*, and then leisurely strolled out of the temple, as was proper on the Sabbath. But the rabbi detained the old man. "Sit down, Mr. Goralsky. Now we can talk."

To one of the men who asked if everything was all right, he said: "Perhaps you'll be good enough to tell Mr. Goralsky's chauffeur that we're going to sit here and talk for a little while."

"You know, Rabbi, I'm a little bothered," Goralsky said when the man left. "This is the first time that I ever rode on the Sabbath, and yet I led the prayers and you even called me up for a Reading."

"It's all right, Mr. Goralsky, believe me. Now tell me, have you notified your lawyer?"

The old man shook his head. "For a lawyer there'll be plenty time. My Benjamin he also says I should call the lawyers. In the old country, in the *shtetl*, we didn't know about lawyers. When we got into trouble—and what kind of trouble? Like opening your store a little too early on Sunday—did we get a lawyer? We went to see people who could help us: somebody who knew somebody or knew a relative of somebody should do a favor. Now, I'm sure the police don't come down and take my Benjamin to the station house just to ask him he should help them. No, they got it in their minds that my Benjamin had something to do with this Hirsh dying. They must have on him a suspicion." He gave the rabbi a searching look to see if he would deny it.

"Yes, I think you're right, Mr. Goralsky."

"But this is impossible, Rabbi. I know my son. He's a good boy. He's big and he's strong, but a heart he's got like a girl—so gentle. When we were in the chicken business, he would never do the slaughtering, on the nonkosher part of the business, I mean. For the kosher part, naturally we had it a *shochet*. I know him, I tell you. Years ago when I was younger, I used to be disappointed in him. A father always wants his children should go to school and become educated. He left school early. Sure, it was hard times and I could use his help, but believe me, Rabbi, if he had a head on him and been good in school, somehow I would have kept him there. But he didn't want to study. It came hard for him. And this was a big disappointment to me. And next door, Hirsh had a son, this Isaac, who was a regular *gaon* and won all kinds scholarships. But later on, I used to think, maybe I didn't do so bad with my Benjamin. This Isaac Hirsh never set foot in a synagogue after he grew up. Then he became a drunkard. Then he married a Gentile. Then they even said that he took his own life."

The rabbi shook his head.

"I know that wasn't true now. I'm only telling you what I was thinking. And my son, who didn't even finish high school, he grew up a fine, kosher young man, and it turned out he even had a head for business. There was even an article they wrote on him in *Time* magazine how he was such a wonderful businessman. Believe me, they're making a mistake, the police. My Benjamin, what interest would he have with this Isaac Hirsh, and after so many years?"

"Well, you've got to understand the situation," the rabbi said. "This Hirsh is comparatively new here and kept to himself. He didn't have any friends to speak of, and no business dealings with anyone who had any connection with him. They found out about your son having known him when they were boys together and about the partnership later on. And then when he made such a point about not wanting Hirsh's body in the cemetery—"

The old man clasped his thin hands together. "God forgive me—that was my fault, Rabbi. He knew nothing about these things. It was from what he heard me say."

"Yes, I know, but there was also the matter of his getting Hirsh the job at the Goddard Lab. He wrote a strong letter of recommendation—"

"See, doesn't that show you what kind of heart he's got, my Benjamin? Never was he friendly with Isaac Hirsh, even when they were boys. I don't blame him. Maybe he got it

170

from seeing my disappointment in him. Maybe I was harsh with him. Even when I realized that he was such a good son, could I tell him to his face? A girl, a daughter you can pat her on the head and pay her compliments, but a son?—"

"Yes, I understand. But you see, because of all this, it's only natural for the police to want to make sure there wasn't some recent connection between your son and Isaac Hirsh. I would earnestly advise you to consult with a lawyer so he can take care of your son's interests."

"No." The old man shook his head. "With a lawyer it's already official. He goes to a judge; he makes a motion; he gets a paper. Right away, it's public and it's in the news-papers. My son is not just anybody. He's an important man. The newspapers would make a big tumult about the police questioning him."

"Then what are you going to do?"

"That's why I come to you, Rabbi. I understand that you and the chief are good friends."

"I'm afraid we haven't been lately," said the rabbi ruefully. "But even if we were, what could I do?"

"You could talk to him. You could find out what they are looking for. You could explain to them. Please, Rabbi. Try."

And Rabbi Small did not have the heart to refuse. "All right, I'll talk to the chief, but don't expect anything. Please take my advice and get your lawyer."

"The lawyer I can get later, but first I want you should talk to him. I don't mean you should work today, Rabbi. It's the Sabbath, but maybe tonight?"

"A man's reputation is at stake. If you can ride on the Sabbath I can work on the Sabbath." He smiled. "Besides, for a rabbi, the Sabbath is his regular workday."

35

The rabbi's call came just as he was leaving. "I've got to see you about Goralsky."

"Sorry, Rabbi," said Lanigan. "I was just on my way out."

"But it's extremely important."

"I'm afraid it can't be done. I have an appointment with Amos Quint and Ronald Sykes at the Goddard Lab in about twenty minutes. I'm hoping we can come up with something that will wind this thing up."

"I'm sure you're making a terrible mistake, Chief. You've got your mind fixed on Goralsky, and you're going to do him a great injustice."

"Look, Rabbi, I've got to run along. I'll try to get over to you later."

"But later could be too late."

"I can't imagine anything that won't keep."

"Rumor won't keep. You've got Goralsky down at the station house. Before long everyone in town will know."

"All right. But the best I can do is meet you at the lab. You can sit in on the discussion if you want. I guess I owe it to you. That is, if you don't mind riding on the Sabbath."

"For this I would make an exception. But I don't like to leave Miriam alone at this time."

"Bring her along."

"Well, if you don't mind—we'll be there."

He hung up and called to Miriam to get ready. "We're going to meet Lanigan at the Goddard Lab."

As they drove along Route 128, Miriam said, "Do you think Chief Lanigan really has a case against Mr. Goralsky?"

"Who knows? I haven't spoken to him for a week or more, until just now. They may have found something I don't know about, but then they probably would have arrested him outright instead of just taking him in for questioning. I'm sure they can work up a plausible motive. The trouble is, the way Lanigan views this case, they could work up a plausible motive against almost anyone."

"How do you mean?"

"Well, he's decided that it wasn't the result of elaborate planning, that since it involved just walking away no great motive is necessary. Anyone could have that kind of motive—his neighbor who doesn't like the way he keeps his lawn—anyone. It's much the same with the rest—weapon, opportunity. Goralsky could have been there because he wasn't at the temple. Well, a lot of other people weren't at the temple. And of course Goralsky drives a car. Yes, Lanigan could make up a case that would justify holding him."

"But he'd be sure of being acquitted, wouldn't he?"

He shrugged his shoulders. "Suppose he were, would that be the end of it for him? Suppose they don't even bring him to trial but release him, everyone will know he has been arrested. Even if they issue some sort of statement, what can they say? Mr. Goralsky has been released because of insufficient evidence? That wouldn't signify he was innocent, only that they'd been unable to find the evidence they needed to connect him with the murder. And if he went to trial and was acquitted, it would be the same. No, he can be cleared completely only if they find the actual murderer. Well, more often than not, they never do."

The car slowed down.

"Why are you stopping here?"

"I hadn't intended to." He pressed down hard on the accelerator, but instead of responding the car slowed down still more. He shifted into second, went a few feet and stopped altogether. He tried the motor, but it did not catch.

"What's the matter, David?"

He grinned foolishly. "I don't know."

"Well, there's a how-d'ye-do. What do we do now?"

"There was a cutoff back there about a hundred yards. Probably the one that leads to Morris Goldman's garage. We're on an incline. Maybe I can coast back—"

"On 128? With cars zipping along at sixty miles an hour! You'll do no such thing."

"I'm not keen on it myself. I suppose I better ease her back onto the shoulder of the road and raise the hood. That's a sign that you're in trouble. The state troopers will be along in a minute, they patrol this road constantly. . . . What's the matter?"

Her fists were clenched and she was biting her upper lip. Her forehead suddenly was bathed in perspiration. After a moment, she smiled weakly. "You might look at your watch and time the next one. I think you're about to become a father, David."

"Are you sure? That's all we need right now. Look, don't worry and don't get excited. Just sit tight and I'll flag down a car."

"Be careful, David," she called as he got out.

A moment ago the highway had been filled with cars, but now not a car was to be seen. He drew out his handkerchief and took up a position in the middle of the road. Presently he saw a car in the distance and began to wave his handkerchief. To his tremendous relief, the car slowed down. It passed, swung over to the side of the road, and then backed up to within a few feet of his car. When the driver got out, the rabbi saw it was Dr. Sykes.

"Why it's Rabbi Small, isn't it? You in trouble?"

"My car stopped."

"Out of gas?"

"I don't think so. No, I'm sure it isn't that. I've been having some trouble—"

"All right, I'll call a garage just as soon as I get to the lab. I'm supposed to meet the police chief there. Conked out right in the middle of driving, eh? Could be that your—"

"Look, my wife is in labor."

"Oh, boy, that's bad—" He eyed her in consternation. "Maybe, I— Say wait a minute! Why don't you take my car and I can hoof it to the lab. It's only a few hundred yards up the road."

"It's very kind of you, Dr. Sykes." The rabbi climbed into the bucket seat of the little sports car and grasped the wheel. He looked uncertainly at the array of dials on the dashboard and then at the grinning face of Sykes leaning on the open door.

"Stick shift with four speeds forward. She'll do a hundred easily. I had her gone over not long ago and she's tuned like a fine watch."

The rabbi nodded at the sticker on the doorjamb. "Yes, I see. *Chai.*"

"What's that?"

"It's a Hebrew word. It means life."

Sykes looked at him doubtfully, and then over at Mrs. Small and seemed to understand. "Right. You both have it on your mind. Well, let me help your lady out."

"No."

"What's the matter?"

The rabbi had stepped out. "No, I couldn't. I wouldn't dare drive it. I—I wouldn't know how. We'd end up in a ditch. Look, I've got a better idea. Why don't you drive on to the lab and tell Lanigan about our situation here. He'll come and get us. Oh, and you could also have someone call the doctor—Dr. Morton Selig. He's in the book, and tell him what happened and that I'm on my way to the hospital."

"All right if you're sure you'd rather."

He climbed into the car and gunned the motor with a deafening roar. "Good luck and my best to your lady."

"Nothing to be worried about, you two," Lanigan remarked over his shoulder to the couple in the back seat. "When I first joined the force, I was on the ambulance trick and I wouldn't care to venture a guess at the number of women I drove to the hospital. We used to take them over to Salem in those days—didn't have a hospital of our own in the town. I don't claim to be an obstetrician, but in my experience the first child always took a long time."

"The pains are coming every ten minutes now."

"Plenty of time. It's when they start coming fast, every couple of minutes or every minute. It's when it's a second or third child they're apt to pop. And don't think I haven't delivered babies either, or helped to. So you couldn't be in better hands."

He was obviously talking to distract them, and the rabbi recognized it and was grateful. He sat with one arm around his wife and gave her his hand to clutch whenever the pains came. Every so often he would wipe her forehead with his handkerchief.

They reached the outskirts of the city and Lanigan glanced back at them. "You know, if you like I could pick up a motorcycle escort. That way we could get through a little quicker."

Miriam answered before the rabbi could speak. "I don't think it will be necessary." She blushed. "The pains appear to have stopped."

"Doesn't mean a thing," said Lanigan. But he slowed down and proceeded at a more moderate pace until they reached the hospital. "I'll stick around, until you know what's what, Rabbi."

Thanking him the rabbi helped Miriam out of the car and supported her up the steps. Though she needed no assistance, she enjoyed his solicitude. With some embarrassment they explained to the reception clerk that the pains had stopped.

The nurse at the desk informed them it was not uncommon and arranged for Mrs. Small to be escorted to her room. The rabbi remained in the waiting room, where after some ten minutes he was joined by Dr. Selig, a pleasant young man of his own age, who seemed to exude both assurance and reassurance.

"The pains have stopped for the time being. It's quite common. Sometimes the girls get a little lazy, or maybe they just change their minds. If they didn't, they wouldn't be women, ha-ha. Well, we'll keep her here for the night anyway. Even if the pains start in again it will be hours, so there's no sense in your waiting around."

"But she's all right?"

"Oh, perfectly. Nothing for you to worry about. You know, Rabbi, in all my practice I've——"

"I know, you've never lost a father."

"Rabbi," the doctor was reproachful, "that was my line."

"Sorry. Can I see her now?"

"I'd rather you wouldn't. She's being prepared and we've given her some sedation. Why don't you just go home. I'll call you just as soon as anything begins to happen."

36

The rabbi climbed into the front seat beside Lanigan. "The doctor says it will be hours."

"I thought as much. I'll drop you on my way back to the lab."

"It was very decent of you to come and get us, Chief," said the rabbi. "Things were pretty rough there for a few minutes until Sykes came along."

"I understand he offered you his car and you refused. Those little foreign jobs are actually no different from ours, except you have to shift a little more often and they respond to the wheel a little quicker than you're used to. But you would have got the hang of it before you'd driven a quarter of a mile."

"Oh, I had no doubt I could drive it. I just didn't want to be indebted to a murderer for the birth of my child."

"Murderer? Sykes?"

The rabbi nodded soberly.

Lanigan stepped on the brake and brought the car to a halt at the side of the road. "Now. Let's hear it."

The rabbi settled back in his seat. "The man who drove Hirsh home had to be on foot. That's basic. If he'd been driving, and stopped to take the wheel of Hirsh's car, he would have had to leave his own. You had alerted the state troopers, so they were patrolling the road. An empty car would have been spotted. Chances are that it wasn't a hitchhiker, because they're expressly forbidden on Route 128. There are signs posted at each entrance, and the state troopers would pick up anyone they saw."

"So."

"But the people at Goddard regularly leave their cars to be serviced or repaired at Morris Goldman's garage because it's just a few hundred yards from the lab. They drop off their cars in the morning and walk along the embankment of 128 to get to work. At night—and Goldman's, like most garages, stays open late—they walk back, pick up their cars, and drive home."

"Everyone knows that."

"Well, to get to the lab from the garage, you have to pass the turnoff where Hirsh was parked. It's just about halfway."

"Yes, you can see the turnoff from the lab."

"Right. Well, now I know that Sykes had his car serviced at Morris Goldman's garage that Friday, because when I got behind the wheel I saw one of his lube stickers on the doorjamb. It was dated the eighteenth. That was Friday."

"It still doesn't place him on foot. After all, he could have picked up his car after work—before Hirsh returned to the lab after his dinner."

The rabbi shook his head.

"Why not? You yourself said Goldman's stays open late."

"But not that Friday night. It was Kol Nidre. He would have closed well before six. And we know Sykes was at the lab that late because he phoned Mrs. Hirsh and left word that her husband was to call him when he got in."

"That doesn't mean he couldn't get home. He could have called a cab—why not?" as the rabbi shook his head vigorously.

"You can ask Miriam if you wish. The nearest cab company, the only one for practical purposes, is the one in Barnard's Crossing. And when Miriam had me stop off there the proprietor told us the only calls he got that evening were to take people to the temple."

"All right!" Lanigan sounded exasperated. "But it's all conjecture."

"No, Sykes had no car all weekend."

"How do we know that?"

"He didn't pick up his car Friday. And he couldn't pick it up on Saturday, because that was Yom Kippur and Goldman was closed. And I know for a fact he had no car on Sunday."

"Oh?"

"You see, when he came to my house to arrange for Hirsh's funeral, he arrived and departed by cab. Why would he do that if he had his car? Yet we know he had it on Monday, because he drove it to the funeral."

Lanigan was silent for a minute. "So your theory—and it's no more than a theory," he said finally, "is that Sykes sat around waiting for Hirsh to call back. When he didn't, he started out on foot to get his car, saw Hirsh parked in the turnoff on 128, and offered or Hirsh asked him, to drive him home and—"

"And Hirsh passed out on the way."

"But why would he want to kill him? Sykes was probably his closest friend here in Barnard's Crossing. He went to bat and covered up for him half a dozen times. I got that from Amos Quint who admitted he would have fired Hirsh long before if Sykes had not interceded for him."

"And why would Sykes have to intercede for him?" the rabbi demanded.

"I don't understand."

"Quint never spoke to Hirsh except on the day he hired him. Everything there went through channels. Whatever communication there was between Hirsh and Quint passed through Sykes. Now if Sykes didn't want Hirsh fired—if he was such a good friend—why mention his mistakes to Quint in the first place? Why go to bat for him? Quint is no scientist, he's an administrator. If Sykes wanted to cover for Hirsh, all he had to do was refrain from mentioning his name and Quint never would have known. But evidently there were errors— at least half a dozen, according to you. Now suppose they were the fault not of Hirsh but of Sykes? It would be mighty convenient to have Hirsh there to take the blame."

"All the more reason for not wanting to kill him. Why give up a good thing? In any case, Quint was going to fire him Monday, so Sykes would be off the hook."

"Then there's your answer!" said the rabbi triumphantly. "This time apparently there was an important mistake—one Quint couldn't overlook. We know he always made a point of seeing a man he was going to fire. He saw him, told him just why he was firing him, and that ended it. Isn't that the way you reported it? So he tells Hirsh the reason for his dismissal, and Hirsh says, 'Oh, no, sir, it was Ron Sykes that did that; I discovered the error.' There's a confrontation, Hirsh shows his work notes. . . ."

The chief folded his hands behind his head and leaned against the car seat, absorbed in thought. Then he shook his head. "It hangs together, Rabbi, and it sounds plausible, but you're just guessing. It's all surmise and conjecture. We don't have a bit of proof."

When the rabbi spoke, his tone denoted both certainty and finality. "Just ask Sykes how he got home from the lab Friday night. Just ask him that."

"Yeah, I'll do that." He smiled. "You know, Rabbi, somehow or other, you do manage to take care of your flock."

"You mean Goralsky and Brown?"

"Oh, we didn't really have anything on Brown. We were just floundering, looking for some line we could follow. You know why he left the temple early? He was ashamed to tell you, but he made a statement to us. He had a business deal on—a big policy, and the customer insisted on getting the papers signed that night."

"I suspected it might be something like that."

"I guess from your point of view it was a pretty terrible thing for him to do."

The rabbi thought for a moment. "No, I don't think it was terrible. In a way I'm rather pleased."

"Pleased that he ran out on your Yom Kippur service to consummate a business deal?"

"No—pleased that he was ashamed of it."

37

Sunday morning, the Schwarz forces were standing around unhappily in the corridor just outside the Board meeting room.

"Do you think the rabbi will show up today?" asked Marvin Brown.

"I doubt it," said the president. "Stands to reason as an expectant father he'll be at the hospital."

Herman Fine came up and joined them. "I understand the *rebbitzin* went to the hospital yesterday. Maybe we should hold off on the rabbi's letter of resignation at least for today. I know I for one would feel funny—"

"Are you kidding?" demanded Schwarz. "The resignation is definitely out. I guess you didn't hear what I just told the boys. I ran into Ben Goralsky after the minyan this morning, and for about twenty minutes all he could talk about was how wonderful 'the little rabbi'—that's what he called him—how wonderful he was. You'd think the rabbi saved his life."

"Maybe he did," said Marvin Brown. "You hear about how if a man is innocent he won't be convicted, but every now and then some guy will confess to a crime some other guy

179

has done twenty years in prison for." He ran his hand under his collar. "Don't think I wasn't plenty worried about the same thing. Besides, even if he got off, how about his old man? A thing like that could kill him."

"All right, the resignation is out," said Fine. "And it's okay by me. So what do we do now? I say we ought to go the whole way and do it up handsome. Mort should read the letter, explain it was due to a misunderstanding, and call for a vote from the Board refusing to accept it."

"Like hell."

"What d'you mean, Mort?"

"I mean I'm certainly glad Ben Goralsky got off, and I'm willing to give the rabbi some credit. Still it's one thing to forget about the resignation, because then we could kiss the Goralskys goodby. But I'm damned if I go begging to the rabbi. There'd be no living with him after that. If we ever disagreed on anything again— Watch it, here come Wasserman and Becker."

"Good morning, gentlemen, I got good news. I just called the hospital and they told me the *rebbitzin* had a boy."

"Hey, that's all right."

"That *is* good news."

"How's the *rebbitzin* feeling?"

They all gathered around, asking questions.

"Look, fellows," said Schwarz, "are we going to stand out here and *schmoos* all day? Let's get the meeting started."

"Yeah, let's go."

"What do you plan to do about the rabbi's letter?" asked Wasserman as they moved toward the door.

Schwarz looked at him in surprise. The group halted to listen.

"What letter, Jacob? What letter are you talking about?"

The men looked at each other and some smiled.

But Becker's face got red. "What are you trying to pull, Mort? You know damn well what letter Jake is talking about. You planning some—"

Wasserman put a restraining hand on his friend's arm. "Becker, Becker, if Mort doesn't know about the letter, that means he never received it."

"Why, was it something important?" asked Schwarz.

Wasserman shrugged his shoulders. "I guess not. Probably something routine—just routine."

38

"The missus home yet?" asked Lanigan.

"Tomorrow," said the rabbi happily. "I take them home tomorrow."

"I was hoping I'd have a chance to see the boy."

"He looks like a little old man, so wrinkled."

"They all do for a few days. Then they begin to round out and get fat."

"I suppose so. The doctor said it was a fine healthy child, but you couldn't tell by looking at him. He looked like a plucked chicken."

"They're just like puppies. They've got to grow into their skins."

"Well, you've made me feel better already," said the rabbi. "Say, why don't you and Gladys drop around tomorrow? You'll be able to see him then."

"Oh, we intend to. But I was passing and thought I'd be able to sneak a preview. I've just come from the D.A.'s office. He made a deal with Sykes's lawyer for second-degree murder."

"Second-degree? But that's unpremeditated—"

"I know, I know. But the D.A. still thought it best."

"But you had a confession."

"We had a confession but not for premeditated murder. When he confronted Sykes, we carefully refrained from mentioning the wiped fingerprint. We told him we knew he was without his car over the weekend; we told him what we'd uncovered about the work in his department at the lab. And I guess we sort of hinted Hirsh's death was probably accidental, and that if he cooperated fully with us it would go a lot easier for him."

He reddened and looked away from the rabbi's direct glance. "It's common procedure. It's done by lawyers regularly right in the courtroom. If you can trap your man into admitting his guilt—what's wrong with it? It wasn't as though he was innocent."

"I'm not quarreling with you."

"Well, he admitted that he'd come across Hirsh as you

suggested and drove him home. Also that Hirsh passed out within minutes after they'd started. He claimed he tried to wake him up when they got to Hirsh's house, but he couldn't budge him. So he decided to leave him there to sleep it off. Only after he'd got home did it occur to him that perhaps he'd forgotten to turn off the motor. By then he was afraid to walk back and see."

"And what about the way he used Hirsh to cover up his own mistakes?"

"He admitted that. As a matter of fact, he gave us a complete picture of what happened at the lab. I guess he was smart enough to realize that we'd find it out eventually, and it would look better for him if he were completely candid with us. It's only a fool who tries to cover up and then finds he has to keep retreating as we learn more and more. It appears that the original brainstorm was Hirsh's. He issued the preliminary report in both their names, but then Sykes assigned Hirsh to other work and carried this on by himself. He claims he wasn't trying to steal the credit; that Hirsh just was not as enthusiastic about his own idea as he was. But he discussed it with Hirsh off and on, and sometimes had Hirsh check his figures.

"Then Hirsh discovered an error. Sykes told him not to say anything yet, with an idea that he'd admit it gradually in a series of progress reports. One would say that unexpected difficulties had cropped up. Then he'd issue another to the effect that a great deal more work and time were needed. And finally, he'd put one out that would make it clear it was a dud. I guess Hirsh might have gone along, except that his name was on the first report and that the research was being done for Goraltronics."

"Hm—that's interesting. Is that your idea, or did Sykes say Hirsh was concerned about Goraltronics?"

"No, I got that from Sykes. Evidently, Hirsh felt some sort of obligation to Goralsky for having got him the job. He even hinted that if Sykes didn't tell the truth he was going to speak to Goralsky himself. Maybe he was just bluffing, but Sykes didn't know. Goralsky had got him the job, so naturally he had every reason for taking the hint seriously. So late Friday afternoon he went to Quint and told him the truth. He claims he was going to admit he was to blame, but Quint was so upset that he lost his nerve. When Quint assumed it was Hirsh's fault, he did not correct him. You can understand how Quint felt because he knew about the merger and the stock going up and all that. He wanted to call

Hirsh in and fire him right then and there, but Sykes lied and said Hirsh had gone home early because of the holiday. That's kind of ironic, isn't it?"

"It's even more ironic than you think," said the rabbi. "Sykes, when he came to visit me that Sunday, remarked that Hirsh would have been alive if he had been a normal practicing Jew."

"That's no lie. Anyway, we typed up his confession and he signed it," Lanigan went on. "Then we sprung the wiped fingerprint on him. We thought that would break him. You see, if we had mentioned it at the beginning he would have realized it was first-degree murder and probably would have refused to talk. This way, at least we had a confession for the major part and if he broke we'd have it all. He clammed up. Refused to say another word until he conferred with a lawyer."

"But you had your case anyway."

Lanigan shook his head gloomily. "After his lawyer got through talking to the D.A., we didn't have much of anything. The fingerprint—or rather the missing fingerprint—would have been peppered by defense counsel. He would have shown that we had men all over that car. He would have argued that one of us could have wiped it accidentally with his sleeve. And the confession? They could say it was obtained under duress."

"And getting home from the lab—how could that be explained away?"

"Easy. He started out to walk to the garage and someone gave him a lift. He doesn't remember the make of car and the driver didn't give him his name. After all, no one saw him near the Hirsh house."

"Peter Dodge did."

"Peter—the minister? When did you see him?"

"He dropped in this morning. He got home from Alabama yesterday."

"And he saw Sykes?"

The rabbi nodded. "He takes a walk every evening, and it leads him past Bradford Lane. He had planned to drop in on Hirsh for a talk, but as he came to the corner he saw the house was dark so he went right past. But he did see Sykes —he's sure that's who it was—walking down Bradford Lane in the other direction toward his home, of course. At the time he had never met the man and just assumed it was someone taking a walk like himself."

"Why didn't he come forward and tell us?"

"Why should he? He didn't know that there was murder involved."

Lanigan began to laugh. "Well, there you have it, Rabbi. We've mismanaged this case from the beginning. We just had bad luck all the way. When we were unable to get in touch with Dodge down in Alabama, we asked the police to pick him up for us so we could question him. The minute they found the police were looking for him, the Negroes hid him, of course—one place to another, I don't suppose he even knew why. Then when he finally returned to his hotel, the Birmingham police did pick him up and called to ask if they should hold him and we told them no, to let him go. After all, we had our man by that time.

"Well, I don't suppose it makes any difference really. But it just shows how much luck counts in solving a case. We had bad luck all the way, and then when we finally hit on the right solution it was still a matter of luck. I mean, Sykes happening to stop and offer you a lift so you were able to see that lube sticker—that was a tremendous stroke of luck."

"Well, we believe in luck, you know."

"I suppose everyone does to some degree."

"No, I mean we believe in a way you Christians don't. Your various doctrines—that God observes the fall of every sparrow, that you can change your misfortune by prayer—it all implies that when someone has bad luck he deserves it. But we believe in luck. That is, we believe it is possible for the truly good man to be unlucky, and vice versa. That's one of the lessons we are taught by the Book of Job.

"Still, I'm not so sure it was all luck. The whole case was permeated with the feeling of our holy day. Subconsciously, I imagine, I thought a great deal about the relations between Hirsh and Sykes, and why Sykes would want to cover up for him. And that's why the explanation occurred to me so readily when I saw the date on the lube sticker. You see, the whole pattern of the crime was laid out before me in our Yom Kippur service."

"How do you mean?"

"Well, part of that service deals with the ceremony of the selection and sacrifice of the scapegoat by the High Priest in ancient Israel. It was even the subject of my sermon. In it I referred to the sacrifice of Abraham, which is the portion of the Scroll read on the day of the New Year, the beginning of the Ten Days of Awe which culminates in Yom Kippur. And that was the whole point of the situation there at the Goddard Lab. In spite of his disassociation from the

Jewish community, Hirsh nevertheless played what in the past too often has been the traditional role of the Jew."

"You mean—"

"I mean he was the scapegoat. His very name should have suggested it to me."

Lanigan was puzzled. "Hirsh?"

The rabbi smiled sadly. "No, Isaac."

39

Rabbi Small paced back and forth in the living room. He was practicing the delivery of his Chanukah sermon, and now and again he would glance at his audience—his infant son, firmly wedged into a corner of the divan. Once he interrupted his discourse to call to Miriam in the kitchen, "You know, dear, he follows me. He's actually focusing on me."

"Of course, he's been doing it for days."

"'. . . so we must consider the miracle of the lights not only as an example of the intervention of the Divine power—'"

The infant began to pout.

"You don't like that? I don't care for it too much myself. Suppose I say, 'We are too much inclined to respond to the miraculous—'"

A whimper.

"How about, 'The real miracle of Chanukah is not the burning of the cruse of oil for eight days rather than for the expected one; it is that a tiny nation could challenge the power of mighty Greece—'"

A cry.

"No?"

The infant took breath and then, his face red and contorted, emitted another wail at full volume.

"That bad, eh?"

Miriam appeared in the doorway. "He's hungry. I'd better feed him."

"Perhaps you'd better," said the rabbi. "I'll try it on him again after he's eaten. Maybe he'll be more receptive on a full stomach."

"You'll do no such thing. After he's fed, he's going to bed. Aren't you, Jonathan?" She nuzzled him, and the cries died down to an uncertain whimper and then stopped. "Besides, I think you've got a visitor."

It was Moses Goralsky. Through the window, the rabbi saw the old man being helped out of the car by the chauffeur but then refuse further assistance with a shake of the head. Clinging to the handrailing he mounted the steps to the door.

"Come in, Mr. Goralsky. This is a pleasant surprise."

"I have a question, a *sheileh*. To whom should I come if not to the rabbi?"

He helped the old man off with his coat and showed him into his study. "I'll do the best I can, Mr. Goralsky."

"You know, when my Ben was in trouble I came to the temple to pray."

"I remember."

"So you know when I recite the prayers, they're in Hebrew. I can say the Hebrew, but what I'm saying, this I don't know, because when did I have a chance to learn? We were a poor family. My father—he worked plenty hard in the old country just to feed us. So after I learned the prayers, he took me out of the *cheder,* you know, the school, and already I was helping him in his work. That's how it was with most people those days."

"Yes, I know."

"So because I don't understand what the words mean, that means I'm not praying? I have thoughts in my head, while my lips are moving, and by me this is praying. Am I right or wrong, Rabbi?"

"I suppose it depends on what the thoughts are."

"Ah-hah. Now that Saturday, what would my thoughts be? They would be about Ben. I asked God He should help him. He should make the police they should find out the truth so they should let my Ben go."

"I would say that was praying, Mr. Goralsky."

"So while I was praying, I made a promise. If my Ben goes free, I thought, then I would do something."

"You don't have to bribe God, and you don't have to make bargains with Him."

"Not a bribe. Not even a bargain. I made with myself a promise—a—a vow."

"All right."

"Now here's my question, Rabbi. Do I have to keep my promise?"

The rabbi did not smile. Hands in his pockets, he strode

up and down the room, his forehead creased in thought. Finally he turned and faced the old man. "It depends on what the promise was. If it was something impossible, then obviously you're not bound. If it was something wrong or illegal, again you're not bound. In any case, where you made the promise to yourself it's up to you to decide how committed you are."

"Let me tell you, Rabbi. Months ago, I was talking to Morton Schwarz, the president of the temple, and I said I wanted a remembrance for my Hannah, which she had died a few months before that. After all, I'm a rich man now, and my son is rich. And my Hannah was with me all the time we were poor. Even when I got rich, she couldn't enjoy it because already she was sick, in bed most of the time, on a diet so she couldn't even eat good. So this Morton Schwarz he asks me what I had in mind. The temple could use an air-condition system, maybe a new organ." The old man shrugged his shoulders. "I'm going to make an air-condition system in remembrance of my wife? Where will her name be? On the pipes? And an organ is better? I had to fight with myself a long time before I went to your temple because there was an organ there. So should I give the temple an organ in my wife's memory? So I said, 'Mr. Schwarz, I don't want a piece of machinery, and I don't want any organs. I had it in mind something like a building.' *Nu,* that's all I had to say, and that's all he had to hear. He tells me he had it in mind to build like an addition to the temple, a special sanctuary which it would be used only for praying, not for meetings or regular business. I told him I was interested."

"Did he tell you how much it was likely to cost?"

"The cost I didn't care. The money, I can take it with me? Or I got to provide for Ben? Schwarz says more than a hundred thousand; I said even two hundred thousand."

"Well—"

"So then later he shows me a drawing, and he explains how there will be like a gallery so you can stand there and talk when you want to leave the service for a little rest, or after the service, a place you can linger." He hunched his shoulders and spread his hands. "Believe me, Rabbi, at my age, you're interested in lingering. You're not in and you're not out—sort of halfway."

"And then did he show you the model?"

"He showed me."

"And?"

"And the model—" he grimaced, "already I wasn't so

crazy over. The building by itself—nice, but attached to the temple, it was already not here not there. The temple—it's plain, it's straight; and the new building, it's fancy. But I'm an architect? What do I know about buildings? So I wasn't sure, but that day when I was praying for my Ben, I made it a promise that if they let Ben go I would give the building."

"And your question is whether you're bound by your promise?"

"That's the question."

"And your objection is that the two, the new and the old, don't go together?"

"Not only that, Rabbi. This I could stand already. But all my life, I'm a businessman. Do you know what is a businessman, Rabbi? A businessman, when he spends a dollar he got to get for a dollar merchandise. Makes no difference for what he spends. If he spends for charity, he got to get for a dollar charity. You understand?"

"I think so."

"So to me it seems like this building is mostly wasted. Do we need an extra building for the temple? To put up a building just to put up a building, just to spend the money, it's not in my nature."

"Suppose the building were separate from the main building. Would you feel better about it?"

"So what would you use it for?"

"It could be a school," the rabbi suggested slowly. "Or even a community center."

"You need a separate building for a school? If you took the school out of the temple and put it in a separate building, for when would you use the temple? For a couple of days a year? It would be a waste. And a center? Here in Barnard's Crossing you need a center for the boys to play basketball? In the city, where nobody had a yard and was lots of kids and was dangerous to play in the street—all right. But here, you need a place for kids to play?"

"Perhaps you're right—"

"Remember, Rabbi, just to put up a building, should be a building—this is foolish. Better in this place should be God's grass and flowers."

Then it came to the rabbi. "You're right, Mr. Goralsky. But there is one building that we do need." He looked at the old man and spoke carefully. "We could use a chapel for our cemetery. Oh, it wouldn't be as big as the plan calls for, but it could be the same general design. And it would be es-

188

pecially fitting since your wife was one of the first to be buried there—"

Goralsky's lined face broke into an old man's smile. "Rabbi, Rabbi, this time you got it. The same design, maybe a little smaller, this would be a nice building for the cemetery. And even a fence, I would be willing to put it in, and flowers and maybe trees. The Hannah Goralsky Memorial Cemetery. It could be like a garden." Then his face fell. "But my vow, Rabbi. I made a promise for an addition to the temple here in Barnard's Crossing. In my own mind, I even saw Morton Schwarz's building—"

"But did your vow concern this particular arrangement of buildings? You made a vow to donate a building to the temple, a memorial to your wife—" He stopped as the old man shook his head.

"Look, Rabbi, you think I made a vow like I was swearing before a notary? I, Moses Goralsky, do hereby promise. . . . No. Was going through my mind all kinds of pictures, feelings, ideas—not so much words, you understand. But I know what I promised," he added stubbornly.

The rabbi nodded thoughtfully. Of course the old man did not verbalize his vow. And he was old enough and rich enough to hold himself to its strict observance, even though he was also shrewd enough to realize that the alternate plan, the cemetery chapel, would be much more useful and appropriate. The rabbi rose from his chair and began to stride up and down the room, while Goralsky waited with the patience of the very old.

The more the rabbi thought of it, the better the plan seemed. No less than Marvin Brown, he realized the importance of the cemetery to the congregation. And it would give Morton Schwarz his building—not exactly as he had planned it, but near enough. And it would permit the old man to set up a lasting memorial to his wife's memory. The problem was, how to permit Mr. Goralsky to do what he actually wanted to do.

He paused in front of the bookcase and his eyes wandered over the large leather-bound tomes that comprised his copy of the Talmud. He selected a volume and took it over to his desk. He leafed through the pages until he found the passage he wanted and swiveled around to face Goralsky.

"I told you at the beginning that if your vow involved doing something wrong, that you were absolved. Do you remember?"

"Of course. *Nu*, so is putting up Schwarz's building a sin?"

189

The rabbi smiled. "For this one particular case, Mr. Goralsky, I shall rule that the law of *shatnes* applies."

"*Shatnes?* But isn't that about clothing—that you shouldn't mix linen and wool?"

"That's the way it's usually construed. But the regulation is mentioned in two places in the Bible, in Leviticus and in Deuteronomy. Why in two places? When the Bible says the same thing twice, it can mean either that the regulation is very important or that it can have another significance. In Leviticus the regulation is joined with an injunction against letting cattle of different kinds breed together and also an injunction against sowing with mingled seeds. In Deuteronomy the regulation is joined with an injunction against sowing a vineyard with different seeds and an injunction against plowing with an ox and an ass together."

His voice took on the Talmudic chanting intonation. "Now if the two passages were exactly the same, you could argue that what is intended is that the regulation is important and should be strictly applied. But where the rule is given, and in each case accompanied by two other rules, and the two from Leviticus are not the same as the two from Deuteronomy, we can interpret this to mean that the precept is intended to forbid various mixtures of two things of different kinds."

He leaned back in his chair. "So you will say, where does it stop? We use many mixtures of diverse things: shoes made of leather and rubber, houses of wood and stone. If we go beyond the specific regulations, then we must have some kind of a test. What then would be a logical test? Why, obviously, if it seems wrong to you. For what other purpose did God give us our intelligence if not to use it? Your initial objection to Schwarz's design was that the two buildings were of two different orders, and it seemed wrong to join them together. It bothered you from the very first. So my ruling is that this is an example of *shatnes,* and hence forbidden."

The old man scratched his head. Then his wrinkled old face cracked into a smile and he beamed in fond admiration at the young rabbi. "And in the cemetery would be all right—it's separate. It's a *pilpul,* but you know something, Rabbi? Suddenly, I'm feeling all right."